CHRISTMAS TRIAD

A SMALL TOWN HOLIDAY ROMANCE

K.C. CROWNE

DESCRIPTION

This Christmas, three Navy SEAL brothers are delivering BIG forbidden packages to one *very* lucky girl.

The Wolf brothers were my childhood friends.
All three of them hot as sin.
Duncan, Evan and Jay. Each with their own unique charm.
Now, there're back in my life...
Older, stronger, and hotter than ever.
I simply can't handle the undeniable desire between all four of us.

But skeletons from my past want to cause harm.
And my former step brothers are ready to bring down the law.

In the midst of the madness, I find myself wanting more than just friendship.
How will I ever choose between the three of them? *And what if I don't have to?*

Dear Reader,
This is a steamy reverse harem holiday romance loaded with all things taboo. Snuggle up next to a warm cup of hot chocolate and enjoy this naughty present fit for any lover of forbidden attraction.
XOXO
-K.C.

CHAPTER 1

DREAM

The perfect, crisp air rushed into my lungs as I stepped off the ferry. The town of Charmed Bay, the sleepy, coastal California city where I'd grown up, stretched along a big curving beach and overlooked the ocean. My life over the last few months had been crazy, but the sight of home managed to put a small smile on my lips.

More than that, it was winter – my favorite time of the year in California. The sky was clear and blue, and the air, while crisp from being on the coast, was not nearly as cold as other parts of the country. It wasn't too hot nor too cold. However, I barely had a moment to appreciate the cozy blanket of nostalgia that had wrapped around me at the sight of my hometown.

"Dream!"

The familiar voice of Clarissa Watts, my best friend from high school, cut through the soft hush of the waves on the shore and the occasional cry of a seagull in the air. I turned my attention to the small crowd of people greeting the ferry's passengers.

It didn't take me long at all to spot her – especially since Clarissa was in the process of hurtling over the small barrier that separated the landing dock area from the greeting area. Once Clarissa was over, she stuck out her arms, a big, toothy smile on her cute as a button face. Slender and pretty with her usual big, thick braid of oak-colored hair flying behind her, Clarissa was a wild blur as she rushed over to me, a shriek of excitement shooting from her mouth.

"Holy *crap!*" Those were the only words I managed to get out before Clarissa threw her arms around me, squeezing so tightly I thought my eyes may pop out of my head.

"Oh, my freaking *God*, it's so good to see you!"

Her enthusiasm was infectious. We screamed and hugged, and I felt the sting of a few tears in my eyes.

"It's so good to see you too!" Under normal circumstances, I would've been thrilled to see my best friend in person rather than on Facetime like we were used to. But with everything that had happened recently, I was even more in need of my supportive friend.

We squeezed each other one last time before letting go and stepping back. I gave Clarissa a once-over. She was just as pretty as ever, her braid back in its usual spot draped over her right shoulder. Clarissa had always been more of the free-spirited type, and her style reflected it. She wore jeans and an oversized cardigan, a pair of pink sneakers on her feet. Even though I couldn't see them myself, her arms were decorated with eclectic tattoos – lots of them new since I'd seen her last, at least that was what I was told

Her expression quickly turned grim.

"Um, I'm sorry about what happened."

I shook my head, not wanting to get into it just yet.

"Thanks. But part of the reason I'm here is so I don't have to think about it."

I nodded toward the dock, the other passengers on the ferry greeting friends and family. Together, Clarissa and I got moving.

"I know, I know," she said. "And we can talk about all that as much or as little as you want. I mean, you've probably done enough thinking about it already. But I still want to put it out there that Adam is a total prick, and I hope he gets hit by a bus." She cocked her head to the side and made a cute little smile.

I laughed in spite of myself. "I appreciate the sentiment, gruesome as it might be."

We headed down the dock, the sea air in my lungs invigorating me more and more by the second. After two years of living in Chicago, it was almost as if I'd forgotten what fresh air actually smelled and tasted like. Sure, I did kinda already miss the hustle and bustle of my block in Wicker Park, but I was happy to be back home.

"OK!" she said, clasping her hands together. "You're back. And you're here for as long as you want, right?"

"Not exactly. I mean, I did tell my manager at the advertising agency that I'd be working remotely for the time being. She didn't seem too bothered – said I could do it for as long as I wanted so long as my work stayed satisfactory."

Clarissa sighed and shook her head, a knowing smile on her face. "I swear, you're wasting your talents there. You're an amazing artist and you're creative as hell. You're gifted, Dream! You could do whatever you want. The worst thing I can possibly imagine is you spending the rest of your life doing touch-ups to ads for fast food websites."

I raised a finger, trying to come to my own defense. "Hey, *you* try living in one of the most expensive neighborhoods in the country without a nine-to-five. Not exactly easy."

She shrugged. "Then don't live in one of the most expensive neighborhoods in the country. Cost of living is nice and relatively low here in Charmed Bay – at least as far as California goes - there's a reason I'm able to make ends meet while running Blueprint." Clarissa was referring to Blueprint Coffee, the hip coffeeshop downtown where she'd been working ever since we were in high school, and eventually took over when the owners retired a few years back

Part of me wanted to deny what she'd said, but I really couldn't because she was right. Clarissa had managed to maintain her easy, breezy, boy-chasing lifestyle while never leaving town. Hell, she'd managed to even get her associate degree taking classes part-time at the community college, though she had to live with her parents for a few years. Charmed Bay was a tiny, coastal community in Northern California, far enough away from the higher cost of living areas in San Francisco or Los Angeles.

"Listen," she said. "I know you had all these big ideas about moving out of your hometown to some metropolis and making it big. I get it, I do. But look how it worked out for you."

I formed my mouth into a flat line. "Wow, you really want to just put it all right out there, huh?"

"It's still fresh, I know. But Dream, I can't think of any sign that your life is ready for some serious changes other than your fiancé, sorry, *ex*-fiancé, cheating on you."

My heart tightened at just the thought of it. She didn't even have to say his name; merely the word was enough to bring the horrible emotions that I'd experienced over the course of the last seven years roiling back. Clarissa must've sensed this. She stopped and I did too, followed by her placing her hand on my shoulder and regarding me with an expression of concern.

"Shit, I'm sorry," she said. "I know a big part of the reason you're here is to put all that crap with Adam behind you, not to have me play it back in totally grisly detail."

Adam. The name of the man who'd turned my life upside down for the worse.

"It's fine," I said. I started walking once more, taking her hand from my shoulder. "If anything, it was my fault for letting things go on for that long. Seriously, I can't believe that I almost married a guy who'd been having multiple affairs on the side. Mostly, I can't believe that I was naïve enough not to realize it was happening."

"You weren't naïve, Dream," Clarissa said as she formed up at my side. "You saw the good in him. You've always been like that, and it's one of you best traits."

"It's the trait that ended up biting me in the ass."

"You can't think that way. I mean, you know what they say about hindsight."

"This goes beyond hindsight. The stuff I let him get away with...

like how he always gave me crap whenever I talked to you. Seeing a text on my phone from you was enough to get him pissed off."

"God, what a creep."

"Seriously – he was convinced that you were a bad influence. He thought that because you like to date but not get into anything serious meant that it'd rub off on me."

"Especially since *he* was the one cheating on *you*! Total bullshit!"

"And you know the worst part? When I finally got the nerve to confront him about all the behind my back stuff he'd been up to, he just shrugged and was like, 'Hey babe, sometimes a guy needs a change of pace, you know?' Isn't that the most disgusting thing you've ever heard? I had his phone in my hand, a picture of some nineteen-year-old in nothing but a thong that I'd found in his messages. I showed him and he didn't even care!"

I raised my finger again, leaning into the full-on vent I was about to launch into.

"And it's not like I was snooping through his texts to find this stuff. The jackass hadn't even bothered to turn off the photo previews on his lock screen. All I had to do was press the text and it came up. He didn't have enough respect for me to hide it."

We continued along the dock, passing by the tourists taking pictures with the ocean behind them or coming in and out of the souvenir shops. The scent of fried seafood was in the air, my stomach rumbling in anticipation of all the delicious food of my hometown that I was suddenly craving.

"Even worse than that," I said, really getting into it. "The most hypocritical bullshit of it all, was how he was totally, one hundred percent opposed to not just texts from you, but texts from...well, you know who."

Clarissa's eyes flashed, a wry, knowing smile forming across her face.

"You mean those sexy brothers you've been crushing on since the day you and I were old enough to have crushes?"

"Clarissa!" I hissed, my face going a deep red. "That's not what I was going to say!"

She shrugged, the smile still on her face as we hurried up the wooden steps that led to the parking lot.

"Just because you weren't going to say it doesn't mean it's not true. And you know that I'm right."

I narrowed my eyes, trying to ignore how fast my heart was beating at the mere mention of the Wolf brothers.

"I don't know that you're right," I said, coming to my own defense. "I mean, seriously, they're like brothers to me Hell, they were almost my brothers."

She let out a loud, totally amused laugh at my words. "It's funny how you say they're almost like your brothers like you all came out of the same mom or something. Dream, they were your stepbrothers, by law, for such a short period of time, I don't even think that counts. You guys never lived together like siblings or anything, it totally doesn't count – And you're not blood related, in case you need a reminder. And I didn't want to bring it up, but that's not even the case anymore now that your mom and their dad are done-zo. Their marriage was so short lived, I almost want to believe your mom is part Kardashian."

I sighed, but I also couldn't help but laugh. It was drama on top of drama with my mother and the Wolf brother's dad, not that I was terribly surprised. A couple years back, while I was in Chicago and the brothers were busy with their military careers, our parents decided to get married. I had grown up alongside Duncan, Evan and Jay, we'd been close friends for as long as I could remember, so it made things immensely weird when my mom called me and told me she was marrying their dad, rich and handsome Bradley Wolf. The fact that I'd gone from secretly mooning over the Wolf brothers to being related to them through marriage had been more than weird. Thankfully, as Clarissa had said, the marriage had been short-lived, not even making it to the one-year mark, so we never had to spend any family holidays pretending to be, well, family.

Now the Wolf brothers were back to being just some guys in

town, and I was still in the process of wrapping my head around it all.

"It's the last thing I want to think about right now," I said. It was a lie, and I knew it the second the words came out of my mouth. After all, fantasies about the Wolf brothers had been a common theme when I'd have some fun with myself under the covers with my vibrator of choice.

"OK, OK," she said. "I know this is all weird for you – I won't make it more so. But the fact of the matter is that they're all back from the Army and are here in town."

I shook my head, quickly correcting her. "Only Duncan was in the Army – Green Berets, to be specific. Jay and Evan were both Navy SEALS."

Clarissa laughed. "Wow, you writing their Wikipedia entries or something?" She grinned and gave me a playful shove. I smiled too but was a little embarrassed to have been so on-the-spot with the right info. It didn't exactly make the case that I hadn't spent more than a little time thinking about them over the years.

"Well, they're all back now. I've seen them around town and..." She closed her eyes and made the face someone might make after taking a bite of the best steak they'd ever had. "Mmm-*mmm*! They're looking good as ever."

I just shook my head and chuckled. She nodded toward her car, an off-white Volkswagen Beetle, the back covered in bumper stickers for local bands and various progressive political causes.

I couldn't help but laugh at the sight of it, how much it reminded me of driving around with her after school back in those days when we didn't have a care in the world.

"You're still driving Sue Ellen?" I asked, coming to a stop next to the car and letting the bag I was carrying drop to the ground.

"Of course!" she said. Clarissa leaned her butt on the hood then hopped onto it, smiling broadly and spreading out her arms as if she were posing for a pinup picture. "You think I'd ever give the old girl up?"

I laughed at the sight as she slid off the hood and came over to me, scooping my bag off the ground as she went around to the back of Sue Ellen and opened the trunk. After tossing the bag in and shutting the lid, she turned her attention back to me.

"You're traveling light for someone who just moved home," she said as we climbed into the car.

Clarissa turned on the engine, *Dreams* by Fleetwood Mac blasting from the speakers for a moment before she quickly turned the volume down.

"Everything else is getting shipped," I said. I sighed as Clarissa pulled out of the parking space and started out of the lot. "Not like I've got much to my name. God, I can't believe I'm starting over like this."

She put her hand on my shoulder and gave me a squeeze.

"I know this isn't the direction you planned on your life going. But look!" She swept her hand in front of her, to the town of Charmed Bay spread out before us. As we reached the top of the bluff, we could see the whole place, the crisscross of streets, the parks, the big, cliffside mansions overlooking the sea. "You're back home, you're going to be staying with your best friend, and you don't have a thing to worry about."

"Aside from figuring out what I want to do with my life. Oh, and not to mention dealing with my mom."

Clarissa swept her hand through the air, dismissing it all as if I hadn't said a thing worth giving a second thought to.

"You'll get it all sorted out in time. But for now, all you need to think about is relaxing, breathing in the fresh ocean air, and getting ready for the holidays." She moved around and snapped her fingers as if dancing to an invisible beat.

"Ugh, the holidays, with everything going on, I completely forgot about them," I moaned.

"But you always loved Christmas," Clarissa said.

"I did, yes, but that was before my life imploded." Still, I forced a small smile onto my lips, not sure of it all. Without thinking, I slipped my phone out of my pocket and checked the group text that I had with the Wolf brothers. The four of us didn't talk every day or anything like that, but we'd had the chat going for a few years now. I scrolled up, the most recent messages all about me coming back to town, the ones above that all inside jokes and emojis.

"So, here's what I'm thinking." She pulled onto the small road that led to her cliffside apartment complex. "First, we get in and settled and have a little something to drink. You tell me all about Adam, get it all off your chest. And then, when you're ready, we head into town and grab some burgers and custard from Red Kettle Diner."

That brought a smile to my face. The Red Kettle Diner, famous all up and down the coast for their triple-smash burgers and frozen custard, had been one of our favorite places to hang during high school.

"Then, after that, we do whatever we want! Correction – *you* do whatever *you* want."

She pulled in front of the four-unit apartment complex that she'd called home for the last few years, turning off the engine.

"Because right now, you're here to start a new chapter in your life. And it's going to be the best one yet."

With one more toothy smile, she threw open the door. Salty sea air rushed into the car, and I didn't waste any time getting out. Clarissa hurried around Sue Ellen and opened the trunk, taking out my bag and hurrying over to her front door.

As she did, I leaned back against the side of the car and looked out onto the ocean, the view from the edge of the cliff spectacular. The beach was down a few hundred feet below, the Pacific Ocean stretching out into infinity.

Clarissa was right about one thing – my life sure as hell wasn't where I'd planned it to be. However, in spite of it all, in spite of the uncertainty, I couldn't help but feel hopeful. Excited, even.

The feeling got even more intense as I found myself thinking of a certain three brothers. I smiled as I gazed out onto the ocean.

The holidays were going to be very interesting.

CHAPTER 2

DUNCAN

The steak hissed as I flipped it over on the grill, juices dripping down and falling into the flames below. My stomach was growling like freaking crazy. I'd put in a hard hour at the gym, and some steak and beer sounded like heaven on earth.

I placed the can of Bud that I'd been sipping against my forehead, the cool, wetness of the can nice as hell in contrast to the heat coming off the grill. I was grateful for the warmer than usual winter this year, not that Charmed Bay ever got that cold to begin with. But it was milder than usual, which meant being able to grill outside.

"Yo, Dunc!"

I glanced up to see my younger brother Evan. He was lounging in one of the chairs in the backyard of my place, some Arctic Monkeys blasting from the Bluetooth speaker on the table.

"Dude, I've been telling you for ten years not to call me that stupid nickname."

Evan, who stood 6'1, his hair a shaggy, sandy-blonde and his eyes the same green as our mom, flashed me the same, broad, goofy grin he always did when he was screwing around. He had his hands weaved together behind his head, the big Navy SEAL tattoo on his right pec on full display as he relaxed.

"But it always gets your attention, doesn't it?" he teased.

"You know, there's different kinds of attention. And the kind you're getting from me now is the kind that's going to end up with me dragging your sorry butt off that chair and tossing you into the pool."

He let out his usual loud laugh, bounding out of the chair and coming over to me, beer in hand.

Evan was the goofball out of the three of us, always cracking jokes and pulling pranks. He was lively and energetic to the point that most people had a hard time believing that he'd been in the service. But he had – and he had the medals to prove he'd been a hell of a SEAL.

"You're a big talk, Dunc," he said, spreading his arms and acting like he was about to grab me off my feet. "But let's see if you've got the actual moves to pull it off."

I smirked, moving out of the way as he rushed toward me.

"You want your steak burned, dude?" I asked. "Because this is how you get your steak burned."

Another laugh sounded from him as he craned his neck to look over my shoulders and check out the progress.

"Looking good, looking good. That one's mine, right?" he stuck out his finger toward the largest.

I snapped the tongs at his finger. "Be careful, or I might barbeque your ass next."

He grinned, tossing his empty beer can into the trash near the grill before fishing a fresh one out of the cooler.

"Hey, you guys want to keep it down?" The voice belonged to Jay, the youngest of us three. He was on one of the other lounge chairs near my heated backyard pool, his eyes hidden behind his mirrored aviators.

Jay had dark hair and dark eyes, and like Evan and me, he was tall, broad-shouldered, and built. On top of that, he was what the girls in high school referred to as brooding. Which to me was a funny way to say, "prickly as a porcupine." The girls seemed to love it, climbing over one another for a chance to be the one to tame him, or whatever crazy plans they'd had in mind.

He also had a mouth on him and was always getting into trouble with teachers or local cops.

The guy was as smart as they came, though, getting grades that always managed to blow Evan and mine out of the water – and ours were nothing to sneeze at. He could've gone off to any Ivy League school he'd wanted, but he'd enlisted like Evan and me, him going into the Navy with Evan. A good thing, too. With the amount of trouble he was known for getting into back in high school, part of me had been certain he'd need the sort of straightening out that only some time in jail could provide.

"Oh, sorry," Evan said, affecting a playfully sarcastic tone to his voice. "If you want, we could move this barbeque to the library. Might be a little quieter there."

"Funny," Jay replied. "Real cute."

He lifted his glasses to show his narrowed eyes before letting them drop back down onto the bridge of his nose. Jay was usually up in his own head, lost in his thoughts, but there was something different about him that afternoon, something more on his mind.

I had a feeling what it was.

I finished up the steaks, plopping them onto the red plastic plates I'd brought out.

"*Finally*," Evan said. "I'll grab the other stuff from inside – should be ready by now."

I carried the plates over to the small table by the pool, setting them down and moving aside the book on military history - this one about the Napoleonic wars - to give us a little more room. Evan hurried into my house, the place ranch-style like most of the other homes on the cliffside. Moments later he returned with a couple bags of chips and a tray of steaming food.

"Hell yeah!" he said as he set down the tray. "There's got to be like, ten pounds of cheese on his mac."

The tray was filled with delicious, gooey-looking mac and cheese that was a diet killer, but one we partook in on occasion. The top was dusted with breadcrumbs, and my stomach rumbled at the sight of it.

Jay sat down in one of the chairs, taking in the sight of the mac and cheese.

"That's all you guys," he said. "One bite of that is another quarter mile I need to tack onto my daily run."

Evan scoffed, already shoving his serving spoon into the mac and scooping out a big portion, the orange and whites of all the different kinds of cheese dripping and stringy.

"More for me," Evan crooned as he plopped the mac onto his plate. "Want some chips?" He pushed a bag of kettle chips toward Jay.

"I'll pass. Steak's fine for me."

Evan shook his head. "Check out Mr. Discipline over here. What's the point of working out every day if you're not going to cut loose every now and then?"

I said nothing, my eyes fixed on the mac and cheese. Evan and Jay set to work on their meals, Jay cutting into his steak and popping the bite of still bloody meat into his mouth.

"Uh, you alright over there, Dunc?" Evan asked. He waved his big hand in front of my face. "Macs for eating, not staring at."

I shook my head, coming back to the moment.

"This is weird."

Evan and Jay both cocked their heads in confusion as I said the words.

"What's weird?" Jay asked.

"The breadcrumbs?" Evan guessed. "I mean, it's not the health-iest thing to eat, but it tastes pretty damn good. You know, gives it some texture." He followed this up by shoveling a massive forkful of the food into his mouth. "Oh *man*." He rolled his eyes into the back of his head as he chewed. "So freaking good."

"Not the breadcrumbs, dude," I said. "This." I swept my hand toward the mac and cheese. "The fact that this was Trish's recipe. I mean, she was kind of a snobby pain in the ass, but she could make a mean mac and cheese. I just never would have expected she'd be a decent cook. Always preferred someone else do it for her."

Evan swallowed down another enormous bite of mac and cheese. "Yeah. And Dad had to go and fuck it up by cheating on her. Not even married for a year."

"The only thing surprising about that," Jay replied, "is how you honestly think relationships last longer than it takes for one person to get bored of the other."

In addition to being rough around the edges, Jay had what you might call a cynical outlook on love. Namely, that he didn't think it was real. He and Evan and I had all gone through our fair share of women over the years, breaking a few hearts here and there. Jay's MO had always been to end things when the woman "caught feelings," as he liked to describe his take on love and romance.

"Just the way Dad's always been," I said. "Straight-shooting man, works hard, always goes to church, talks on and on about the importance of doing the right thing. And then he cheats on his wife with some twenty-three-year-old he met off a dating app? What the hell was he thinking?"

Another smirk from Jay. "Kind of cute that you think the image dad created for himself is anything close to what he's really like."."

I reached over and gave him a shove. Jay only chuckled in response.

"And you guys know about Dream, right?"

Jay stopped eating, and so did Evan. Just the mention of her was enough to put us at attention.

"She's back in town, you guys know," Evan announced, a broad grin on his face.

"Of course, we know," Jay replied. "We're all in the same group text with her, remember?"

"Yeah, yeah," Evan said. "But I want to know why. Not like we pry into each other's personal lives, but she got kind of weird when I asked her about the reason why she was moving back."

"Something with Adam," I said. "And I'm guessing whatever it was, it wasn't pretty."

Jay shook his head, taking off his sunglasses and showing off the flash of anger in his eyes.

"If he did something to hurt her…" he trailed off. "I don't even want to say what's on my mind. Never liked that prick. Not a surprise that he'd do something shitty to one of the few good people in this world."

My brothers and I, we all had a relationship with Dream that could best be described as complicated. We'd known her since we were kids, the four of us consistently being in one another's lives in one way or another. Hell, we were even there for her when she lost her dad in a car accident when she was ten. After that happened, the guys and I made a silent pact with one another to look out for her, make sure we did whatever we could to keep the scary parts of life far away from her.

Puberty hadn't been kind to Dream. She'd gone from cute kid to gawky teenager, complete with braces and gangly limbs and glasses as thick as a pane of glass. She'd still been pretty in her own way, of course, but she wasn't exactly the belle of the ball in high school.

That all changed, however, around the time that Dream hit seventeen. She had her braces removed, switched to contacts, and her long, gawky body filled out in all the right places. In short, she'd become a knockout. My brothers and I did our best to not notice what was happening in our own home, but it was damn near impossible. Dream had always been like a kid sister to us, but it took us all by surprise when our dad married her mom. They just eloped one day, didn't invite us since we were all away in the military. It made things weird with Dream for a bit, so in a way, I was relieved that the marriage failed - even if I had been hopeful for both her mom and my dad finally finding love. anyway.

Long before our parents got married, we were fiercely protective of Dream. Not a guy in school dared go near Dream for fear of getting on our bad sides. And sure, it hadn't hurt that we'd all made sure word got out that we'd take care of any guy who did her wrong. Hell, it didn't even matter that I'd already graduated when she was a freshman. Our intentions might've been good, but it didn't work out so well for Dream – not a single guy had wanted to risk asking her out.

No surprise that Adam Myles, shifty little shit that he was, would wait until the three of us had been deployed on the other side of the globe before he made his move. Even less of a surprise that he'd fucked it all up.

"Yeah," Evan said. "Dude better stay in Chicago if he knows what's good for him."

I raised my palms, trying to bring some calm to the situation. Between Jay's angry nature and Evan's wild side, I often found myself playing the cool head.

"Easy, now," I said. "We don't know what happened between those two. Let's see Dream and find out if she even wants to talk about it before putting a bounty on Adam's head."

Jay's jaw worked as he kept his mouth shut. I could sense that, while he planned to listen to me, he was already thinking about what he'd do once he got his hands on Adam.

"Fine, fine," Evan agreed. His worried expression vanished, replaced by his usual happy-go-lucky smile. Great thing about Evan was that he never stayed preoccupied for long. "We definitely need to make plans to see her, you know? It's been how long? Years?"

"Yeah, way too long," I said, leaning back and putting my feet up on the table. "Be nice to catch up with her."

"Heard that her friend, Clarissa, is doing a big Christmas thing," Jay said. "Hopefully she sticks around in town long enough to go."

I nodded, sipping my beer.

"Might be weird," I muttered. "After all these years and what happened between our folks."

They both nodded – I didn't need to say another word.

"The perils of living in a small town," Jay proclaimed. "Everyone knows everyone or has dated each other or some other kind of thing."

Evan regarded me with expectant eyes, slight concern on his face.

"Yo, Dunc...you gonna eat that steak?"

I let out a snort of a laugh as I realized I hadn't taken a bite since we'd sat down.

"Hands off, bud – this one's all mine."

I sliced into the steak, my mind going right back to Dream as a red pool formed on my plate. I stabbed the meat, bringing it to my mouth and chewing.

Dream. How many times had I thought of her over the years, thought of what it'd be like to get her into bed with me? It'd been so wrong to think about – she was like a sister to me.

But we were adults now, and our parents weren't together anymore. Maybe it wasn't so taboo after all.

CHAPTER 3

JAY

I was thinking about her again. How the hell could I not? Dream was back in my life, and there wasn't a doubt in my mind that she was as beautiful as ever. Hell, a quick check of her Facebook was enough to confirm that.

"Earth to Jay!"

Evan waving his hand in front of my face was enough to derail my train of thought. Probably for the best – last thing I needed was to let my mind linger on thoughts of Dream.

"What?" I asked, the word coming out in a slight snarl. It wasn't anything personal – not like I was mad at Evan. That's just how I talked sometimes. Probably one of the reasons I'd had the reputation in town of being "prickly," as Duncan liked to say.

I was in the hot tub, my arms draped over the side as I watched the sun set over the western horizon. I'd always loved nature - preferred it to people most of the time, to be honest. The sunsets of Charmed Bay never failed to impress.

Nothing like your brother's giant hand in front of your face to spoil the moment, however.

"Need to ask you a favor." A slightly sheepish grin was on his face.

"Let me guess – you had a few too many and now you need a ride home?"

He laughed. "That's it. I've only had three, but I don't want to risk it, you know?"

"Sure, sure."

With that, Evan gave me a thumbs up. I glanced over my shoulder, spotting Duncan seated at the table, his left hand holding a beer on top of his propped-up knee and his right resting on the book he was reading. The Bluetooth was still playing music, some early Led Zeppelin drifting out of the speakers.

The evening together was typical for the three of us. We were all different in our own way, but that didn't mean we didn't love spending time with one another. Since it wasn't often that we were all in the same place, what with our crazy schedules in the service, we were all determined to enjoy one another's company now that we could Losing our mom all those years back had taught us that you can never take family for granted.

I watched the sun dip lower and lower into the Pacific, the sky turning a deep, twinkling purple above.

"Yo!" I said, calling over my shoulder at Duncan. "Thinking it's time to peace out. I want to get an early night's sleep in and hit the gym tomorrow."

Duncan checked the time on his phone. "Not a bad idea. Might go with you, unless you were thinking of doing a solo thing."

I shook my head. "Nope. Thinking seven."

"Works for me," he said. "Someone's got to make sure you're not slacking."

He flashed me a grin and I let out a laugh, splashing a little water in his direction. It'd always been wild to me how much Duncan looked like our old man. He was tall, with dark, close-cropped hair, and a serious face. But unlike the old man, he was as gregarious as they came. Everyone in town knew the Wolf brothers, but everyone especially knew Duncan. He'd always been one of those guys who always made things happen, was always setting up social events and connecting people to one another. He was a nice balance to a guy like me, who preferred to keep to himself.

"I'm coming too!" Evan chimed in as he stood on the edge of the deep end of the pool, preparing for a jump.

Without waiting for a response, Evan jumped into the water, curling his huge body into a cannonball right before hitting the surface. The guy landed like a boulder, water splashing all over the backyard. He bobbed his head up from under, the usual big grin on his face.

Evan and I helped Duncan clean up, the three of us finalizing our plans to meet at the gym in the morning. Once that was taken care of, Evan and I headed out for the night, both of us giving Duncan a hug before he shut the front door behind us. Evan's car, a bright red Jeep, was parked in his driveway. My black BMW convertible was on the street. Moments after saying our goodbyes to our big brother for the night, we were on our way.

I drove through the winding roads of Duncan's neighborhood. The area was a mix of small, ranch-style homes like Duncan's and huge mansions – one of which was our childhood home, and where our dad still lived. Evan's place was downtown, close to the bars and all the rest of the action. My own pad was nearer inland, by the local parks where I loved to go for runs, or just to get away from it all.

"Man!" Evan said as he rolled down the window and stuck his arm out. "That was fun! Nothing like throwing back some beers with your bros, right?" He flashed me another huge smile. Evan and I... well, we didn't have the same energy level. But in spite of my closer to the chest way of doing things, his friendliness and enthusiasm was still pretty damn infectious.

"Yeah," I said with a nod. "It was a nice night."

Evan nodded in response, then pursed his lips. I could tell there was something on his mind.

Just because he was more fun loving than most people didn't take away the fact that he was smart as a whip. The three of us had all scored in the ninety-fifth percentile on the ASVAB, which meant that the military had all but rolled out the red carpet for whatever positions we'd wanted.

So, he was always thinking. That moment was no exception.

"You know what I've got on my mind?"

"What's that?" I asked.

"Well, more like who I've got on my mind."

"Dream."

The word came out of my mouth without any thinking involved. Truth be told, she'd been on my mind, too, ever since I'd found out that she was coming back to town.

He grinned at my response. "So, you're thinking about her too, huh?" He ran his hand through his shaggy hair. "God, I don't know what it is about her. But I can't get her out of my head."

"I've got a suggestion – it's because she's hot as hell."

Evan chuckled. "I know. I mean, shit, how could anyone not notice that about her right away? But it's not just that. There's something more to her, something special. It's something that I don't know how to describe, exactly."

"Yeah, I know what you mean." Silence fell over the car, as if both of us were trying to puzzle out that certain something about her.

"It's like...it's like it's hard to be around her, like everything she does pushes me over the edge," he said, breaking the silence. "I know it's been years since we saw her, butI can't think straight when I'm near her."

I left Duncan's subdivision, driving toward downtown. The streets became more crowded on both sides of us, lined with apartments and businesses, and plenty of people out for an evening stroll in the warmer-than-usual weather.

"Well, you're going to have to get used to that," I said. "Because she's going to be back in town for a while – and so are we."

"It might be temporary with her, right?" he asked. "Might just be that she and Adam are having some relationship drama and they need some space apart."

I shifted in my seat, gripping the wheel tightly at the mention of Adam. Just like the mere mention of Dream's name made my heart beat faster and my cock twitch to attention, hearing Adam's name was enough to send a pulse of hot anger through my body. The guy had always been a prick, nowhere near good enough for Dream. To hear that he might've done her wrong...

I pushed it all out of my head. Focusing on that would be a sure-fire way to get me to drive like a maniac.

"Could be," I said. "Either way, I'm guessing she's going to be here for Christmas, at least. That means you're going to have to get used to her being around, for a little while anyway."

He smiled. "I'm looking forward to it. Do you think she actually thinks of us as family

? You know, since our parents were, well, you know."

"I don't know. Technically she's not related to us anymore. It was all a legal thing, and not like we were raised together or anything. I doubt she ever thought of us as her brothers. Did you think of her as a sister? I mean, not just in a protective 'little sister' way either, but like a real sister?."

"Not really." He shrugged.

"So I don't see what the big deal is. Nothing has changed between us. Dream is the same to us as she always was."." As soon as I said the words it occurred to me that it would be damn near impossible to think of Dream like anyone else. She was too special for that.

He ran his hand through his hair again. "I still think it's a bit screwed up. Here I am, here *we* are, talking about her like she's just any other woman. But she's not. It's Dream - the girl we swore to protect growing up, and it feels wrong wanting to date her. But damn, she sure knows how to push me over the edge. And you know the worst part?"

"What's that?"

"She's not even trying! All she has to do is show up and be herself and it's enough to make me go insane. God, imagine if she actually tried to seduce me!"

I chuckled, trying to keep my thoughts off how I felt the same way. Wasn't sure why, but I felt the urge to hold my tongue. What was I supposed to say, that I wanted her too? The situation was strange enough already.

Evan went on. "But none of that matters, right? If she's back in town and dealing with all sorts of bullshit courtesy of Adam, doing anything with other guys is probably the last thing on her mind. Especially if that other guy happened to be one of us."

We reached downtown, the tight grid of roads flanked with dozens of businesses and brick apartments. There were parks and fountains and everything else a quaint small town needed. It wasn't long before I was in front of Evan's pad. He lived on the top floor of a mixed-use building, the bottom floor occupied by Red's, a bar we frequented. It was still pretty early, but Red's was already hopping with clientele – likely upperclassmen from the local college.

"Maybe it's not so crazy," he said, speaking as if thinking aloud. "Like you said, our dad and her mom are done. We might have a special bond, but we're not actually family. What'd be so bad about going after her?"

I couldn't hold back any longer. I smirked, then spoke.

"If that's the case," I said. "You're not going to be the only one to want her."

Evan turned to me and cocked his head, as if he wasn't sure he'd heard me right. Then he laughed.

"Thanks for the ride, bro. You know, I think I'm gonna grab one more at Red's. You down?"

"Nah – driving, remember?"

"Oh yeah. And thanks again, by the way. See you tomorrow morning, bright and early – right?"

"Yeah, bright and early."

He reached over and gave me a friendly swat on the back before bounding out of the car and heading into Red's. Through the window, I watched as he spotted people he knew at one of the tables, greeting them with a big smile and throwing his arms out as if he wanted to pull them all into a bear hug.

I put the car into gear and pulled back onto the road. As I drove home, I knew one thing for sure – I couldn't wait to see Dream Stokes again.

CHAPTER 4

DREAM

I opened my eyes that next morning to warm sunlight pouring in through the bay windows in Clarissa's apartment, the soft hush of the water down on the shore as the sound drifted up along the cliff-side, and the plaintive cry of seagulls as they glided over the ocean. I took in the sight of Clarissa's place - the décor full of plants and art as quirky as she was.

I woke up to all of that – plus the blaring alarm I'd set on my phone.

"*Nooo,*" Clarissa moaned. "Turn it *ooofff.*"

My hand shot out to where my phone rested on the coffee table. With a quick press, the alarm was silenced. I sat up on the couch where I'd slept, Clarissa curled up on the nearby loveseat. Last night we'd stayed up late, watching some gory 80's horror movies while eating our burgers and ice cream, with a little bit of wine here and there. I wasn't hungover at all - didn't drink nearly enough for that - but my body still cried out for more rest after my cross-country trip.

But no rest for the weary, as they say. I had to be up bright and early that morning.

"Hey, you're the one who wanted to sleep on the couch knowing I had to be up at the butt crack of dawn."

Clarissa sat up and rolled her shoulders, her blanket still wrapped around her.

"Why'd you have to be up so early anyway?" she asked. "Don't tell me your job's making you check in at normal office hours or something."

The couch cried out to me, practically begging me to curl back up onto it and steal a few more hours of sleep. That, however, was most definitely not in the cards. So, I threw off the blanket and put my feet on the shag rug underfoot.

"Nope. It's my mom, remember? She wanted me to come over for breakfast."

Clarissa tilted head her back and let out an *ahh* of remembering. "That's right." She opened her mouth to say something. Before she could get a word out, something on her phone caught her eye. She grabbed it and read something on the screen, her eyes flashing with surprise.

"What's up?" I asked.

"Noah, my opener at work just texted me, said he's feeling sick and doesn't know if he can make it through his shift." The way she said the words 'feeling sick' made it sound as if she didn't entirely believe him. Her thumbs went to work, typing out her response. "He's lucky I wasn't sleeping in on the one day I scheduled off for myself this week." Once the text was sent, she set down her phone and got up. "Looks like we're both making an early morning of it. Go on and get dressed – I'll get some coffee going for you."

"Thanks so much."

She grinned. "That's what roommates are for, right?" The smile broadened after she spoke the words. "Roommates. God, I can't believe we're only just now living together. We could've done it right out of high school, but *someone* had to go off to Washington State for her graphic design degree." She playfully wagged her finger at me as she hopped off the couch and went over to the kitchen to start some hot water for the coffee.

"Well, consider this making up for lost time," I said with a smile, realizing how lucky I was to have a friend who'd put me up like that.

Clarissa opened her cupboard, revealing shelf after shelf of coffee bags from work. She took one down and began scooping some into a French press.

"Speaking of which," she went on. "I know you were all jazzed up about getting your own place, but if you wanted to live together long-term, there's tons of amazing apartments right by the beach. And not just *kind of* on the beach like this place, but actually *on the beach*. I can pull some places up on my laptop for you to look at when you get back..."

As she went on, my phone lit up with a text from my mom.

Hope you're up and on your way over. Hate to think you'd sleep in for our breakfast.

I let out a grunt of annoyance.

"What?" Clarissa asked.

"Nothing. Just the standard checking up on me text from my mom. I don't know why, but her texts always come across like she thinks I'm an irresponsible idiot."

Clarissa bounded over and read the text over my shoulder. "It's because she puts periods at the end of all her sentences. It's a boomer thing – they don't know how serious it sounds."

I laughed, setting my phone down. "That could be it. But also, the way she's always staying on top of me, making sure I'm on task."

"Could be because she knows you've been through some serious stuff. I know your mom can be a little...icy. But I don't have any doubt that she loves you like crazy. She's just got her own way of showing it."

A sunny answer like that was classic Clarissa.

"Anyway, I'll do your coffee to go. And before you ask, *yes*, you can borrow my car."

"Wait, how are you going to get to work?"

She smiled over her shoulder as she made her way back into the kitchen.

"We live in California, remember? It's pretty nice out today – I'll ride my bike into town."

"You're such a sweetheart. I'll get a car before too long. You forget that in most of the country outside of three big cities you actually need one to get around."

"All in good time, my dear – just like everything else that you're worried about. Now, get up and get ready! You don't want to keep Mom waiting."

I laughed as I pushed myself off the couch and hurried into the bathroom to wash up and get ready for the day. After throwing on a pair of jeans and a nice top, I stepped into some white low top Chuck Taylor's just in time for Clarissa to hand me her car keys and a coffee thermos.

"Good luck with Mom," she said. "Try not to let her get under your skin, you know?"

We said our goodbyes, making some tentative plans for lunch downtown after she got back from work.

Moments later I was behind the wheel of Sue Ellen, my gut tightening in anticipation of seeing my mom in person for the first time since, not only what had happened with Adam, but the drama between her and Brad. We were both in the wreckage of relationships that hadn't worked out, and I had no idea what things would be like when I saw her.

My relationship with my mother was strained to begin with. She and Dad had been a perfect balance. He was warm and good-natured and a little goofy, whereas Mom was a little more clearheaded and practical. But with Dad gone, it seemed to me like Mom had let the bad traits take over. Clear-headed and practical had given way to cynical and materialistic. And on top of that, losing her husband had only made her more dead set on me finding a man, despite my having other priorities in life beyond getting an expensive rock placed onto my finger.

And even after I'd gotten engaged, she hadn't let up. It was like she'd been nervous about my ability to "seal the deal," to become Mrs. Adam Myles. So, me breaking off the engagement and coming home as single as I'd been when I'd moved to Chicago, left doubt it wasn't going to go over well.

As I pulled into the ritzy, beachfront neighborhood where Mom lived, I knew I needed to just rip the Band-Aid off and get it over with. The huge villas of the expensive area loomed over me on both sides, the luxury cars in the driveway a stark contrast to the paint worn Bug I was driving. But I still preferred Sue Ellen to any dumb BMW. I was happy with my life, happy that I had my independence. If Mom couldn't see that, well, then it was on her.

My little pep talk worked. At least, until I pulled into the half circle driveway in front of her huge house. As my eyes tracked up and down the three-story home, sleek and modern with glass walls that made it look like something out of LA, I couldn't get over how *good* she was living. Sure, she'd had a pretty big payout from Dad's insurance policy that she'd made some smart investments with, but the home I was looking at was far more than what that should've afforded.

I killed the engine and stepped out of the car. The beach was close enough that the crash of the waves on the shore was a low roar, and the smell of sea water was thick in the air. I stepped up to the front doors and prepared to knock. But as I raised my fist, a familiar voice piped in.

"There you are, Dreamy." It was Mom, her voice coming in through a speaker somewhere. I looked around and the only thing I could find that might've been the source was a small electronic device on the wall to my left, a blue ring in the middle.

"Uh, Mom?"

"I can see you through the camera. Come on in, the doors open."

"Good. Because I'm getting some major 2001 vibes talking to you through this thing."

Mom said nothing in response to my dorky joke, the blue light turning off.

I opened the door and stepped inside, the interior of her palace of a home just as impressive as the outside. The space was expansive, with lots of whites and light grays dominating the décor. Many of the glass floor-to-ceiling walls were open, sea air flowing through the home.

It was nice – I had to admit. I'd never much gone for fancy homes and all that, but Mom sure knew how to treat herself.

"In here, Dreamy."

I followed her voice through the house, eventually stepping into a gigantic, open kitchen. The room was decked out with top-of-the-line appliances, copper pots hanging over the island in the middle. The windows looked out onto the beach, and the kitchen bar was topped with fresh fruit and bagels and tons of other good stuff.

Seated at the kitchen bar was my mom, Trish.

"There's my little one."

She set down the tablet she'd been looking at and stood. Mom looked great for her age – not that being in your mid-fifties was old, of course. She had a slender, toned body and was dressed in her usual Lululemon leggings and matching top, both a bright pink, with Nikes on her feet. Expensive jewelry glittered in the sun as she stood up. She had the same blonde hair as me, though hers was in immaculate beach waves instead of my simple ponytail. Her hazel eyes were the exact same shade as mine. One look at the two of us together left no doubt that we were related.

She strolled over to me, a clean-smelling perfume wafting behind her. Mom wrapped her arms around me, pulling me close against her. It was all very standard mom – a warm, slightly over-the-top greeting that I knew would be followed by a barrage of pointed questions.

"Hey, Mom. I like the pla—"

I didn't get a chance to finish before her hazel eyes flashed, as if she'd just realized something.

"I had this amazing spread delivered from downtown and I

completely forgot the coffee. Hold on." She craned her head and called out. "Analyn? Come in, would you please?"

In an instant, a trim but muscular, pretty woman in her thirties appeared, her skin and hair both dark.

"Yes, Miss Trisha?"

"Would you mind making a pair of coffees for me and my daughter? A bit of cream for both."

"Of course." She smiled and prepared to turn.

"I'm Dream, by the way," I introduced myself.

"Nice to meet you, Miss Dream," she said.

I smiled right back at her. "Just Dream is fine. And you know what? I think I can make my own coffee."

Mom's eyes flashed. "No, you won't. Analyn, please go ahead and prepare them."

Another nod and Analyn hurried over to an expensive looking espresso machine and went to work with quick hands.

"Mom, you hired a maid?"

Mom scoffed as she led me over to the kitchen bar to sit down. "We prefer the term housekeeper. Believe me, I didn't plan on it. But Amber down the road and I were having lunch and she told me about how she'd hired someone to help out around the house and how much it changed her life. She told me to try it for a few weeks and see how I liked it, and now I can't imagine getting through a day without Analyn's help. Not to mention, I'm sponsoring her Visa from the Philippines. It works out for everyone, you know?"

Analyn hurried over and placed two steaming mugs of coffee on the bar.

"Thank you, Analyn," Mom said. "I'll let you know if we need anything else."

With a silent nod, she turned and was gone.

"Go on," Mom gestured to my cup. "She makes an amazing cup of coffee."

It felt weird to be waited on like that, and it made me want to get to the heart of the matter.

"How the hell can you afford all of this?" I asked. "I don't even want to guess how much it cost."

"Surprisingly less than you might think. The previous buyer was a motivated seller."

"But still," I said. "How?" Right after I said the word, I noticed there was something different about Mom – her lips. They were huge. "Did you get *filler?*"

Mom smiled, then flicked her eyes over to the food. "Eat up. We've got quite a bit to discuss, it seems."

I sighed, my stomach grumbling to remind me that I hadn't had breakfast yet. I went straight for the everything bagels, grabbing one and preparing to smother it with some nearby cream cheese.

"You chose the most carb-loaded thing here," she said. "That sort of habit is going to catch up with you if you're not careful."

I narrowed my eyes, opening my mouth wide and taking a huge bite of the bagel.

"You know," I said after I chewed and swallowed. "Most moms would give it twenty minutes after seeing their daughter for the first time in a year before calling her fat."

"Oh, stop being so dramatic. You're not fat, which is why I want to keep it that way. You're on the market again, remember? Last thing you're going to want is an extra twenty pounds in all the wrong places."

I followed this up with another bite of my bagel.

"*Sooo* good," I said with my mouth full for extra effect. "Nothing like carbs."

Mom flashed me a wry smile. "Cute. But someone's got to look out for your future. Seems to me that you're failing on that front."

"Wait," I asked, setting down my bagel. "What's that supposed to mean?"

Mom lowered her eyes and tilted her head toward me in a "come on, now," expression.

"You know exactly what I'm talking about. You were engaged to a handsome, wealthy young man and you threw it away. Now you're back to square one, living on your friend's couch. Why you're not living with me, I can't understand. There's more than enough room for you here."

"Maybe because Clarissa doesn't chew me out every time I eat a carb."

"In other words, she enables your behavior. Let's see how far that gets you."

I snorted. I'd been in Mom's house for less than twenty minutes and I was already getting pissed.

"What happened?" I asked, wanting to change the subject. "With you and Bradley?"

Mom smiled slightly, as if more amused than anything else.

"It turns out Mr. holier-than-thou had a taste for younger women. I came home to him, believe it or not, in bed with some woman less than half his age. Some LA model he'd bought here." She swept her hand toward the house. "But Bradley was at least prudent enough to know his squeaky-clean reputation would be tanked in this town if all that were to get out. He bought me this house and signed over enough of his investments to make sure I'd be able to live comfortably for the rest of my life."

"And you're the one who wants to tell *me* how to have a happy relationship, huh?"

Mom smiled again. "Happiness has nothing to do with it. You need prudence. That means securing your future, making sure you never want for anything. After how well you did in high school, I had hopes that you'd accomplish this through a good career. Those hopes were dashed when you decided to major in art or whatever."

My blood pressure was rising. "I majored in graphic design because it was my passion, and I was good at it. And I have a good job."

"What, making online advertisements? Good luck cracking high five figures in that line of work."

"Believe it or not, Mom, some people have ambitions other than earning a ton of money. Or, in your case, getting it in a divorce settlement."

Mom flashed another fake grin, clearly not bothered by my words.

"That's fine. You want to live your little starving artist lifestyle, then go for it. But you need a husband who's making some money to bankroll that kind of thing. All you had to do was stick with Adam for long enough to make it legal. You divorce down the road, then fine. But you couldn't even stick it out for that long. Tell me, what was so bad about him that you couldn't marry him?"

Mom didn't know how Adam acted when I'd confronted him. She didn't know the anger I'd seen in his eyes, that pure rage that I'd never seen before. I'd lied to Clarissa, told her that he'd handled it casually, but that had only come later.

First, there had been anger – anger that had made me scared.

"Maybe give him another chance," Mom said, shrugging as if merely tossing the idea out there.

The idea that I would give a man like Adam another chance was the last straw. I burst out of my seat and stuck my finger in her face.

"You left Brad because he cheated on you, right? And you think *I* deserve to be treated the same way?" The cheating was only part of it, but I wasn't about to get into the rest. I was too mad for that.

Mom shrugged again. "Sometimes you have to make sacrifices for the sake of your future."

That was it. I couldn't take it anymore.

I turned and stormed out of the kitchen, ignoring Mom's protests. As soon as I was back behind the wheel of Clarissa's car, tears streamed down my face.

Just like that, the wounds that had only begun to heal were ripped wide open.

CHAPTER 5

EVAN

Thank freaking God I had a workout that morning. The gym was always great for taking my mind off shit.

And I had plenty on my mind.

The three of us were at Jake's Gym, the open-air beachfront place where we'd been working out since we were old enough to do a bench press. It'd been something of a rite of passage for all of us that, when we hit ten, Dad would take us here and show us the ropes.

The old man had some crazy ideas about things, but exercise wasn't one of them. He'd managed to give us all a passion for fitness that had stuck well into our adult lives.

Grunge music played on the speakers; the place alive with dozens of people getting their morning workouts in. Duncan was on the lat pull machine; Jay was doing his preacher curls. I was taking a quick water break when a few gym bunnies in skintight leggings passed me by, all smiling and making it obvious as hell they were into me.

I smiled back, but it was more out of being polite than anything.

Something - some*one* - else was on my mind.

"You alright, dude?" Duncan glanced back at me from where he was seated on the lat press machine.

Duncan was clean-cut, all-American style. He was tall and broad-shouldered, with dark brown hair. He was dressed in a sleeveless shirt, the bald eagle of his Army tattoo stretched across his big bicep.

"Huh?" I was in a daze. I shook my head and came back to the moment.

Duncan nodded in the direction the girls had gone. "Those three were all over you – I could see it in the mirror. I've been out in public with you enough times to know that by this point you'd be trying to get all three of their numbers at the same time."

"Right," Jay agreed with a grin. "All for yourself, and none for us."

"But you look like you're a million miles away, man. What's up?"

A quick glance between Jay and I let me know he had the same thing on his mind, too. We had a silent conversation, both of us trying to figure out if we ought to bring up what we'd been talking about last night.

I decided to do it. My brothers and I never kept secrets from each other, and I wasn't about to start then.

"Want to get some fresh air?" I asked, nodding toward the outdoor part of the gym where the basketball and sand volleyball courts were.

Duncan was confused, his forehead crinkled. "Uh, sure. Let me wipe this thing down and hit the head and I'll meet you out there."

"Sounds good."

I nodded to Jay, who hopped off his preacher curl seat and gave the spot where his butt had been a quick wipe down before joining me on the way outside. Guys were busy playing basketball, six girls in bikinis busy with volleyball.

The girls were total babes, but just like the ones inside, I wasn't interested in them.

There was another woman on my mind who was taking up that part of my brain.

Jay dropped onto the bench next to me, the two of us saying nothing for a time while we people watched.

"You really want to do this now, huh?"

I let out a snort. "You don't? Dude, you're the one who started this whole thing last night on the way back to my place."

Jay raised a dark eyebrow. "You mean after you'd spent the entire ride going on about her?"

I opened my mouth to speak but knew there was no point. The cat was out of the bag.

"Doesn't matter now, does it? She's back in town and you and I both want her. And I'd bet anything that Dunc wants her too."

"Dunc wants who too?" Duncan spoke from behind us. He dropped onto the bench and leaned forward, his dark eyes flicking between Jay and me. "What the hell have you guys been talking about? Or *who*?"

His face flashed with realization. Then he sat back, the three of us turning our attention forward.

"Dream."

We all said the same name at the same time, silence hanging in the air.

Then we started laughing.

"Makes sense we'd all been thinking about her," Duncan said. "I mean, she did just get back in town. But why the hell were you guys being so conspiratorial about it?"

I laughed. "*This* asshole," I gave Jay a playful shove he didn't appreciate, "told me last night when he dropped me off that he was into her."

"You skipped the part where you were going on about her the whole way to your place," Jay responded. "But the how doesn't matter. What does is that all of us are into the same woman."

"That's not the only part that matters," Duncan said. "We're into the same woman who's been off-limits for as long as we've known her, because we were supposed to be looking out for her - not hooking up with her."

"It's weird as hell," I said. "But that makes it kind of hotter, you know? She's forbidden fruit. And I'm ready to take a bite."

Duncan groaned at my words. "So, you guys spent the drive talking about how much you both want Dream."

"Not exactly how it happened," Jay said.

Duncan shook his head. "Man, older brothers really got to do all the thinking for you guys, huh?"

"What're you talking about?" I asked.

"Did you two stop to think *why* she was back in town?"

I scrunched my forehead, trying to figure out what he was getting at.

Then it hit me. I let out an *ohhh* in realization.

"She's here because she just broke up with Adam," Jay said, nodding his head slowly. "Meaning, there's a damn good chance she's not even thinking about getting involved with someone right now."

"Right," Duncan replied. "Here you guys are getting all wrapped up in how much you want to get her into bed. But don't forget she's a person with her own wants."

"And she's as independent as they come," Jay agreed. "One of her best features, really."

But I wasn't about to be discouraged. "Hey, what if she needs something to take her mind off all the bullshit she's just gone through with Adam? You know, come back to town and have a little fun."

Duncan nodded slowly, as if considering the idea. "Maybe. She's the only one who can decide that. But even if she was in the mood for a rebound, there's still the issue of there being three of us and one of her."

"She's a big girl," Jay said. "She can choose who she wants."

"And we're all going to be OK if she picks someone who's not us?" Duncan asked. "You know how competitive we all get. Especially with one another."

I grinned, sitting back and letting an idea play in my mind.

"Oh no," Jay groaned. "Evan's thinking. Never good when this happens."

"Nah, you guys are going to like this one."

"What is it?" Duncan asked.

"Well, here's the deal. We all want Dream. Let's forget about the fact our parents were married - briefly - we've all been wanting her for the last ten years, right? Long before our folks even noticed one another."

"Sure," Jay admitted.

"Then why don't we all have her?"

"You're kidding," Duncan said. "How the hell are we supposed to do that?"

"It's not like we haven't done it before. Remember Emily Davis back from my JROTC camp?"

"When we found out that we were all dating her at the same time?" Duncan asked. "How the hell could I forget?"

"Right!" I exclaimed. "We were all into her, and none of us cared. Emily didn't even care – if anything, she was happy to have the attention from all three of us. We got what we wanted, and she got what she wanted. Everyone was happy."

"But that was a weird, one-off thing," Jay admitted. "Emily was fun, but she was, ah, different. I doubt Dream's anything like her."

"Yeah, but do you know that for sure?" I asked. "It's 2021 – times are different. People are cooler with, uh, unconventional arrangements like that."

Duncan laughed. "Loving how this conversation started out with us talking about how we're all into Dream then ended up with us considering the idea of sharing her. What if she's not into that?"

"Then so what?" Jay asked. "If Dream's down with all three of us, then cool. But if she wants one of us or *none* of us, then c'est la vie, right?"

"Yeah," I agreed. "All I know is that I'll be kicking my own ass if I don't try, even if I have to compete with my own brothers. And wouldn't it be nice if we didn't have to compete with each other?"

Duncan grinned. "Alright, I think this could work. If she wants it. But we'd be cool if she chose just one - or even none - of us too, right?"

I nodded. "Of course. And we won't be too pushy about it, let her have some space, and she can come to us on her own time, and we can just see what happens."

Jay seemed to think it over for a second before saying, "Alright, I'm game. We don't have to compete for her, we'll see who she wants, and we can always share if it comes down to that. After all, Dream is a special woman."

"If it gets you even considering dating someone, then she certainly is," Duncan said with a wink toward Jay.

CHAPTER 6

DREAM

Clarissa and I were having lunch over at Cherry's Tomatoes, a hip little salad joint near Blueprint Coffee. The place was packed with the lunch crowd, mostly students from the college. Over Thai chicken salads, I regaled Clarissa with everything that had happened with Mom during breakfast.

"I don't get it," Clarissa said as she stabbed a piece of Mandarin orange. "Why did she buy the bagels if she was just going to make some comment when you took one?"

I laughed despite how pissed off I was, but the moment quickly passed, and I was right back to being annoyed. "Mom's weird like that. I wouldn't be surprised if she put them there as a test or something. She was always playing weird games with food when I was a kid."

"Well, whatever's going on with her, you don't need to worry about it. You've got a place to stay, and as long as you're crashing on my couch you can eat whatever the hell you want."

Her words brought a smile to my face, making it abundantly clear just how lucky I was to have a friend like Clarissa.

"You know, when I first stepped foot in that huge house part of me was like, 'why don't I take a bedroom here?' Don't get me wrong – I totally appreciate what you're doing for me. But there's going to come a time when you get sick of me crashing on your couch."

"Maybe," she said with a shrug. "But when that happens, I'll have put the pressure on you to get a bigger place with me." Clarissa followed this up with a smile and a cheeky tilt of her head before stabbing a big piece of tofu with her fork.

"Of course, she knew all the buttons to push. She even gave me crap about my art, how she was convinced I'd be a starving artist and I needed a husband to afford the lifestyle *she* thinks I should be living." I let out a grunt of annoyance, resisting the urge to toss my fork onto the ground.

Clarissa didn't say anything in response. Instead, she gave me a curious look, like she was trying to figure something out.

"What?" I asked.

"When *is* the last time you painted? I mean, I only ask because you were freaking awesome back in high school. Seriously – you were, like, the best painter in town."

I blushed hard. I'd never been able to take compliments very well.

"No way. I wasn't even close to being the best painter."

"Well, either way, tons of people thought for sure that you'd be famous off your art. So, you sticking with it?"

I glanced down, shifting in my seat.

"It...Adam..." was all I could say.

"What happened?"

I sighed, glancing away and trying to figure out where to begin.

"Back when he and I started dating, when we came back into each other's lives in Chicago, he loved that I was a painter. At least, that's what he said. I came to find out later that he didn't give a damn at all."

"Oh God. How'd you find out?"

"When I moved into his place, he told me that he'd clear out the storage unit that I'd rented when I'd come to town. He brought all of my stuff over, minus the boxes of my paintings. Turns out he'd thrown them away."

"What?" Her eyes went wide with surprise and anger. "He *threw them out?*"

"That's about how I reacted. His excuse was that he didn't know what was in the boxes, that they looked like nothing. But part of me was sure he'd done it because he'd wanted me to put that part of my life behind me. After all, he was the one who pushed me into getting a job at the design firm."

"What a prick," she said, shaking her head. "Total underhanded crap."

"I tried to stay on top of my art, getting some supplies and setting up a little spot in the apartment where I could practice. But he'd always make some comment about my stuff getting in the way, how much of a mess it was. It was a 'death by a thousand cuts' sort of thing. How was I supposed to relax and get into the zone if I had to hear him scoffing and see him rolling his eyes every five minutes?"

"I tried to find other ways to channel my need to create art. I volunteered at children's hospitals doing face painting, which was a blast. And I even worked at a couple of renaissance fairs doing costume painting."

Clarissa smiled. "That sounds like fun."

"It was. But you'll never guess what happened."

Her smile vanished. "Adam."

"Yep. He never outright forbade me from doing those things, but he'd make his comments. He'd say I was spending too much time on my hobbies, that I wasn't being present in our relationship. He'd say that there was no way I'd be promoted at my job if my head was in all my volunteer work."

Clarissa narrowed her eyes and shook her head. "Total manipulative bullshit. It's classic stuff; I learned about it in the abnormal psych class I took in college. People like him want to separate you from anything that isn't them. They want to be your whole world and get threatened by anything that seems like it might infringe on that."

It all sounded so familiar.

"That's right," I said. "If it were up to Adam, I'd be stuck in the apartment watching TV until it was time to work. Then off to the office and back home to do it all over again. Oh, not to mention sex on demand." Saying the words sent a shiver up my spine. The idea that I'd done anything like that with a man like him was almost unbearable.

Then my mind went to other matters, like the night he screamed at me with rage in his eyes, his fist slamming into the wall so hard he cracked the plaster, his anger so intense that I worried he might cross a line that a man had never crossed with me before...

Clarissa reached over and took my hand. "You don't have to worry about any of that anymore. You made the tough, but right call to leave Adam. The hard part's already done." She smiled warmly, a smile that I couldn't help but match with one of my own.

"Thanks. But it feels more like the hard part has just started. I have to make a new life, try to put together something from the wreckage of the one I left behind."

"It'll be fun!" Clarissa said with a smile. "Look, you've got a job, your health, and a totally supportive, totally charming best friend to help you through it!" She grinned, letting me know she was teasing about the last part. "But seriously – you're here, and you're doing what you need to do. You want to know what I think?"

"What's that?"

"That you're overwhelming yourself with all this talk about rebuilding your life and figuring out what to do. Right now, I think you've earned a little cutting loose."

I scrunched up my brow. "What kind of cutting loose?"

"*That* kind."

She grinned and glanced over my shoulder, with a slight nod. I turned to see what she was looking at, realizing right away. A tall, handsome man in a sharp, business casual outfit was at the counter, a warm smile on his face as he thanked the cashier and turned away with his salad.

He turned in our direction, our eyes meeting. The warm smile appeared again; this time charged with sexual energy as he checked me out. His salad in hand, he strode past our table and sat down a dozen feet away, slipping a MacBook out of his leather briefcase and opening it.

"Now, I realize you might be a little out of practice after being in a relationship for so long," Clarissa said. "But if you need a reminder, that's what it looks like to get checked out." She glanced over my shoulder in the man's direction again, chewing on her lower lip.

"That's what's awesome about Charmed Bay – this place is a hot spot for tourists and grad students and people working remotely like you. That means not only are there a ton of guys here, but it's a constantly changing supply." She tilted her head back, as if giving the matter some serious thought. "That's what I think you need."

"Random guys?" I asked. "I don't know about that. I mean, I know you like to keep things fresh. But Adam...he's the only guy I've ever been with."

Clarissa's eyes flashed with surprise. "Then we definitely need to get you out there."

"I know," I said. "I should be playing the field or whatever. But I don't know if I can do that. Sex for me...it has to be special. I'm sure that sounds naïve but it's how I feel. I need a connection, a real connection that's not just based on something physical."

She nodded in understanding. "Sure, I get that. But don't under-estimate just how fun it can be to have something just physical. And with Adam, well, you know the old expression about how the best way to get over someone is to get under someone else." She glanced over her shoulder one more time, making eyes at the guy. He was glancing back, but it wasn't clear if he was looking at Clarissa or me.

"How about this," she said. "Tonight, after work we can hit up Red's. They've got awesome drink specials on Wednesdays, which means that the place is always packed with every sort of guy the town has to offer. We can go there, grab a few, and...see what happens. If you meet someone, awesome. But if you get there and decide that you're not ready for it, then no pressure. But you at least owe it to yourself to give it a shot, right?"

She was making sense. Meeting guys seemed like the last thing I wanted to do but being around people did sound nice.

"I'm telling you, you're always worrying about other people, putting everyone else before you. If you ask me, I think it's time for you to do what you want for once. Live a little, you know?"

I considered the idea, taking a few more bites of my salad. Before the conversation could go on any further, my phone buzzed in my back pocket. I raised my butt and slipped my phone out, giving it a look.

"Shoot," I said. "It's an email from my boss seeing if I can meet for a zoom call in an hour."

"Huh?" Clarissa turned back to me, breaking from making eyes with the guy again. "Oh, then we can head back home."

An idea occurred to me. "You know what? I think I want to walk, clear my head and think about some of this stuff we've been talking about."

She cocked her head to the side. "You sure?"

"Yeah. It's a nice day out, you know? Sunshine and movement are always good when you've got things on your mind you need to get straight."

Clarissa glanced over her shoulder one more time before turning back to me with a smile on her face.

"In that case, I might have to find another dining partner for lunch."

I laughed, getting up. "Go for it. See you back at the house, OK?"

She winked before glancing over at the guy, who was eyeballing her just as hard as she was him. I got a to-go box for my salad, bagged it up, and was soon on my way.

Downtown Charmed Bay was abuzz with daytime activity, people coming in and out of the various stores, zipping around on scooters, cars coming and going. The sun was shining, and the air was perfect, with a tinge of salt to never let you forget that the beach was nearby and just enough crispness to remind you that it wasn't summer even though the sun was shining brightly

My mind went back to the conversation with Clarissa, how she wanted me to get out there and have some fun with other guys.

But I wasn't into other guys. In fact, whenever I let my thoughts drift to that subject, the same three people always appeared – the Wolf brothers.

And not just one of them, all of them. The three of them had been my dirtiest little secret fantasy ever since I was in high school. But I'd always known there was no way it could actually happen. After all, they were brothers.

Not *my* brothers, not technically. Still, even as a teen I knew it was wrong to think about.

However, I reminded myself that there was nothing wrong with a little taboo fantasy. What warm-blooded woman didn't fantasize about more than one man at one time? The fact that they were brothers just made it even hotter for me, even though I knew it could never happen for real.

The image of all four of us together appeared in my mind, a tightness forming between my legs as I walked home. I imagined all of them, their glorious, powerful bodies on display as they worked to please me, making me come over and over, their big hands moving all over my curves and breasts and everywhere else...

A horn honked, pulling me back into the moment. I was standing in the middle of Shay Street; a car stopped a few feet from where I stood. The extremely annoyed guy behind the wheel honked again, sticking his arm out of the window and waving to move me along. I raised my palm and mouthed "sorry!" as I hurried off the street.

My heart was racing, but as soon as the danger had passed, I was thinking about them again. Sure, there'd be guys at the bar tonight to choose from. Probably lots of hot, smart men who most girls would do anything to get a chance with.

However, there were only three I wanted – the same three who'd been haunting my dreams for as long as I could remember.

CHAPTER 7

DUNCAN

R ed's was packed with the sort of crowd that had been coming there every Wednesday night since long before I was sneaking in there with a fake ID back in the day. The place was a standard college town sports bar, rock music coming from the speakers and the bartenders working their asses off refilling pitchers and pints for the twenty and thirty-somethings lined up at the bar.

There were definitely some gorgeous women among the crowd. Lots of cute as hell college girls in tight jeans and short skirts with their hair down and inviting smiles on their faces. Just about every one of them cast at least one glance over at my brothers and me, their eyes moving from one to the other to the other as they considered which one of us they wanted most.

We were used to it. Hell, it was almost funny by that point. That night, though, there was only one woman on my mind.

Dream.

I scanned the crowd as I sipped my beer, hoping to spot her. The odds of her being there weren't great, I knew. Dream had never been the partying sort of woman. She had friends in high school, but she'd always been more inclined to spend her evenings home working on her art rather than going out and causing trouble like my brothers and I often did.

Even though I didn't want to get my hopes up, I kept looking.

"What about her?" Evan asked, nodding toward a slender blonde standing near the bar, looking around aimlessly in the way that people tended to do when standing at a bar waiting for a drink.

"She's cute," Jay said. "But...I don't know." There was a distinct lack of enthusiasm in his voice.

"You don't know what?" Evan asked with a grin. "She's gorgeous and she's been glancing in our direction ever since we walked in."

Jay sipped his drink, staring off into space.

"I don't know," he repeated.

Evan scoffed, shaking his head before taking a pull of his own beer.

"Don't make that noise at me," Jay said. "If you're so keen on the woman, why don't *you* go over there and say something? She's looking at you just as much as she's looking at me."

"Don't feel like it," Evan replied. He didn't hesitate for a second, but I could sense he'd shot out the words without thinking them over.

"Don't feel like it?" Jay asked with a grin. "Dude, you're acting like I'm not your damn brother and can't see right through your BS. Since when the hell have you not felt like going after whatever beautiful woman happened to be nearby?"

"Since tonight. I'm here to chill out, have some beers, and relax with my brothers. Not every night has to be about girls."

Jay laughed, and I could tell right then he wasn't about to let up.

"Not every night has to be about girls, which is why you're pushing me to go after her. Bud, I'm getting the distinct impression you've got some, ah, ulterior motives with what's going on here."

Evan shrugged. "Think whatever you want. Sue me for trying to get my brother set up with a gorgeous woman."

I flicked my glance up at the blonde, her eyes still going back and forth between the three of us. There was a tinge of impatience on her stunning features, as if she couldn't figure out why the hell not one of the three guys that she was all but putting herself on display for weren't coming over to say a word.

Finally, some broad-shouldered college guy in loose jeans, a faded T-shirt, and backwards hat, stepped from the crowd and positioned himself in front of her. I watched as he put the moves on, tilting his head toward the other side of the bar. The girl smiled in a way that made it clear she was happy to talk to him, and eager to go sit down where he wanted.

Before she did, she leaned to her right to take one last look at us. The expression on her face seemed to say, "you sure?"

None of us took the offer, however. Disappointment flashed on her face for a moment before she turned back to the college guy. He stuck out two fingers to the bartender, and within seconds a pair of drinks was on the bar in front of them. He took one, she took the other, and then he put his hand on the curve of her hip and led her into the crowd, and they were gone.

"Well look at that," Evan commented. "Totally blew it. What, you afraid to shoot your shot or something?"

"Worry about your own business," Jay replied in the slight snarl his voice took on whenever he was irritated.

"Just messing with you, man!" Evan said, clapping his hand down on Jay's shoulder. "Go after the girls, don't go after the girls – doesn't make any difference to me."

Jay narrowed his eyes slightly, as if still trying to figure out what was going on.

Just at that moment, Dream stepped out from among the crowd and stopped whatever argument was happening in its tracks.

Damn, did she look good. Some of my earliest memories of Dream were of her in the grips of her awkward phase when her limbs were all kinds of gangly and her mouth was more braces than teeth. She was cute back then, sure, in a "kid sister you want to look out for" kind of way.

When she'd finally come out of her little awkward phase she'd emerged as a *woman*. She was slender and petite - couldn't have been more than five feet and a few inches - but curvy in all the right places. Her blonde hair, thick and silky, was pulled back into her usual ponytail that showed off her model pretty face with hazel eyes, fair skin, and lots of freckles. Her lips were full and naturally red, the kind of lips that were impossible to notice without wanting to kiss.

Dream's chest was smaller, not that it mattered, but she more than made up for it with what had to be the most perfect, round ass I'd seen in my life. More than a few times I'd had to chasten myself for having highly unacceptable thoughts about what that ripe, round ass would look like bouncing on my cock, moans pouring from those lips as I drilled her hard from behind, my hands cupping her no doubt perfectly shaped tits.

I hated those thoughts, as much as I secretly loved them. After all, what kind of a way was that to think about someone you thought of as a little sister?

Even the thought of it then was enough to stiffen my cock. Dream was dressed in a tight little black skirt that showed off her luscious legs and a cropped green blouse that gave a hint of her flat middle.

Not one of us said a word as we all clapped eyes on her hard.

Dream seemed lost in the bar, her petite figure slipping through the crowd as she tried to find someone. An expression of slight worry painted her features. But the worry vanished the moment she laid eyes on us. A huge, beaming smile spread across her face and she let out a happy squeal that cut through the din of the crowded bar. Before my brothers or I had a chance to react, she was already running over with her arms stretched out, her nipples poking through the thin fabric of her shirt.

"Oh my *God!*" she rushed over to the table and made a beeline for me – likely because I was the closest to her. She threw her arms around me, squeezing me as hard as she could.

Damn, did it feel good to have that tight little body against mine. It made my mind race with all sorts of things I wanted to do with her.

"Well, well," I said, a genuine smile spreading across my face. "If it isn't our long-lost step-sis." I stuck my tongue out at her, letting her know I was teasing her.

"And if it isn't my three-strapping step-bros," she proclaimed, playfully rolling her eyes and putting her hands on the curves of her hips and looking us all up and down. "That just sounds so weird, even in jest."

"Yeah, good thing our parents were together after we already grew up," Evan said. He put his foot on the stool across from him and pushed it out. "But first, where the hell is *my* hug?"

He sprang up and headed over to her with his usual friendly smile on his face. They hugged, and when it was done, she turned her attention to Jay.

"Now, I know PDAs have never been your thing..."

A wry smirk formed on Jay's lips.

"I think I can make an exception for you," he said. Jay rose and Dream quickly wrapped him up in a big hug. I gestured to one of the bartenders and raised the empty pitcher, sticking out two fingers with my free hand. A few seconds later the bartender was setting two pitchers of some local lager on the table along with Dream's glass.

"Oh my God," she said, her eyes jumping from one of us to the other to the other. "You have no idea how glad I am to see you guys. I mean, I was looking forward to seeing you all anyway, but this is perfect timing."

I was confused, and judging by the looks on the other guys, they felt the same way.

"How do you mean?" I asked as I picked up her glass and prepared to pour. I didn't get a chance. She quickly plucked the glass from my hands with her slender fingers and poured her drink herself.

"Bossy as ever," Jay said with a grin as she poured.

"I prefer the term strong-willed," she said with a wink in Jay's direction. "And what I mean is that I showed up here with Clarissa. You guys remember her, right?"

"How could we not?" Evan asked. "You guys were attached at the hip all through high school. And she dated about half our mutual friends."

She hadn't dated any of us. Clarissa had shown interest, of course, but the three of us had all known better than to get involved with Dream's best friend.

"Well, she's still up to her old tricks. We came to the bar tonight and within, like, ten minutes, she'd already picked out a guy and made her move. She told me that it was my turn, and that I'd have better luck if she wasn't attached to my side...so yeah, here I am."."

That's right – she'd broken up with Adam. I didn't want to say anything. No doubt that was all still raw.

"She's got a point," Jay agreed. "You want to get back in the dating world, you're going to have to put yourself out there."

"Right," Evan chimed in with a smile. "And you know what they say – the best way to get over someone is to get under someone else." He grinned, as if he were pleased as hell with his words. Then his expression went sour. "Wait, that's kind of a crude thing to say to someone you used to think of as a little sister."

Dream chuckled. "Not really. Not like I hadn't heard it from Clarissa already anyway, and besides, we're all adults here. I'm no longer that gangly kid you had to scare the boys away from. And it's not like our parents are still married, so we aren't actually related or anything." She bit her lower lip and batted her eyelashes, almost leading me to believe her little speech was to send us a message - that we could think of her like a grown woman, a woman that was available to us. Or maybe it was wishful thinking."

Evan reached forward and gave her hand a squeeze. "Just because our parents aren't together doesn't mean we don't sometimes feel protective over you. We've got a bond between us that's not going anywhere."

I shared the sentiment, of course. My eyes went down to Evan's hand on top of Dream's. A tinge of something ran through me. It took me a second, but I quickly realized what it was.

Envy. I wished that was my hand on Dream's.

I pushed that thought away quickly.

"Anyway," I said as I topped off my beer. "Been too long since we've all been in the same room. I think we're overdue for a little catching up."

She smiled. "I agree. It's been too long."

With that, the night was on. Over drinks we all shot the shit just like we used to. We talked about what we'd been up to over the last few years, but with a major exception – none of us pressed the issue with her and Adam. If she wanted to bring it up, that was one thing. But nobody wanted to be the one to drag up raw feelings if she didn't initiate it first.

The night was fun. We slipped right into our old banter, swapping jokes from our ongoing text conversation and busting each other's chops about how we were back in the day.

Once I got a few drinks in me it was impossible not to flirt with her – at least a little. I'd laugh at her jokes, touch her hand, and she'd touch me right back.

It felt like we were entering dangerous territory and I wasn't sure how far I should wade.

CHAPTER 8

JAY

I was having fun – I had to admit it. Usually, big crowds and loud bars weren't my thing. A good night for me was hanging out at my place outside of town, sipping a glass of whiskey while some Johnny Cash played, my thoughts unspooling.

However, there, with my brothers and Dream, I was having as good a time as I could imagine. The drinks were flowing, the conversation was great, and when the country music started on the speakers, I knew it was only a matter of time before Evan felt the urge to get up and do what he did best.

A thud sounded out as Evan put his big hands on the table.

"I don't know about you guys, but I'm feeling the need to shake my ass."

Dream laughed. "You want to dance? You guys know I suck at dancing, right?"

"No way," Duncan said. He leaned back in his seat, a freshly poured beer held in front of his chest. "I refuse to believe a woman like you doesn't know how to move on the dance floor."

"A woman like me?" she asked, raising her eyebrows in mock surprise. "Now, what's that supposed to mean?"

It was hardly the first of such comments that had happened during the conversation. Sure, the guys and I had tried to keep ourselves in check, but once the booze settled there was no holding back the flirting.

"A woman as good-looking as you," Duncan said, not holding back in the slightest. "What do you think I meant?"

That got a laugh out of Dream. "That's nice of you to say. But I don't think there's any correlation between how good-looking someone may or may not be and how decent they are at dancing."

Evan sprang out of his seat and hurried over to her. "Those are a lot of words you just spent time saying when you could've been dancing. Now, come on!"

Before she had a chance to react, Evan effortlessly scooped Dream out of her seat, a surprised squeal shooting out of her mouth.

"What the hell are you doing, Evan?" she asked with a light-hearted laugh. She was trying to sound indignant, but the smile on her face as Evan threw her over his big shoulder betrayed how much fun she was having. Evan, head and shoulders taller than just about everyone on the dance floor, carried her over and set her down, Dream laughing her head off.

I watched as Clarissa, still dressed in the hippie style clothes she wore back in high school, a few new tattoos on her arms, stepped out of the crowd with a tall, good-looking guy at her side. Soon, they were all dancing together.

"Well," Duncan said as he polished off his beer. "Be a shame to let Evan have all the fun, right?"

"You get started without me," I said. "Never been much of a dancer."

"Oh yeah," Duncan replied with a grin. "You're more the flower-in-the-corner type. Almost forgot."

"Screw you," I said through a small smile. "Got a little shit to think about. I'll join you later."

"You'd better." Duncan raised his finger to me as he went into the crowd. Duncan, being the social dude he'd always been, was greeted warmly by the dozens of people on the dance floor. No doubt he was friends already with half of them.

I hadn't been lying when I'd said that I had stuff to think about. Namely, I had the Dream situation to wade through.

She looked good and she was right - she was no longer the gangly kid we had sworn to protect growing up. I'd noticed that we'd dodged some serious topics during our conversation – mainly the ones of how our parents had broken up, and how she and Adam were done.

Made sense to not get into the heavy stuff right away, and I couldn't help but notice that there had been some major changes in our dynamic since we'd all last seen each other.

Sooner or later, we were going to have to talk about it all.

I sipped my beer, watching my brothers and Dream and Clarissa dance to the music. Evan and Duncan passed Dream back and forth, each of them putting their hands on her hips in a way that was just over the line of what was appropriate. Or maybe I was just jealous.

Right as I hit the halfway point of my beer, I watched as something strange happened. Dream, standing at the bar as some shots were poured for her, slipped her phone out of the back pocket of her tight, short skirt. She had a smile on her face when she checked the screen. But that smile lasted exactly as long as it took to see what was on her phone.

Whatever it was, it caused the color to drain right out of her face. Without even taking the shots, she hurried from the bar and through the crowd. I watched as one of the exits to the back alley opened and her petite figure slipped through.

Something was wrong. Without thinking twice about it, I jumped from my seat and hurried across the place, swiping the shots she'd ordered from the bar as I weaved through the crowd. I wasn't sure if the guys had seen me, but I didn't care. All that mattered to me was that something was wrong with Dream, and there wasn't a chance in hell I'd be letting her go through it alone. As I made my way through Red's, I felt a wavering that let me know I was a little drunker than I thought.

The shots in hand, I opened the exit with my hip and stepped out into the alley. The air was perfect – just the right amount of cool air, the stars twinkling above, the music and commotion from inside quieting to a low murmur the moment the door clanged shut.

I glanced around. No one was out there but a couple of smokers, both busy with their phones.

Then I spotted Dream.

She stood with her back against the brick wall of the bar, her eyes on the sky above. If she noticed that I was there, she didn't say anything.

"You forgot something," I said as I approached with the shots.

"Huh?" Dream snapped back into the moment, her eyes going to me, then the shots in my hands. When she realized what was going on, a smile took hold. "Oh, hey Jay. Sorry, just a little jumpy right now."

"Whatever it is," I said, handing one of the shots to her, "I bet it's nothing a little..." I leaned in and sniffed the drink. "*Fireball?*" I laughed.

"What?" she asked. "You too good for a shot of Fireball?"

"Nah. Just reminds me of back when I first joined up. I'd go out with the guys when we were on leave, and they all wanted to drink Fireball. I guess it's the booze of choice for under-twenty fivers who want to get drunk as quick as they can."

"Well, good – because that's what I need."

"Right," I said. "Now, let's find something to toast to, and—"

I didn't get a chance to finish before she raised the shot then brought it to her lips. Dream tilted her head back and the booze was gone in the blink of an eye.

"Now," she said. "You'd better hurry and finish that before I steal it."

Something was definitely wrong, but I wasn't about to press yet. Instead, I leaned back against the wall.

"Then I'll do the toast – to our... reunion."

That got a small smile out of her. With that, I threw the drink back, the cinnamon whiskey burning on the way down. I let out a satisfied *ahh* as the booze settled, knowing it was bringing me to just the right amount of tipsy. For a few moments, neither of us said a word as we watched the stars above.

I was soon ready to break the silence.

"So," I said. "You want to talk about what happened in there?"

"Huh?" There was genuine confusion in her voice.

"I saw you on the dance floor. You got a text or something on your phone and then you rushed out of there like your ass was on fire. What happened?"

She pursed her lips, as if having a quick internal debate.

"And don't even think of lying to me," I said, raising my finger. "You've never been good at it. Remember the time you took my car to go to Taco Bell and tried to lie to me about it? And even when I found a clump of their shredded lettuce on the driver's side floor you still stuck to your story?"

She laughed, which was my goal. "I know, I know. What can I say? I was starving and needed some study fuel." But the smile didn't stay on her face for long. "It's Adam."

Just the mention of that prick sent my blood into a hot boil.

"Fucking prick," I snarled.

She didn't respond. I realized right away that my words weren't helping.

"Just that…I know he didn't treat you right. Hard to keep myself measured when I know that."

She frowned and nodded, accepting the point but not adding to it.

"Anyway, it was nothing, really. Just a text from him talking about some stuff that I'd left at the apartment. I can tell he's trying to pick a fight with me about it, but I'm smart enough to not take the bait. It's just that, I don't know, I'm out here trying to have fun, to put all that behind me. But all it takes is a message from that asshole to put me in a sour mood." She shook her head, as if frustrated with herself. "Sorry to lay all this on you."

"Wouldn't have come out here if I didn't think there might be some venting involved. And I don't mind it one bit. Always been more of a listener than a talker."

That got a smile out of her. "Well, I've got more stuff that you can listen to. Not sure what you heard, but Adam and I are done, as I'm sure you've guessed. And I'm moving back for good."

My heart did a little jump at this bit of information.

"What happened with him?" I asked. I knew it wasn't my business to pry into, but I couldn't stop myself. Dream wasn't my stepsister anymore, but that didn't mean I wasn't still intent on looking out for her.

She frowned again, glancing away as if she wasn't sure she wanted to get into it.

"It's kind of a long story."

"I'm not in a hurry."

With that, she took a deep breath and went into it. She told me about how controlling Adam was, how he kept her on a short leash and barely let her leave his sight. And then she told me about how he cheated on her over and over, acting like it was no big deal. She explained the fight they'd had, the one where he'd slammed his fist into the wall and scared her enough to make it obvious to her that she needed to leave.

By the time she was done, I was furious, my jaw working, my teeth clenching. I had to use all my restraint to keep my rage in check. Last thing she needed was more anger. For a hotheaded guy like me with a hair trigger, however, keeping it pushed down was no small task.

"It's over," I said. "You're back, you're here with friends and family. Whatever shit went down in Chicago, you don't have to worry about it now."

She smiled. "I'm glad. Knowing I've got friends close at hand..."

"You've definitely got that."

Dream sighed. "And to know that you support me – that's another thing."

"Through thick and thin."

She smiled at me. "My mom's got a different take. She thinks I'm crazy to have gotten rid of a guy who could've provided for me. I mean, as if I *want* some guy to just give me his credit card and let me spend my days having brunch or whatever. She acted like I should've sucked it up because he'd be able to provide 'all the things I needed in life'."

"Except for the important stuff," I said. "Like happiness and trust. And partnership."

She nodded eagerly as she turned to lean her shoulder on the wall and face me. "You get it. Mom doesn't, but you do."

For a moment, I considered commiserating with her about my dad, telling her about all the boneheaded things he'd done to show that his priorities were as screwed up as it gets. But I didn't. She was smiling, and I didn't want to dampen the mood. Not to mention the fact that sharing my feelings about stuff like that wasn't exactly my favorite thing to do.

As she stood there under the starlight, looking gorgeous as ever, there was something else on my mind – something other than talk.

I wanted to kiss her. Just imagining my lips on hers was enough to send a rush of blood to my cock. Maybe it was the booze making my head all muddled, but I could swear from the way she looked at me, the way she was inviting me with her body, that she wanted it as much as I did.

What would happen if I were to do it? Would she hate me? How many lines would I be crossing, lines that I wouldn't be able to step back over?

Dream shivered and wrapped her arms around her body.

Without thinking, I stepped closer to her and wrapped my jacket around her shoulders.

"Thank you, but you didn't have to--" she said.

"No, I did. You're cold."

I didn't move away from her, I was staring down into her beautiful eyes

She didn't move back either.

"Well, whatever happens, I'm glad you're back," I said. "Always good to have people who you can count on around."

Not only did she not move back, but she inched closer. She was so close, in fact, that her nipples grazed against my chest each time she took a deep, full breath. I felt like I was losing more and more control by the second, like there was nothing to do *but* kiss her.

Either way, I wasn't imagining things.

I had to stay strong. I couldn't give in to what I wanted. Once I tried to kiss her, there'd be no going back, and there was a damn good chance it'd cost me one of the most important relationships in my life.

"I'm glad I'm back, too," she said. Dream flicked those hazel eyes up at me, and when she did, I knew I was in some major trouble.

Whatever was going to happen next, it felt out of my hands.

CHAPTER 9

EVAN

Where the hell was she?

I was in the middle of grinding on the dance floor with some cute girl I had no intention of doing anything more than dancing with. I was having fun, but it was getting close to the time to move on.

I turned around, looking for Dream. She'd gone off to the bar to grab a couple of shots of Fireball - my favorite - and hadn't come back. In the middle of my dancing, I'd tried to spot her.

The girl I'd been dancing with, a tall brunette with a nose ring and an arm covered in tattoos, turned around and wrapped her arms around my neck, smiling at me in a way that made it clear she was mine for the taking. Hell, the way she was looking at me made me think I could've nodded toward the bathroom and had her naked in one of the stalls in less than a minute.

However, sex was the last thing on my mind. Even if I weren't looking for Dream, I wasn't in the mood. It felt like other women just didn't hold the same appeal now that Dream was back in town.

The brunette gave me the look, the one where they narrowed

their eyes and curled up one side of their mouth, the one that said, "alright, let's cut the crap and get into bed."

"So," she said. "Want to get out of here?"

It didn't matter that she was offering herself up to me like a main course – I was starting to get worried about Dream. I glanced over my shoulder and spotted a college-aged guy about my height dancing alone. I recognized him as the guy who'd been hitting on the brunette before she and I had started dancing. Without a word, I ducked out from under her arms and turned to the guy.

"Yo, dude – mind holding my place?" Before waiting for his answer, I put my hand on his shoulder and weaved him under the girl's arms. The brunette looked a little surprised but didn't seem too bothered.

"Uh," said the guy. "Want to dance?"

She smiled. "Sure."

Just like that, I was free, and I immediately began looking around again for Dream. Red's wasn't huge, and it didn't take me much time at all to cover the floor.

I didn't see her anywhere. As I took a break to lean against the bar and collect my thoughts, I spotted a pair of guys opening a side door and stepping into the back alley. I couldn't think of any reason why Dream would want to go out there, but it was the one place I hadn't checked.

I hurried toward the door and opened it, stepping out into the cool night air. A few people were out smoking, but further down the alley I spotted someone familiar.

Scratch that – I spotted *two* someone's familiar.

Jay and Dream were getting close – *very* close.

What the hell was going on?

I was relieved that I'd found Dream. But that didn't answer the question of why she'd run out here, or what she was doing with Jay.

One way to find out.

"Well, howdy, kids!" I shouted, stepping around the pair as they spoke in hushed tones to one another. "Hope I'm not interrupting anything!"

Their eyes flashed and their mouths opened into "O" s of surprise, letting me know I very much had interrupted something.

What it was, I had no damn idea.

"What the hell are you doing, Evan?" Jay growled, anger in his eyes. "Why the shit would you sneak up on us like that?"

I shrugged as I placed my hand on the brick wall and leaned against it. As I stood there, I realized that I was tipsy. Not full-on drunk, I still had my head on straight, but enough to where my already low inhibitions were even lower.

"Just saw you guys having a private conversation and figured I'd join in. We're all family, right? I mean, not technically. But you know."

"Well, you ruined the damn moment, dick," Jay grumbled. His eyes flashed with surprise, and I realized that he'd just said something that he hadn't intended to say.

"Oh, so that means there was a moment to ruin, huh?" I asked. "What were you guys getting up to out here anyway?"

Dream still looked startled. I'd known her for long enough to see that she wasn't in the middle of some emotional crisis, so I didn't feel too bad about jumping in. But as I stood there looking her up and down, I couldn't resist how I felt about her at that moment.

She was stunning – just hot as hell. Her sexy legs were barely covered by the tight skirt she had on, and the little hint of midriff from her cropped shirt was enough to make me wild with desire. It was strange, really. I'd spent years trying to ignore how I felt about her, but right then and there it was as if I'd decided I was tired of pretending.

I wanted her, and I didn't care that Jay was standing there to witness it.

"Listen, Dream," I said. "I have to tell you something."

She cocked her head to the side in curiosity. "What's that?"

I swept my hand up and down her body. "You look fucking amazing. In fact, it's damn near criminal for you to be showing up looking like this when you had to know there was a damn good chance we'd be here."

This time not a single word came out of her mouth. Instead, she regarded me with a blank expression that made it clear she couldn't believe what she was hearing.

Hell, *I* could hardly believe what I was saying.

"What the hell are you talking about, Evan?"

Maybe I should've kept myself in check, stopped it there. But I couldn't. Truth was that I'd meant every damn word that had come out of my mouth, and I wasn't done.

"I mean, shit! Look at you in that outfit and, oh my God, the way you were moving out there."

Part of me expected a slap. Hell, maybe I would've deserved it.

I'd never been the kind of guy to hold back when it came to how I felt. With Dream looking as good as she did, I wasn't about to start.

She didn't slap me. In fact, her expression softened. Then a giggle sounded from her lips.

"God, Evan, you're such an ass," she said with a big smile on her face.

"Yeah, Evan," Jay said. "Not the time for this shit."

Jay was acting...strange. Sure, he was doing the right thing sticking up for her, keeping himself measured to see how Dream reacted. I was the brash, uninhibited one of the group but Jay was more on the hotheaded side. If I'd been anyone but his brother, I was sure I'd have been rewarded with a slug to the jaw for doing what I was doing.

Through his narrow-eyed skepticism, there was no doubt he wanted to see if she was offended, or if she was welcoming what I was saying.

"You're too much, Evan!" she shouted through laughter. Then she placed her hands on my chest and gave me a shove. She didn't manage to budge me even an inch.

"Yeah, maybe. Do you want to know just how too much I can really be?" I asked lasciviously.

The smile faded from her face, and she stared up at me with wide eyes, her mouth opened slightly. She dragged her tongue slowly over her lips in a way that was unmistakably inviting.

I decided to take things one step further. I placed my hand on her hip and pulled her close, bringing her against me. My cock was stone stiff by this point, and I let her feel my length through my jeans. Jay watched in silence.

"Listen, Dream," I said. "I'm into you, and I'm done pretending I'm not. I want you. And I can tell you want me."

"But..." she trailed off.

I had a sense of what she was about to say. So, I put her mind at ease.

"You don't have to pick only one of us, just so you know. You want all three, you can have all three. We've already talked about it, and we agree. And it starts with this kiss."

"Kiss?" she asked. "What kiss?"

I was tired of talking. I leaned in and showed her exactly what I meant.

When I kissed her, she kissed me right back.

CHAPTER 10

DREAM

It was, without a doubt, the most surreal thing I'd ever experienced in my life. I was outside of the bar, my head swimming with Fireball, and none other than Evan Wolf's lips on mine.

Sure, I'd spent more than a few nights wondering what it would be like to kiss him...and Jay...and Duncan. But it had always been a scenario I was certain would stay in fantasyland; something that would never actually happen in real life.

Nope. It was happening. His big hands were on my hips, his mouth flush against mine. He tasted like whiskey and delicious musk, the perfect flavor to wash over my eager palate. The way his cock felt pressed against my body...it was all I could do to imagine what it would feel like inside of me.

The kiss was amazing, and it wasn't long before we opened our mouths, our tongues probing for one another's as we both sank deeper and deeper into what was happening. The rest of the world around me was a total blur, nothing existing but his lips and his hands and his tongue and his cock.

Jay. An awareness of what was going on, of who was there, came to me like an electrical jolt. My eyes opened in panic. What was happening? What was he doing? Was he just standing there while his brother made out with me?

I didn't have to wonder for long what Jay was thinking. A second pair of huge hands lightly fell onto my upper back. My body went stiff with shock as I realized what was going on.

They were both touching me.

Evan's hands remained on my hips as Jay pulled me against him, making me the meat in a delectable Wolf sandwich. Jay's hands continued moving, his fingertips tracing over the inward lines of my upper back, then down to my hips, finally settling onto my ass. He pulled me close, letting me feel his hard cock through his jeans as Evan continued pressing his against me from the front.

Two cocks. I'd never imagined experiencing the sensation of feeling two rock solid pricks against me at the same time. It was enough to make my heart jackhammer in my chest, my wetness to soak through my panties. I could hardly contain how excited the brothers had made me.

With both sets of their hands on me made me realize just how big these two guys were. I was 5'2, according to my last checkup, and the brothers loomed over me. Each was easily a head taller, their sizes like two of me rolled into one. I felt so small between them both, but in spite of that, they each handled me with care, firm yet gentle all at the same time.

Now that I was used to Jay's touch, I allowed myself to fall back into the kiss. Evan's tongue met mine again, and Jay's hands began to rub my ass through my skirt. It felt so good, so perfect that I decided to let whatever was going to happen...happen.

Evan continued kissing me, his hands inching around to my front and stopping at my belly, my middle twitching with anticipation at his touch. Where would he go? Surely, he wouldn't move up my skirt there in the alley behind Red's.

He didn't. Instead, he decided to tease me some more, his fingers sliding over my taut belly and venturing up my shirt and under my bra. By this point my nipples were solid as pebbles and it wasn't just from the cold either, my chest was rising up and down.

Evan's tongue continued to mingle with mine as Jay placed his lips on the base of my neck, my skin breaking out in goosebumps as he moved his mouth over me. Evan had reached up under my bra, taking my breasts into his huge hands and teasing my nipples with his fingertips. It was impossible to say how good I felt in that moment, being there between Jay and Evan.

I had no idea how far they were planning on going, but whatever they had in mind, I was along for the ride.

"Dream!" A familiar voice in the distance snapped me back into the moment. "You out here?"

I opened my eyes and stood up straight. Evan's hands stayed on my breasts, Jay's on my ass.

"Clarissa," I said, the name coming out in a sharp stab.

"Yo, Dream! Don't tell me you ditched me!"

"I have to go."

"You don't have to do anything," Evan said, an inviting smile on his face. "You can stay right here."

"Yep," Jay agreed as he placed his lips on my neck one more time. "Just stay right here." As he said the words he reached his hand between my legs, squeezing my bare thigh and hinting at what he might have in store for me if I were to stay.

I couldn't. I was turned on like mad, but I knew, through the booze and the passion, that I needed to give this some serious thought. I couldn't go from seeing them for the first time in years to... doing whatever it was they had in mind for me. I needed time to process what was happening, what it might mean.

"I really want to," I said. "But this is...too intense. I have to go."

I slipped Jay's jacket off my shoulders and let it fall into his arms. Without waiting for a response, I ran. Panic had taken hold and the last I saw of the brothers were their wolfish smiles over my shoulder as I hurried down the alley. Soon I was in front of the bar, the deep red neon light of the "Red's" sign washing over the small group of people smoking and chatting near the entrance.

Among them was Clarissa. Her eyes snapped onto mine, relief washing over her stressed-out face as she realized it was me.

"Dream!" she shouted as she ran over. "Are you serious? You up and vanish in the middle of a crowded bar? Do you have any idea how worried I was?"

"I'm sorry!" I spoke. The words came out strangely, like I was under the influence of some sort of strange drug.

Then again, I could still feel the press of Evan and Jay's lips on my body, the sensation of their cocks through their jeans against my skin. Maybe I was under the influence of *their* drug being their kisses and their touch.

Clarissa stepped back, her hands on her hips as she looked me up and down.

"Well, what's your excuse? I'm keeping the hottest guy in there waiting because I wanted to make sure you hadn't gotten thrown into the back of some human trafficker's van or something." She cocked her head to the side, giving the matter some thought. "OK – the hottest guy aside from the Wolf brothers. But that goes without saying."

The Wolf brothers. Just the mention of them was enough to make my heart beat faster once again, my blood to run hot. I had to tell Clarissa what had happened, where I'd been.

But outside of the bar wasn't the place to do it.

"Come on!" I grabbed her hand and led her back inside. The place was a wild blur, and I didn't want to look around for fear of laying eyes on Jay or Evan.

Moments later we were in the women's bathroom, the two of us locked in a stall while chatter from the gaggle of girls in front of the mirror filled the air and gave my words cover.

"Alright," Clarissa said. "Tell me what happened."

I closed my eyes, took a deep breath, and spoke.

It all came out in some wild stream of consciousness, just one word tumbling out after another. Clarissa listened with wide eyes and rapt attention; her jaw slacked.

"You're *kidding!*" she shouted, putting her hands on my shoulders and giving me a slight shove. "Both of them?"

"Don't say it out loud!"

She laughed. "What, you think that one of them is going to be here in the ladies' room or something?"

"No jokes," I said as I leaned back against the wall behind me. "This is all so weird, and I just got wrapped up in the moment and..." Another thought hit me. "Clarissa, they're *brothers!*"

Clarissa pursed her lips and rolled her eyes. "Are you kidding me? They are obviously okay with it if they came on to you like that, so why should it bother you? If you ask me, you'd be an idiot not to go for it."

"Are you serious?"

"Dream, this is a once-in-a-lifetime thing. You had two gorgeous men smashed up against you, both of them ready to do whatever you wanted..." She shuddered with delight. "Just the idea of it's enough to make me hot."

"I can't. I mean, I don't know." I stood up straight, a realization occurring to me. "I need to go. I need to get home right now."

Concern took hold on her face. "Yeah, sure. We can go now."

"No, you stay here. I feel like I need some serious alone time to think about all this."

"You sure? 'Cause I can leave right now, no problem."

I smiled slightly, happy to know that I had a friend there for me. "It's OK. I just need a good night's rest."

Clarissa pulled me into a tight hug. "I know you might feel overwhelmed by all this, but if you let a chance like this slip through your fingers..."

By that point, she'd made her thoughts on the matter more than clear. She led me out of the bathroom and through the bar. Like before, I kept my head down to avoid being spotted by the guys. But then I accidentally laid eyes on Duncan. He was, as I always remembered him back in the day, all laughs and smiles and in the center of a big group of people.

But where were Evan and Jay?

It didn't matter, I decided. I rushed out the door and quickly called an Uber. Luckily, in a place like Charmed Bay, one didn't need to wait long for an Uber to arrive. Moments later the car was in front of Red's and I hurried inside, my head still spinning.

I was glad to be alone, glad to be with my thoughts and no one else. As soon as the commotion of the bar faded, the words Evan had said right before he'd kissed me played once more in my mind.

"You don't have to pick only one of us, just so you know. You want all three, you can have all three. We've already talked about it, and we agree. And it starts with this kiss."

What, exactly, had that kiss started?

I had a feeling I was about to find out.

CHAPTER 11

DUNCAN

Two things hit me when I woke up that next morning – the first being the wicked hangover slamming in my head.

The other was the look on Dream's face as she'd left Red's.

Really, "leaving" wasn't the way to describe how she'd gotten out of there. It was more like she'd fled. I'd been chatting with a few casual acquaintances from back in the day when I'd spotted her, and though I'd tried to catch her attention, she'd seemed too preoccupied with getting the hell out of there to notice me.

I threw off the covers and trudged to the bathroom, knowing I needed something for the throbbing headache. As I grabbed a few Aspirin from the bathroom cabinet, I tried to figure out what could've happened to make her run out like that.

A thought occurred to me as I filled a glass of water and tossed back the pills – was it possible that a guy had done something to make her feel uncomfortable? Had some prick gotten grabby with her on the dance floor?

Just the idea of someone pulling a stunt like that with Dream was enough to send a blast of anger through me so intense that it pushed the hangover aside.

Get a grip, Duncan, I said as I closed the mirror cabinet and regarded my reflection. *Don't get pissed over something that you're imagining.*

But stranger things had happened. And if there was one thing college guys *weren't* known for, it was behaving themselves when they were drunk.

I was already feeling better once the water and pills were down the hatch. However, I knew there was only one thing that would really put my hangover down. I stepped over to my nightstand and picked up my phone, seeing a message from Evan.

Garbage plates at Red Kettle! Get your ass out of bed and get there! One hour, bro!

I chuckled as I read the message, seeing that Evan was thinking the same thing as me. He'd sent the text half an hour ago, which meant I had plenty of time to get moving. I threw on a pair of loose-fitting jeans and a white V-neck shirt, stepping into a pair of black Chuck Taylors on the way out.

The Red Kettle Diner, one of my favorite food joints in town since I was a kid, wasn't too far from the house. I decided to walk, figuring some fresh air and movement would be good on the hangover front. Sure enough, when I finally spotted the big red kettle on top of the diner that gave the place its name, I was feeling right as rain. A little food in the belly would have me feeling ready to take on the day.

I opened the front door to the diner, the place filled with natural light from the big glass walls. The restaurant was about half-full, a handful of men and women at the U-shaped counter that curved through the main dining floor.

"Boys are in their usual spot, Duncan." Melody, the middle-aged manager of the place, a woman who I'd known since I was a kid throwing back coffees during study breaks in high school, greeted me with a smile.

"Thanks, Mel," I said. "Mind putting in the usual for me?"

"Had it in when I spotted you coming up," she said with a wink. "And coffee's already on the table."

I smiled and thanked her again as I made my way over to the corner booth where the guys and I usually sat whenever we came in. Sure enough, Jay and Evan were already there, a big carafe of coffee on the table along with a plate of onion rings.

"Hell of a breakfast," I said as I slid into the booth and grabbed one of the mugs.

"Hey," Evan said as I sat. "I've got this hangover cure thing down to a science by this point. First, you drop a bunch of greasy stuff in there to soak up all the booze that's left. Then you dump an extra-large garbage plate on top of it to finally put it to bed. Then you go home, take a nap, then hit the gym when you wake up. By the time that's all done, you're gonna feel like a million bucks."

"Or," I said with a smirk, "you could just show some restraint the night before."

Evan made a "pssh" sound, waving his hand through the air. "Yeah, sure. But where's the fun in restraint?"

He pushed the plate of onion rings toward me, a big bowl of dark orange Red Kettle special sauce in the middle.

"When in Rome," I said, picking up the fattest ring.

I dipped the ring and took a big bite. The breading was crunchy and delicious, and sure enough, the bite had settled like a cloud in my stomach.

"When you're right," I said, "you're right."

Evan let out a quick bark of a laugh before putting his big hand on my shoulder and giving me a shake.

As I went in for another bite, I noticed something strange about Jay on the other side of the booth. He hadn't said a word since I'd arrived, and he had a look on his face that suggested he had something serious on his mind.

"Yo," I said, popping the last bit of onion ring into my mouth then waving my hand in front of him. "What's up?"

Jay glanced over at me for a quick moment before turning his attention back to Evan.

"Oh!" I said, dusting my hands and reaching for my coffee.

"Either of you talk to Dream last night before she left? I was with some people, and I saw her fly out of the place around midnight. It was weird – she looked like she'd seen a ghost."

Jay's eyes stayed on Evan.

"We need to tell him."

Evan chuckled as he dumped a small container of cream into his coffee. "Dude, why are you being so serious? You're acting like someone died or some shit."

"Because it's a big deal and Duncan deserves to know."

"And he will know. I was planning on telling him, like we talked about. Just giving him a few minutes to settle in and get some food and coffee in him first, you know?"

I leaned in. "You guys know I'm right here, right?" I couldn't help but laugh at the absurdity of it all. "I don't know what the news is, or what your plans were for telling me. But I'm going to hear it, and I'd like to hear it now."

"Fine, fine," said Evan. "It, ah, it has to do with Dream."

"Has to do with Dream, how?" I asked. "Did something happen to her last night?"

"You could say that." Evan replied with a sly smile.

"Tell me," I said. "Out with it."

"I'll do it," Jay said.

With that, he leaned forward and spilled it.

He told me everything, told me about how he'd gone outside with Dream the night before, how Evan had joined them, sauntering up all cocky and full of whiskey. He told me how Evan blabbed about how hot he thought she was, how much he wanted to kiss her.

"You didn't," I looked at Evan. "You *didn't*."

Evan kept right on grinning. "I did."

I let out a sigh. Before we had a chance to go on, Mel came over with three garbage plates. The meals, as unappetizing as the name might've been, were like heaven on a plate. Mel had moved to Charmed Bay from upstate New York and brought with her the spin on a breakfast special from that area. It was a huge plate of home fries, gravy, biscuits, sausage, and cheesy scrambled eggs.

Too bad I was no longer in the mood to eat.

"You *kissed* her?" I asked, my eyes wide. Part of me wanted to grab Evan by the collar and smack some sense into him right then and there. But I held back.

"That's not all," said Jay. "We both kissed her."

I didn't know what to do. I let my head hang back, an annoyed groan flowing from my mouth.

"Are you guys serious?" I asked.

"What?" Evan replied. He grabbed the bottle of hot sauce from the condiments and splashed some onto his food. "Didn't we already talk about this? We agreed that we all wanted her, and if she wanted to share then that'd be fine with us. And trust me, she was more than down with sharing."

"Yeah," I said. "Right up until the time she freaked out and ran out of there." My stomach grumbled, and I decided I couldn't resist the food any longer. I shoveled a big forkful into my mouth and chewed. The food was so good that for a moment I'd forgotten all about the incident, letting myself get carried away to grease heaven.

"So, she got a little overwhelmed," Evan said. "She was happy with it while it was happening."

"But have you guys talked to her since then?" I asked. "Checked up on her to make sure she's OK?"

"Nah," Evan answered. "Not yet. I was thinking about it, though."

I closed my eyes again, more than a little frustrated with what I was hearing.

"Dudes, did you think *maybe* it wasn't the best idea to go from zero to sixty like that? Sure, I was thinking we'd talk to her about all this. But not in the alley behind Red's when we were all drunk. No wonder she ran the hell out of there. Poor kid was probably more overwhelmed than she'd ever been in her life."

Evan and Jay shared a look, one that suggested they'd both realized they'd screwed up.

"Fuck," Jay said, setting down his fork. "You're right. Dumbass move."

I nodded. "We're going to be lucky if Dream doesn't keep her distance from all three of us now."

Evan shrugged. "Or she just might want some time to process what happened."

"Could be either. But what we're going to do is simple. We give Dream her space, let her figure it out, then come to us if she wants to go further. And we need to be ready for any answer she gives us. We had all talk about not coming on too hard, letting her come to us if she's interested. Then the first night we see her after all this time you two pounce on her like a couple of horny middle-schoolers at their first make out session."

I sighed and shook my head. I was still frustrated, but my brothers weren't stupid – they'd gotten the point by then.

After I finished speaking, that same worried expression formed on Jay's face yet again.

"Oh God," I said. "Don't tell me there's more."

"There is," Jay said. "But it's not about what we did. It's what she told me about Adam."

"About Adam? They broke up – what more is there to say?"

Jay took a deep breath and spoke. He told me what he'd heard from Dream last night, how she'd told him about how Adam had treated her, how he'd threatened her by punching the wall.

By the time he was done, I was furious.

I wanted to kill Adam. It was a damn good thing I had my brothers to hold me back.

CHAPTER 12

EVAN

A crash sounded out, the table shaking as Duncan slammed his fist onto it. Jay and I instinctively reached forward to grab our waters to make sure they didn't fall over from the impact.

"That fucking prick!" The words came out of Duncan's mouth in a fearsome snarl, one that caught the attention of some nearby diners.

"Easy, D," I said. I was trying to keep calm, but it wasn't easy. Fact of the matter was that I'd never seen Duncan that mad before. Between the three of us, he'd always been the one who'd had the easiest time keeping a cool head. Seeing him like that was strange as all hell.

I couldn't blame him though. When Jay had told me about what Dream had said about Adam, wringing that smarmy little shit's neck had been the first thing to appear in my mind.

Mel hurried over, a worried expression on her face.

"You guys alright?"

I glanced over at Duncan. His jaw worked; his eyes fixed forward in an expression of pure anger.

"We're alright," he said. "Just got some news I'm not happy about." He closed his eyes hard, then turned to Mel with a softened expression on his face. "Sorry to make a scene. It's all good now, Mel."

Worry faded from her face at Duncan's words. "Just let me know if there's anything I can do, OK guys? And I don't just mean bringing you more coffee." She placed her hand on Duncan's big shoulder and gave it a motherly squeeze before departing.

"Fucking hell," Duncan said, his tone lower. I could sense that while he was doing his best not to freak out in the middle of the restaurant, he was still pissed as all hell.

"It's over," Jay piped up. "Dream got away from him. She's back in town and where we can look after her, make sure no asshole like him gets anywhere near her."

Duncan clenched his jaw again. "But he's still out there. Hell – he's *from* Charmed Bay. Odds are good that he'll be back for one reason or another eventually."

"Then we'll cross that bridge when we come to it, dude," I said. It was weird talking to Duncan like that, trying to calm him down. It was usually him taking on that role.

"But if he does," Duncan said, "I'll crack that shithead's skull." There was no doubt in my mind that he meant his words. If Adam had happened to walk into the diner at that moment, he probably wouldn't have made it three steps in before Duncan took him apart limb-by-limb.

He clenched his fists so hard that his hands looked like big stones. Then he unclenched them, closing his eyes, and taking a deep breath.

"I need to go," he said. "Need to clear my head."

Without another word, and without waiting for a response, he shot up and stormed out of the diner. I watched as he stepped through the door and made his way down the road, disappearing down the nearest block.

"Can't blame him one damn bit," Jay said as he topped off his coffee. "When she told me about Adam and what he'd done to her..." His face flashed with anger as he recalled the words. "But yeah, no sense in getting worked up about it – it's in the past."

"He's right, though," I said. "What if Adam comes back to town? Starts some shit?"

Jay shrugged. "Then we take care of it when it happens. And we make damn sure that he doesn't get a chance to hurt her again. He's already shown what kind of a man he is, and we're not going to take any chances."

I shoved down another big bite of food, feeling more restored with each bit I got into me. The physical part of the hangover was going away. But it was beginning to be replaced with regret at what had happened between us and Dream.

"He was right about the other shit, too," I said. "That was dumb. We shouldn't have come onto her so hard and so fast."

Jay smirked over his meal. "*We*? I was out there talking to her. You're the one who sauntered up like God's gift and laid down all those lame lines. You're lucky she's into us as much as we're into her – can't imagine that cheeseball game of yours working on any girl who's not already sold."

I laughed, picking up a small piece of onion ring and whipping it in his direction. He caught it and popped it into his mouth.

"Hey, when I came outside you two were getting nice and cozy together. Pretty sure that if I'd come out a few minutes later *you're* the one who would've made the first move instead of me."

He said nothing as he chewed his onion ring and swallowed.

"Well, so what? What's done is done."

I nodded. "True. And I know what Duncan said, but damn, it doesn't sound right."

"What? The part about waiting for her to come to us?"

"Yeah. Dream's assertive as they come, but it's still a pretty tall order to expect her to seek us all out to make sure we're cool. *We* should be the ones doing it."

Jay glanced aside, giving the matter some thought. "Yeah, you're right. But *we* shouldn't be doing anything. There's three of us, and if we all come to her to talk, she might feel overwhelmed."

"Then what's your solution?"

"One of us reaches out to her. And that one of us should be me."

"You? Why you?"

"Because you're the one who made the first move. You try to talk to her one-on-one again and she might think it's your way of trying to pick things up where you left off. Trust me, it's easier this way."

I shook my head, a little frustrated. He was right, but *I* wanted to be the one to reach out to her, maybe even to apologize for coming on so strong so suddenly.

The important thing was that one of us reached out and put Dream at ease. She had enough to deal with moving back and all the shit with Adam. We needed to make sure she had one less thing to worry about.

"Alright," I said. "Give her a call and see what you can do. In the meantime..." I took the last bite of my meal before pushing it aside and pulling Duncan's half-eaten plate in front of me.

Jay laughed. "You ever think about anything other than food?"

At that moment, Dream appeared in my mind. She was dressed in the tight skirt and green top that she'd worn last night.

I grinned. "From time to time."

CHAPTER 13

DREAM

"I don't understand – *body painting?*"

Mom's voice drifted up to me as I poked around in one of the enormous storage closets in her house, looking for my boxes of art supplies. I'd taken an offer to do some face and body painting at the local farmer's market that the town held one every weekend down by the beach. I used to do it when I still lived in town, and it was always lots of fun. I'd make some money, get some fresh air, and practice my art.

After everything that I'd been through over the last few weeks, I needed something to take my mind off it all.

"Why do you say it like that? You're making it sound weird."

"Because it *is* weird," she said. "What are you doing, exactly? Painting landscapes on people's *bodies?*"

"It's not like that. Well, I mean, it's kind of like that. People come in and you paint on them. It's cool – you get to do all these designs on them. And there's always lots of cute kids who want their faces painted."

"I see. Sounds like time you could be using to find something a little more lucrative in town. But that's just one woman's opinion."

I held my tongue, turning my attention back to the room.

I picked up one of the nearby boxes off one of the many shelves, opening it and hoping that my art supplies were inside. Instead, there were many sets of expensive looking swimwear that, judging by the fact that price tags were still on them, hadn't been worn once.

"You know, Mom," I said. "There's this little trick that some people do when storing stuff, it's called 'putting labels on it so you know what it is.' You might want to look into it."

I glanced over my shoulder and shot Mom a smile, letting her know I wasn't trying to bust her chops too hard. Dressed in her usual outfit of expensive athleisure-wear, today's color an eye-catching electric blue, Mom leaned against the entry to the closet with a glass of white wine in her hand.

"Oh, whatever. You're more than lucky that I actually still have all your art things from high school. Never say your mom doesn't love you, right?" she flashed me a smile full of pearl-white veneers.

She had a point. As much as she gave me crap about wanting to be an artist, she *had* supported me in my dreams when I was a kid.

"But what I want to know is why you can't simply get your stuff from Adam's place. Surely, he still has what you left there? Why not just call him up and ask him to ship it?"

I paused in the middle of opening another box, a sick feeling rushing through me at the mere thought of Adam – let alone talking to him.

"It's not like that, Mom," I said. "Things are...they're not good between us. And you know this."

She scoffed. "Yes, likely drama that would be easily resolved by a mature phone call. But what does your idiot mother know."

I chose not to take the bait, instead opening another nearby box.

"Yes!" I let out a cry of excitement as I laid eyes on my body painting supplies. They were all there, just as I'd left them.

"You find them?"

"I did!" I was totally thrilled to have all my stuff in front of me. I picked up the box and hurried out of the room, rushing past Mom then stepping into the kitchen and setting the box down on the bar.

"Now, don't make a mess with all that stuff," she said. "The help can clean it up, but I'd rather them spend their time on more important things."

I said nothing as I pulled out the paints, brushes, and patterns and all the other things I'd need.

"That doesn't look like much," Mom observed. "That's going to be enough to paint at the farmer's market?"

"It'll be enough to get started. And if I need more, I'll just go to the art supply store."

She opened the fridge and refilled her wine from the bottle inside. "Well, sure. But it just seems like a waste knowing that Adam likely has supplies to send you. We can call him right now, in fact!" She reached for her phone on the kitchen island. "Yes, we can call him now and maybe even discuss some other matters in the process. I think that's a great—"

"No!" The word shot out of my mouth as I turned around to face my mother. "We're not going to do that. We're not going to call Adam; we're not going to hash things out. We're not going to do any of that. I made my decision and I'd like it very much if you actually respected what I've decided for once instead of trying to poke your nose where it doesn't belong."

Mom said nothing, her eyebrows arched in mild surprise, the bottle of white wine still in her hand.

"The breakup is still fresh and, as much as I'm sure I did the right thing, it still hurts to think about. There was a time when I thought he was going to be my forever person and, well, that sure as shit didn't happen. I'm doing my best to get over it and it's not helping when you're constantly poking at the open wound. So, stop!"

I felt strange when all the words finally came out of me. I also felt...relieved. Mom just stood there, finally shaking her head before stepping over to the fridge to put away her bottle of wine. After closing the door, she leaned against the fridge and sighed.

"Well, you're not the only one who's been through a rough breakup," she said. "I know what it's like." She glanced away as if she were thinking about something in a difficult way. Then she shook her head. "Handle this situation however you want. But I'm your mom, remember. I wouldn't be doing my job if I were to stand idly by and not offer my opinion on whatever's going on in your life." A small smile formed on her lips. She was being pushy and headstrong as ever, but at least in that moment she seemed to have tried to look at things from my perspective.

"Anyway, I should get all of this home and see what I've got. Farmer's market is tomorrow, so I need to get ready."

Mom watched as I scooped the box off the counter and started out. She followed me, opening the door.

"The farmer's market isn't really my thing," she said as she saw me off. "But maybe I'll drop by. I might even wear my sports bra so you can paint a little something on my belly." She followed this up with another smile, and I wryly chuckled as I heaved the box into the back of Clarissa's car.

Moments later I was on the road. As I drove, I realized that between staying at Clarissa's place and using her car and Mom holding onto my things for me, I was entirely dependent on other people at that moment in my life. I vowed to get things together - to buy my own car, to rent my own place and finally, truly, start this new phase of my life.

I didn't have too long to think it over. My phone rang and I saw that it was a call from Jay. My stomach tightened as memories of last night came rushing back. Part of me wanted to dismiss the call, but the idea of ignoring the guys seemed cruel. Plus, we needed to talk after what went down at Red's.

"Hey." I turned the phone onto speaker and put it in the holder on my dashboard.

"Hey. What's up?" As weird as what had happened last night might've been, it was still good to hear his voice.

"Not much, just driving home from Mom's. You know, I think

this is the first time in a long while that someone's called me who wasn't a robo-dialer."

He chuckled. "Glad to stand out."

There was an awkward pause. It was as if neither of us knew quite what to say.

Finally, Jay cleared his throat and spoke. "Uh, I was calling just to see how you were doing. And...to say I'm sorry for making things weird at the bar last night."

It was a relief to hear the words.

"You're back in town and trying to get settled in and the last thing you need are a couple of horny dudes pouncing on you. It was bullshit, and I'm sorry."

He meant the apology, and I appreciated that. But at the same time, hearing him say the words "pouncing on you" was enough to make my pussy clench. I shifted in my seat, trying not to think about how freaking hot it had been, despite the awkwardness.

"Thanks. It's not your fault, you know. It takes two to tango, after all. Or three, in this case."

He laughed. "Good. And I didn't just call to apologize – I wanted to see if I could make it up to you."

"Make it up to me? How?"

"I don't know. Anything you need help with? Not sure if you're planning on moving, but I've got the truck and—"

"The farmer's market!" I shouted.

"Huh?"

"I'm setting up a booth there for tomorrow evening. If you want, it'd be a huge help to bring my stuff there and help me set up."

"Sure, absolutely. What time?"

"Well, I need to work a little in the morning, and the market starts at one and goes until the sun goes down. I'd need help getting my stuff there then getting it back. I'm sure you're busy, but—"

"Done. I'll do it." There wasn't a trace of hesitation in his voice.

I couldn't help but smile.

"Alright, great. You know where Clarissa lives, right?"

"Pretty sure. But send me the address to be on the safe side."

"You got it. And...thanks, Jay."

"My pleasure."

The call ended right as I pulled up to Clarissa's place. I parked and sent him the address, a thumbs-up response following seconds later.

Then I smiled. My life was crazy, and what had happened with the guys had only made it more so. However, there was something about the Wolf brothers, something that made me certain things were only just getting started between us.

CHAPTER 14

JAY

It was Friday afternoon, and I couldn't believe how excited I was.

Dream had been all I could think about - the last thing on my mind before I'd gone to bed, the first image to appear when I'd woken up that morning. I couldn't remember the last time a woman had captured my attention in such a way – if ever.

As I drove my black F250 through downtown Charmed Bay on my way to Clarissa's place, I did all I could to keep my excitement in check.

Stay focused, dumbass, I told myself. *The whole point of this evening is to do her a solid to make up for what happened the other night. You show up sporting a hard-on and trying to get your hands down her pants that'll just make things worse than they already are. Keep it together.*

My pep talk worked – kind of. My focus was back on the evening, but damn if I wasn't still thinking about her, thinking about all I wanted to do to her and that tight, perfect little body of hers.

I imagined slipping my hands down her pants, moving under the waistband of her panties, spreading her lips and entering her with my fingers. I envisioned watching her eyes close and her mouth open in quiet pleasure, her back arching as I moved in and out of her. And I imagined feeling her pussy clench around my fingers, her gorgeous face tightening in an expression of silent ecstasy as I brought her to orgasm.

Beeeeeep!

I came back to it, looking around and realizing that I was at a green light at the biggest intersection downtown. A row of cars was behind me, and when I figured out that it was me and my daydreaming holding up the show, I quickly stuck my hand out the window and waved in an apologetic way toward the cars behind me before pressing the gas and driving on.

The other drivers quickly passed me, shooting the daggers in my direction that I knew I deserved.

It wasn't a good sign. I wasn't even with Dream, yet I was already fantasizing about what I wanted to do to her. If there was one thing I'd learned in the service, it was discipline. I focused as I drove, using the old trick of paying attention to what was directly in front of me and nothing else.

It worked. That is, until I pulled up to Clarissa's place and the door opened. Dream stepped out with a big, inviting smile on her face.

Damn, did she look good dressed in a pale blue maxi skirt and tight-fitting sweater that hugged her slim body in all the right places. Her hair was pulled back in its usual ponytail, and her eyes sparkled even from that distance. She was dressed modestly, but that didn't mean I wasn't thinking about hiking up that skirt, pulling off her panties, and having her spread her legs over my cock.

"Hey!" she shouted as I pulled the truck to a halt. "Good to see you!"

I hopped out of the truck, and she didn't waste any time hurrying over and throwing her arms around me. Having her body pressed against mine reminded me of the other night, when my hands had been all over her, grabbing Dream's thigh and squeezing the ripe, warm skin.

"Same to you, kid," I said. I looked her up and down. "Happy to have brought the truck, but it doesn't look like you've got much to carry."

She flashed me a wry smile. "It's all inside. Don't worry – nothing crazy."

I chuckled, trying to ignore the incredible sexual tension between us.

"Where's Clarissa?" I asked.

"At work, slinging espressos and all that good stuff."

That meant she was alone. Part of me wanted to say, "forget the farmer's market," scoop her off the ground, and take her inside for the screwing of a lifetime.

"Here," she said, nodding toward the door. "Let me show you where it all is."

I nodded, clearing my throat as we stepped inside the apartment. The place was small but open, the living room and kitchen in the same single room, separated by a bar. The floor-to-ceiling back door gave a really nice view of the ocean in the distance.

"Nice digs," I said.

"Yeah, not too shabby. But they're temporary. You *are* in my room, after all."

"Huh?"

I wasn't sure what she meant at first. With a smile on her face, Dream tilted her head toward the bigger of the two couches, which was draped with several sets of her clothes over the back, blankets folded at one end, and several pairs of shoes gathered on the floor in front of it.

"Ah," I said, getting it. "Well, I'm sure you'll have your own digs before too long."

"I hope so. I love living with Clarissa – don't get me wrong. But she enjoys the company of men, if you get my drift. And she's not shy about expressing it." Another head tilt, this time toward the open bedroom door. "Makes it hard to sleep, you know?"

I chuckled. It was funny but Dream even talking about sex was enough to make me half-hard. I needed to get out of there, and fast. Otherwise, I risked giving in to what I wanted.

Or maybe, what we both wanted.

"Anyway, the stuff?"

She pointed past me, toward a stack of boxes near the front door that I'd missed on the way in.

"That's it. Just those three."

"Oh, no problem at all." Without another word, I stepped over to the cardboard boxes, squatted down and slipped my fingers under the bottom of the lowest.

"Be careful – they're heavier than they look. There's a dolly in the closet if you—"

I didn't need any of that. I lifted the boxes up from the ground and began carrying them outside.

"Or you could do that. Either works."

Once I reached the truck, I hoisted the boxes into the bed and went to both sides to strap them down. A blue tarp covered the back third of the bed, and after getting Dream's attention, I pointed it out.

"See that?"

"Yeah – what is it?"

"Last time I went to the farmer's market I got burned up like crazy. That's a tent you can use for your setup. Trust me – even when it's cloudy, you can still get sunburned, and it can help keep the sun out of your eyes while you work."

"Oh my God," she said, clasping her hands together. "I can't believe I didn't think of that."

Before I could react, she turned and threw her arms around me, giving me a squeeze. Her perky tits pressed against my arm, and sure enough, my cock went hard.

"My pleasure. Now, you ready to do this?"

"Ready."

After double-checking to make sure everything was strapped down good and tight, I opened the door for Dream and helped her up the big step into the truck. Seated in the cab of the massive truck she looked even more petite than she usually did, her legs barely reaching all the way to the floor.

Soon we were off. The beach wasn't too far away and when we arrived there were already dozens and dozens of people there setting up their stands. I parked on the lot and went for the boxes.

"Not a chance," she said, reaching toward my arm. "I'm carrying one of th—" She set her hand down on mine and the moment she did, it was like electricity ran through us. I turned, my eyes locking onto hers. Dream's mouth was open slightly, her expression one of shock, as if she were just as surprised by what was happening between us as I was.

For a long, perfect moment, there was nothing but her and me, her hand on my skin, the sea air thick with salt all around us.

Dream cleared her throat, snapping us both out of the moment.

"Um, what I was going to say was that I'm carrying at least one of these boxes. Not a chance I'm letting you take them all." Before I could react, she opened the truck bed and undid the straps holding the boxes in place. She bent over to grab the nearest one, drawing my eye right to her ass draped in her light skirt.

Once she had the box in hand, I could tell by the strained look on her face that she wasn't quite ready to hold it. She shifted her hands, trying to maintain her grip.

"Now," she said, nodding her head toward the other boxes. "Put one of those other ones on this."

I laughed. "You're out of your mind if you think I'm giving you another one. Come on – we've got to carry this stuff all the way to the beach."

"But—"

"Aren't you painting?" I asked. "Don't you want to keep your arm in good shape for that?"

She shifted the weight of the box from one arm to the other as she considered my words.

"Yeah. I guess you're right."

I laughed. "Of course, I'm right." I leaned forward and grabbed the other boxes along with the tent kit.

"And arrogant, too," she said with a smile once I had it all in hand. "Just like I remember you being back in high school."

I closed the truck up and locked it with a click of the fob. Then we were off.

"Oh, yeah? And what else do you remember about me from high school?"

"Well, mostly that you were arrogant, like I said. And kind of a jerk to other people."

"A jerk, huh?"

"Yeah. I remember you always...snarling at people."

"Only way to get them to leave you alone sometimes."

"And that's what you wanted?" she asked. "People to leave you alone?"

"I had my brothers – who else did I need? And besides, letting people get too close is how you get hurt."

She raised her eyebrows, a small smile on her lips.

"Is that right? Did someone hurt the big, tough Jay Wolf?"

"Nope. And that's never going to happen. Really, it's more about knowing who you are and where your boundaries lay. If you want to enforce that shit, you're going to have to behave in ways that other people don't like."

"Interesting." She said the word with eyes narrowed slightly, as if I'd said something that she wanted to give more thought to at a later time.

We reached the main area of the farmer's market. The place was packed with vendors, people setting up food stands and craft tables, an acoustic band in the center putting together a small stage.

"Wait, hold on." Dream stopped in place, her eyes on something or someone ahead.

"What's up?"

"This place is divided up into little sections. If you want to have a place, you have to get in touch with the farmer's market people and reserve a space."

"Makes sense."

"And I'm in 3F. Right there." With her free hand, she pointed ahead to a small spot with a paper sign in front that read, "3F".

There were already people there, two big guys setting up a stand for what looked to be local whiskey.

"Hold this," Dream said. Before I could say a word, she plopped her box on top of mine and began going through her purse. She fished out a piece of paper and unfolded it.

"Yeah, that's right," she said, tapping the paper. "I'm at 3F."

"Looks like that guy took your space. See? He's in yours and the one next to it."

"Shoot," she said. "Must be a misunderstanding. Let me go talk to them."

Before I could say a word, she was already on her way over to the guys. My first instinct was to jump in and have her back, but I knew Dream well enough to understand that she was as headstrong as they came and loved to fight her own battles.

Hell, it was one of the things I'd always loved about her.

"Excuse me!" she said, waving her hand to get the attention of the men. They both looked up, their eyes shaded under the brims of their trucker caps.

"Yeah?" one of them asked in a gruff voice.

"I think you guys are in my spot," she said. "Well, you're in your spot *and* my spot. So, if you could move, that'd be great."

"These are both our spots," the other guy said. "Talked to the farmer's market people earlier today, told them we'd need two for all our merch."

"That's impossible," Dream said, shifting her weight from one foot to the other as she considered his words. "I got an email from them a few hours ago, the confirmation they send out to everyone who reserves a spot."

One of the men stopped what he was doing, giving Dream a narrow-eyed, hostile glance.

I didn't like it. The way he looked at her made my blood boil, but I did my best to keep myself in check.

"You calling me a liar?" he asked her.

Dream squared her shoulders and stood up straight.

"Maybe I am," she said. "Because there's no way they would promise me the spot and then give it up to you a couple of hours later without informing me. If you ask me, it looks like you guys only reserved the one spot, and then when you realized you'd need two, you just moved on over into mine and acted like it'd be no big deal to take it."

One of the men shrugged. "Either way, looks like you're out of a booth."

The other, a sneer on his face, flicked his eyes up and down Dream's body. "How about this – come share some whiskey with me in the tent and maybe we can work something out." He winked, letting out a laugh that the other guy joined in on right away.

That was about all I could stand.

"Or" I said, stepping up to the booths. "You two can move your little whiskey table over into your spot before I move it myself. And maybe a bottle or two ends up in your ass in the process."

I put my hands on the table, moving a few bottles of whiskey aside as I glared down at both of them. The cockiness they'd shown to Dream just a few moments ago vanished in a heartbeat, cowed fear replacing it.

The guys shared a glance, one that suggested they were thinking the matter over, changing their tune on the spot.

"Whatever," one said. "We can do the tables front to back."

"Yeah," the other added. "Whatever."

I grinned; my eyes still narrowed. "Glad we could work something out, boys."

One of them scoffed as they stepped over to the table that was in Dream's spot. They lifted it up and hurriedly put it back in their spot.

Once that was done, they didn't waste a second getting the barrier put up between the booths, cutting us off from view.

"Pricks." The word came out dripping with venom as Dream began unpacking her things.

"Common type," I said. "Act like they're tough when they think they can pick on someone smaller than themselves. But as soon as somebody their own size, or in my case, a bit bigger, gets toe-to-toe with them, they wilt like lilies in the sun."

Dream pursed her lips. "You didn't have to jump in like that. I would've been able to handle them."

I stepped over to the tent and began taking it out of its pack. "Of that, Dream Stokes, I have no doubt. But I figured I'd be a gentleman and save you the time." I flashed her a smile and a wink, and she grinned right back.

Dream went to work unpacking her art supply boxes. "I had to admit that I was worried when you got in those guys' faces."

"That right?"

"Yeah. I remember how hotheaded you can be. Back in the day you'd throw a punch at anyone who looked at you the wrong way."

I chuckled. "Teenage me was a pain in the ass. Military got most of that sorted out."

She kept on grinning. "You know, now that I think about it, it wasn't just guys looking at *you* the wrong way – it was any dude that looked at *me* the wrong way. One can't help but wonder how many guys back then didn't ask me out because they were afraid of what you might do to them if they did."

"I guess you'll never know," I said with a wink. "And trust me, I might've been all piss and vinegar back then, but I've always had a good douchebag radar. If I scared anyone off, it was in your best interest."

I laughed as the two of us finished setting up. When we were done, Dream had her painting station out in front of the tent, which held the supplies. A handmade sign that read "Body Painting by

Dream" adorned with colorful flourishes that she'd made herself was stuck out in front.

The farmer's market had started to fill out, dozens of people streaming in through the entrances and milling around the stalls. Already I could see more than a few kids grabbing their parents' hands and pointing to Dream's booth, eager to get some face painting done.

"Alright," I said. "You're set up. Time for me to get going. I'll see you in a bit when they close up, OK?"

As soon as I finished my words, however, the whiskey boys next door began to laugh in a loud, obnoxious way. I had a mental image of how rowdy they might be in a few hours, after one too many tastings.

Dream glanced over in their direction, too. "Oh, OK. See you in a bit, then."

I shot one more look in the direction of the whiskey boys.

"On second thought, how about I just stick around? Makes more sense than for me to leave and come back in a couple hours."

Dream quickly nodded, as if she were having the same thoughts about the idiots next door.

"That'd be great. You can grab a beer, maybe even a hot dog if you're feeling really crazy."

"Hell, if I'm feeling really crazy I might have you do some body painting on *me*."

She chuckled. "Careful, soldier – I might hold you to that one." She waved one of her thin paint brushes in my direction, a sly, sensual smile on her lips.

I had a laugh at her words, my cock shifting a bit at the innuendo. But we didn't have a chance to continue the conversation before her first customers arrived. Dream was friendly and warm, helping them into the chairs and pulling out some sample designs they could choose from. The boy went with a tiger, which I told him would've been my choice, and the girl went with a flower pattern.

By the time Dream was done with the kids, the market was damn near packed, a small line already formed in front of her tent. After grabbing a beer from a stand nearby, I ended up playing assistant, helping Dream with her brushes and paints. As the time flew by, as she painted like crazy, I couldn't help but admire it all. Dream was as hard of a worker as they came, giving each customer careful attention as she focused entirely on her painting and fulfilling each request. Kids had their faces painted, college-aged girls left with intricate designs on their bodies, and a few dudes even came for tattoo style painting on their arms.

I sipped my beer and helped when I could, the sun slowly dipping closer and closer to the water. The sky soon filled with burning reds and oranges, the type of sunset you could only find in a place like Charmed Bay.

"And...done!" Dream dabbed the finishing touches of a unicorn design on her last customer, an adorable little girl. "What do you think?" Dream held up a small mirror to the girl's face.

"It's awesome!" she said. The girl threw her arms around Dream, pulling her close for a hug that Dream wasn't expecting, but was happy to reciprocate. "Thank you so much!"

"Happy to do it!" Dream told her.

The girl scampered off to join her parents and that was that. The sun was nearly down, booth runners were taking down their goods, and the last few customers were making their way out. From the booth next to us the whiskey boys, seemingly as drunk as I expected, let out a pair of loud, obnoxious laughs.

"Alright," Dream said. "Time to pack up. But...I kind of want to wait until those jackasses are gone first. How would you feel about going for a walk?"

I stood up, putting my hand on the small of my back and giving it a good crack, then setting down the nearly empty can of my second beer.

"A walk sounds pretty damn good," I replied.

She smiled and we were off. We walked past the whiskey guys, who were passing back and forth one of their bottles and probably about twenty minutes away from getting a ticket for public intoxication. Thankfully, they were too wrapped up in their bullshit to pay much attention to us.

We made our way through the farmer's market, eventually reaching a less packed section of the beach as we chatted, going over the fun of the evening. Before we knew it, we'd walked what had to have been a couple of miles.

"Thanks again for doing all that," she said.

"Helping you with the stand? My pleasure."

"Not just that – dealing with those assholes, too. I'm sure I would've been able to handle them on my own, but it was nice to know you had my back."

"Hey, that's what friends are for, right?"

She smiled, glancing over at me, and tucking her hair behind her ear.

"You know you don't have to look out for me anymore," she reminded me.

. "I'm going to be looking out for you whether you like it or not. I know damn well by this point that you're the type who likes to fight her own battles, and that's great. But you never have to go it alone if you don't want to."

I looked around, noticing that we'd made a curve along the beach toward a section where there weren't any people. It was just us and the waves and the setting sun.

"Here," she said, nodding to an overturned log on the sand. "Mind sitting for a minute?"

"Sure."

We sat down and said nothing for a time as we watched the waves come in. It was damn nice, sitting there with her by my side.

It was more than nice. Being there alone with her was making my cock twitch, making me want more than just her company. As if she knew what I was thinking and wanted to let me know she felt the same way, Dream put her head on my shoulder. I wrapped my arm around her and pulled her petite body against mine.

I wanted her like crazy, and I was beginning to feel like she wanted the same.

Then she laughed.

"What's so funny?" I asked.

"Nothing. Just thinking about what happened the other night."

She didn't need to clarify. But I asked anyway.

"And what about it?"

"It made me feel good to know that you still care," she said.

I couldn't help myself. I put my hand on her thigh and squeezed. "Well, I know you're not a child anymore. Doesn't mean I'm not still going to take care of you."

She turned to me, sexual hunger in her eyes.

"Take care of me, huh? I think I'm going to need to see what you mean by that."

I grinned. "Happy to demonstrate."

There wasn't a chance in hell I'd be able to hold back any longer. I leaned in and kissed those ripe, wet lips good and hard.

CHAPTER 15

DREAM

It was dangerous as hell. We'd kissed before, but this time we were alone – no one to stop us from what we both desperately wanted. Part of me questioned whether or not it was a good idea; another part of me was scared out of my mind about going further with Jay than I already had.

But as soon as those lips were on mine, all I could think about was how much more I wanted, how there was a hunger in me that I couldn't ignore, that only one thing would satisfy.

He tasted too fucking good – just as good as Evan had. There was a bit of beer on his breath, and between that and his stubble there was no doubt that I was kissing a gruff, rough *man*. The kiss began with just our lips, our mouths moving over one another's as our hands explored each other's bodies through our clothing. It was almost hesitant at first, like we'd never kissed anyone else before and weren't quite sure what we were doing.

But if Jay had any uncertainty, it only lasted for a few moments before he took control in the best way possible. He put his big hand on the small of my back as he opened his mouth and sought out my tongue with his. I didn't waste a second before returning the kiss and letting his tongue move inside, teasing mine, his taste washing over me as I felt myself grow wetter and wetter.

His other hand was still on my inner thigh, his skin warm and rough against mine. He moved it up as we kissed, his fingertips slowly pushing up the hem of my skirt. All I could think about was how much I didn't want him to stop, how I wanted to tear off my clothes and have him take me right then and there.

When his hand finally reached between my legs, my body tensed in anticipation. Seeming to sense something was wrong, he pulled away and regarded me with a careful expression.

"You alright?"

"I'm alright." I didn't even need to think twice about it. "There's no one here to stop us like before. We keep going and..."

He nodded. But Jay didn't seem concerned – not even a little. In fact, he seemed even more eager than before.

"We keep going and I'll have you out of those clothes."

His words sent a shiver of sexual energy through my body, my skin breaking out into goosebumps.

"You just might. But is that a good idea?"

"Maybe, maybe not. But being with you is about the only damn thing I can think about anymore. And I've got a feeling you've had me on your mind, too."

He was right about that. However, he didn't have the whole story. I wasn't just thinking about *him* – I was thinking about all three of them, about the words spoken the other night stating I didn't have to pick one.

I pushed that all out of my head, focusing on the moment. I didn't want one more than the other, of course. I wanted Jay and I wanted Evan and I wanted Duncan. One at a time would be perfect.

"Was what Evan said true? About me not having to pick just one of you?"

Jay nodded. "Are you okay with that?"

"I think so... yes."

"Then there's no point in holding back. We're here together. You ask me, we should make the most of it."

My panties were soaked through, and my mind raced with all the things I wanted to do to him – or have him do to me.

He was right. There was no point in holding back.

He put his hand on the curve of my jaw. "You ready?" It was my chance to back out.

"I'm ready."

Our lips were on one another's once more, and this time we kissed with the passion of two lovers who were on the verge of having one another. My hands went to the bottom of his shirt, my fingertips tracing the sculpted notches of his hips before I went up, savoring the sensation of his washboard abs, his middle solid as stone. His pecs were just as perfect, and when I finally reached his round, powerful shoulders, his shirt was nearly all the way off.

"God, you taste so damn good," he said. "Good as I've always imagined."

Confirmation that he had, in fact, wondered what I tasted like sent another thrill through me. Before I could respond, he sealed my lips with another kiss, both of his big hands settling on my hips. He did what I'd done to him, his hands moving up my sweater over my bare skin, the feeling almost more than I could bear.

Jay reached under my bra and took my breasts into his big hands, his fingers teasing my nipples until they went hard as pebbles. I moaned, opening my legs toward him as we faced one another.

"You're sure no one's close by?" I asked, having the presence of mind to open my eyes quickly and glance around. Good thing it's not summer, I thought, the off-season meant no tourists would be enjoying the beach. "People see us, and they might start talking."

He grinned, his hands still caressing my breasts. "Gorgeous, I've got a feeling that by the time this is all said and done, we're going to be giving Charmed Bay enough gossip to last a lifetime."

Jay was right, but I pushed that all out of my head, letting my hand fall onto his cock as I squeezed his thick length through his jeans.

Without any thought on my part, my hands went to work on his button and zipper. I opened them as quickly as I could, a flash of his black boxer briefs all I saw before I reached down into his underwear and took hold of his cock, pulling it out. He was as thick and long as I'd guessed, his head glistening with pre-cum.

He groaned with pleasure as I stroked his length. He was so big, so thick that my fingers could hardly encircle him as I stroked. But the sly grin on his face made it clear he loved what I was doing. He leaned back a bit, giving me space to wrap both of my hands around him, to stroke his thickness up and down.

He only let me do this for a short time, however, before sitting forward and undressing me with a fury. He pulled my sweater off and tossed it aside, exposing the lacy, dark blue bra I wore underneath. Once that was done, he shimmied my skirt off my legs. My panties were a plain white thong, and it was a touch embarrassing that I didn't match. He didn't seem to care one bit. His eyes moved over my barely clothed body like I was the sexiest damn thing he'd seen in his life.

"Come here," he said. Jay didn't give me any choice in the matter. He effortlessly picked me up and placed me in front of him, my bare feet in the sand once I kicked off my shoes. The sand was cold underneath me, holding no heat whatsoever. The air was chilly, but the heat growing inside of me was enough to keep us both warm.

He grabbed the waistband of my panties, rolling my underwear down my legs.

"God, you're fucking gorgeous." His eyes moved over every square inch of me as he placed his hands on my hips, squeezing my curves. Jay was now wearing nothing at all, having slipped off his jeans and underwear, his cock pointing straight up.

"You're not so bad yourself, soldier," I said with a grin.

He chuckled as he guided me toward him, spreading my legs as he brought me down onto his lap. Once I was over his cock, I reached down and wrapped my fingers around it once more, ready to bring it inside of me.

Was I about to have sex with Jay Wolf? Was I about to sleep with a man who once treated me like his little sister, always looking out for me?

I decided at that moment to do a little less thinking, and a lot more doing. I lowered myself down, feeling his stiff, solid head rub against my lips. I moved lower, lower, taking his head and then the first of his many inches.

Then I stopped.

"Wait," I said. "Don't we need protection?"

"Military makes sure we've got a constant clean bill of health," he said. "But if you're worried about the other thing..."

"I'm on the pill."

There was nothing to worry about, no reason not to keep going. The way he felt inside of me was like nothing else. There were the waves, the sun, and the gorgeous man underneath me.

So, I went with it.

By that point I was so slick that Jay, even with his incredible size and my petite frame, was able to slide inside me without much effort. I took him, inch by inch, and soon he was buried deep, his thickness instilling in me a sensation of perfect fullness as my walls stretched to accommodate him.

I held fast for a moment, shifting my hips, and letting my body get used to his size.

"You alright?" he asked, his hands on my hips.

"I'm more than alright. How about you?"

He chuckled. "Just trying to wrap my head around the fact that I've got Dream Stokes sitting on my cock."

It was surreal, but it felt so freaking good that none of the other stuff seemed to matter.

I smiled, leaning in and placing a kiss on his perfect mouth – my way of silently signaling that I felt a little of the same way. It was weird and wonderful and so far, I didn't regret it one bit.

I raised my body up then slowly slid down the length of his cock, his perfect stiffness driving up inside of me and filling me full once more. His cock in me, I rocked back and forth, the curve below his head hitting my G-spot in just the right way to bring an orgasm within sight. I rode him steadily, moans pouring out of me as the orgasm arrived sooner than I'd expected. I grabbed onto his shoulders and leaned forward, pleasure blasting through me in pulsing waves.

He grinned, placing his hands on the curve of my ass as he moved up and down below me, pumping into me from underneath. He moved with the power of a machine, his cock driving up over and over, the intensity so much that I could hardly think straight. My eyes rolled into the back of my head, my hair and breasts bouncing like wild.

I focused enough to look down at him, to see the sensual expression of raw, animal passion on his impossibly handsome face. He might've been underneath me, but in those moments, he was in total control.

The second orgasm approached and rushed through me before I had a chance to prepare. The pleasure was incredible, waves of delight crashing through me just as surely as the waves crashing on the shore behind.

This time Jay came with me. He grunted hard, his cock pulsed inside as he drained himself inside of me, his wet warmth spreading through my body. I dropped onto him, the orgasm so intense that all I could do was rest my head on his shoulder and try to catch my breath.

He wrapped his big arms around me, holding my body flush against his as we rode the high together. When it was over, when our orgasms had faded, our chests rising and falling together, all we could do was sit and catch our breaths, his cock still inside of me.

I listened to the waves, listened to the breeze broken only by the occasional cry of a seagull. It was all so perfect – I didn't want it to end.

"We need to get going." Jay's words let me know that it did have to end. We couldn't simply stay in one another's arms like that forever – as nice as it might've sounded.

"Yeah, you're right." I sat back, taking in the sight of Jay underneath me, his perfect, muscular body there before me. I wanted to burn the image into my mind, never wanting to forget.

"But before we do…"

I didn't have a chance to react. He slipped his fingers into my hair and pulled me close to him, planting a long, lingering kiss onto my lips. I fell into it, my pussy clenching and letting me know that it was ready for him if he wanted to go one more time.

But the kiss ended. Jay lifted me off his lap, then reached down to pick up my clothes.

"We're lucky we haven't been spotted already," he said. "Let's get dressed before our luck runs out."

Without a word, I threw on my clothes and he did the same. We walked back to the market after we dressed, neither of us saying a word to each other. It wasn't the awkward sort of silence, though. It was the peaceful, pleasant sort that could only come with comfort and familiarity. We walked through the sand, occasionally glancing at one another with a smile.

Most of the market, including the whiskey bros, had cleared out by the time we returned. Jay helped me pack my stuff and put away the tent, the two of us carrying it all to the truck when we were done.

We were almost to Clarissa's place before either of us said a word.

"So," I said. "I'm working the market again tomorrow."

He nodded. "Oh, so you want some more help? I can come bright and early if you need it."

"No, that's not why I mentioned it. Clarissa's giving me a ride in the morning. I mentioned it because I wanted to see if you and the guys wanted to come by and say hi. Unless you think that'd be weird."

Jay seemed genuinely confused. "Weird? Weird how?"

"Jay, we just had sex."

He furrowed his brow and cocked his head to the side. "What difference does that make?"

My first instinct was to explain to him exactly why a little detail like that made a difference, but by then we had pulled up to the apartment complex.

"So, what do you think?"

He grinned. "Sure – I think we can make some time."

"Perfect. The markets from nine until five tomorrow. I'll break for lunch around noon, so maybe you and the guys can come by before then?"

Jay pulled the truck to a halt. "It's a date."

With that, he hopped out and helped me load the gear into Clarissa's car for the next morning. Once that was done, he climbed into his truck with a wink.

"See you tomorrow, Dream."

He drove off and I was alone, with only one matter remaining – was it a date with all three of them?

CHAPTER 16

DUNCAN

The horn on Evan's car blasted outside of my house.

"Sheesh, dude!" I shouted from my bathroom. "Easy, already!"

Without even a few seconds pause after the horn stopped, a text message lit up my phone – from Evan, of course.

Yo, we're here! Get your ass in gear, dude! this was followed by five "fire" emojis.

Sometimes I couldn't help but laugh at Evan's exuberance. I also couldn't really blame him. I was just as excited to get to the farmer's market and see Dream as he was.

I took one last look in the mirror, making sure I didn't miss any spots during my shave, then headed out of the bathroom and my house, grabbing my keys, Seahawk's cap, and sunglasses on the way out.

Sure enough, Evan and Jay were out front, the top down on Evan's red convertible, Motley Crue blasting from the speakers. I turned my ball cap around, shaking my head as I approached the car.

"You want to wake the neighborhood, dude?" I asked.

Evan laughed, turning down the music. "Come on, man! It's

Saturday and we're going to have some fun! Now, get your ass in the car. The faster we get moving, the faster we get to see Dream."

He was right about that. To my surprise, just the thought of being able to see her was enough to make my heart skip a beat with excitement. I vaulted over the side of the car, landing in the back. Jay was in the front seat, and he turned his head to greet me with a quick nod.

"Let's *goooo!*" Evan shouted as he turned the volume back up and drove off.

The music was loud enough that we didn't get much of a chance for conversation. That was too bad – I wanted to ask Jay how his time with Dream had gone the evening before. He'd been the one to tell us about the farmer's market, after all.

I tried to get a sense of what was on his mind by glancing at his expression from the backseat. Jay was as hard to read as they came, and with his eyes hidden behind a pair of mirrored aviators, the job wasn't any easier.

We drove on, Evan singing at the top of his lungs to the music. When we pulled into the beach parking lot everyone there turned to stare at the convertible blasting music. Evan found a spot and when he killed the engine it took me a moment or two to adjust my ears to the relative silence.

"You're gonna blast your eardrums out with that shit," Jay chided with a smirk as we climbed out of the car.

"Nah – you listen to it loud, and it makes your ear drums tougher."

That got a laugh out of me. "Dude, that's not a thing."

Evan *pshhhed* and waved his hand through the air as he went over to the trunk to take out a cooler and some folding chairs. Once he passed them out, we were on our way down to Dream's booth. A steady stream of people was making their way down the path that led from the parking lot to the beach, and when we joined them, we saw just how packed the place was. Dozens and dozens of stands were set up, hundreds of people there shopping and eating and enjoying the mild, unseasonably warm morning.

"So," Jay said. "She was down this way if you guys want to follow me. Hopefully the pricks that tried to steal her spot yesterday aren't there this time."

I chuckled at the idea, already seeing how something like that could've played out. No doubt Jay had put the guys in their places right quick.

We headed down into the market, the smells of good food and the pleasant din of the crowd filling the air. Jay took the lead, and it wasn't long at all before we spotted Dream at her booth. She was busy at work painting the cheek of some cute kid, a long line of others waiting for their chance snaking around the nearby booths.

Damn, did she look good. Dream was wearing a pair of tight jeans, hinting at that gorgeous ass underneath, and a long-sleeved top that dipped low enough to show off just enough cleavage to leave a guy wanting more. She smiled brightly as we approached, saying something to the boy she was working on before hurrying over and letting out a squeal of delight.

"There you guys are!" she shouted as she gave each of us a hug.

"What, you think we wouldn't show up?" I asked when it was my turn, savoring the sensation of her petite but curvy body against mine.

"I mean, I knew you'd all come. But I was getting a little anxious, I guess."

Her eyes flicked over to Jay. "Hey!" she said.

"Hey."

A few beats of silence passed, making it more than clear that something was going on between the two of them. I did my best not to laugh, not wanting to bring up anything awkward.

I couldn't help but wonder though if something *had* happened last night.

Didn't matter. Dream was her own woman, and while Jay was my brother, he wasn't under any kind of obligation to tell me every bit of his business. Besides, nothing stayed a secret for too long between the three of us. I'd find out soon enough.

"OK!" Dream said as she led us back to the tent. "This is Noah." She swept her hand toward the boy, a kid with a shaved head and scrappy look to him who regarded us with huge eyes. "And he wanted a tiger on his face. Isn't that right, Noah?"

Noah said nothing, the kid's big eyes moving between the three of us and back again. The kid was clearly unsure of what to make of the three huge men in front of him. I flashed him a grin, dropping down to speak at his level. He had an outline of a tiger's face on his cheek, the colors not filled in yet.

"You're getting a tiger? That's so freaking cool. What kind?"

"The orange kind."

"There's lots of different kinds," I chuckled. "During one of my last tours with the Berets, I saw one that was white. You ever seen a white tiger before?"

"Wait, there are *white* tigers? And hold on, you were a Green Beret?" A big grin spread across his face, and I could sense Noah wasn't sure which of the two details to be more excited about.

"Yep, and yep."

He turned to Dream, who was in the middle of preparing her paints.

"Miss Dream, is it too late to get a white tiger?'

She smiled over her shoulder, holding up a tube of white face paint. "Not at all. Had a feeling you might change your mind."

"What was the white tiger like? Was he mean?" Noah asked, so excited that he was literally on the edge of his seat.

"Let me tell you all about it..."

The kid hung off my every word as Dream went to work painting. Jay and Evan chatted with some familiar faces in line, everyone seeming to want to know what the Wolf brothers had been up to. By the time I'd finished with my story, Dream was putting the finishing touches on the white tiger.

"Want to check it out?" she asked, holding up a mirror in front of Noah's face.

"Yeah!" Noah turned his head to check out his new art. I had to admit, it was good. The detail was amazing, down to the whiskers.

"I think it's pretty rad," I said. "How about you, kid?"

"I love it!" he said, bouncing off the seat. "Thanks, Miss Dream! And bye, Mr. Wolf!"

"Bye!" I said, waving to Noah as he hurried off to show his friends his new face painting. He joined a nearby group of kids his age, eagerly pointing in our direction, making a machine gun shooting gesture with his hands, leaving little doubt what he was telling them about.

I chuckled as I watched.

"You've always had a way with kids, Dunc," Dream said as she stepped to my side. "They practically worship all of you guys."

"Kids are fun," I said. "They're always excited to hear about anything and everything. And they're never afraid to tell you what's on their mind."

"Very true, very true. Anyway, I'm starving. I'm thinking of taking care of the next few people in line then breaking for lunch. You guys want to grab some food and meet me back here in, say, thirty?"

"Perfect," I said. "I'll pull the guys away from the line."

Dream smiled before turning her attention to the next customers. I hurried over to the guys, letting them know the plan. They were down, and we split up to grab drinks and food from around the market. I bumped into tons of people that I knew from back in the day, and it was hard not to lose track of the time in conversation.

Before too long we were all back in front of Dream's tent. Jay picked up some hot dogs, I grabbed a couple of sixers of some local craft beer, and Evan...well, he had two armfuls of just about everything the market had to offer.

"You know there's only four of us, right?" I asked, my eyes tracking along all the food in his arms. He had funnel cakes and pie and pork rinds and churros and burritos and more. Truth be told, it all looked really good.

"Yeah, but we all eat as much as two normal-sized people each," Evan replied with a grin. "And I'm hitting the gym later anyway. Gotta hit those macros, you know?"

I laughed, using my free hand to snatch a bag of pork rinds from his arms.

"Damn, guys," Dream laughed, emerging from the tent. "When you said we were going to do lunch I didn't know you meant buffet style."

"Blame this guy for that," Jay said, tilting his head toward Evan.

"Hey, I'm not complaining. Painting all morning works up more of an appetite than you'd think. Anyway, let me grab your chairs. Got a table in there, too. One sec."

She popped into the tent, and I took the time to glance around at the painting samples she had on the walls, little papers hung up with all kinds of designs customers could pick out. Every one of them was incredible.

Dream stepped out with the folding chairs bundled up in her arms. I quickly set down the beer and helped her, taking the chairs, and opening them up as she went back in for the table. A few moments later we were seated, the food covering the entire surface of the table, each of us with a cold bottle of beer.

"So," I said. "How's the market been?"

"Amazing," she said. "And such a perfect way to spend the week before I have to get back to work." She sighed, as if the mere idea of work was too painful to consider. "It was nice for a few days while it lasted."

"You're working remotely for the time being, right?" Evan asked. "That can't be too bad."

"It's not, really. I'm just being a baby. But the thing about the market is that it's given me a taste of what it's like to earn some money from my art. I used to get the chance to do stuff like this in Chicago, but then Adam..."

She trailed off. The mere mention of Adam was enough to send a pulse of anger rushing through me. Judging by the way Evan and

Jay's jaws clenched, I could sense that they had similar sentiments on their minds.

"Anyway," she said. "It's been nice."

"Then why even work?" Evan asked as he unwrapped one of the huge, California-style burritos he'd bought. "Just quit your job and do this for a living."

Dream nearly spit out her beer. "Funny how you say it like it's that simple – just quit my job and what, live on Clarissa's couch until I can make a living doing face and body painting? Which will never happen by the way. The market for that isn't exactly booming."

"Stranger things have happened," Jay replied. "And look at all this." He swept his hand toward the art surrounding us. "It's a damn crime that someone this talented would have to work for a living doing touch-ups to print ads."

Dream sighed, as if we were talking about something to which she'd already given a ton of thought.

"It's not that simple. The work I do now, it's not ideal."

"Not ideal?" I asked, leaning forward.

"OK, it sucks. But it pays the bills! And more than that, it's an artistic type of job."

"Really?" Jay asked, his tone suggesting he didn't believe her.

"Well, along the same lines as artistic. But right now, I don't have the luxury to quit what I'm doing and chase some silly dream."

"It's not a silly *dream*," Evan countered. "It's what you want to do, right? It's what you were born to do. Nothing stupid or silly about that."

Jay nodded in agreement. "You ask me, what would be silly is if you gave up on your dream because the timing wasn't perfect."

"And what's not perfect about right now?" I asked. "You're making a fresh start. Might as well do the same with your job."

Dream smiled. "You guys need to stop – you're all making way too good of a case for this."

I grinned right back at her. "That's because it's not hard at all to convince an insanely talented artist that she should pursue her art."

She waved her hand through the air, redness appearing on her cheeks.

"Alright, alright – that's enough." Dream was telling us to stop, but the smile on her face made it more than obvious she liked what she was hearing.

The guys and I laughed before diving into our meals. Evan smashed his first burrito, tearing the foil open for the second while Jay and I washed down our bites with beer.

The conversation came to a halt when Dream's friend Clarissa appeared in the crowd. Once she spotted Dream's tent she made a beeline over to us, a worried expression on her face.

"Hey!" Dream said as Clarissa approached the table. "What's up?"

Clarissa bit her lower lip. Whatever was on her mind, she was having a hard time putting it into words.

"It's Adam. He's here."

CHAPTER 17

EVAN

The guys and I looked at one another with the same hard expression. The mere mention of Adam Myles was enough to make each one of us want to drop our beers and burritos and storm through town until we found him, beating his sorry ass to a pulp when we did.

At that moment, however, Dream was our priority. The color drained from her face as Clarissa said Adam's name. She sat there stunned, not sure what to do with herself.

"Adam?" I asked. "As in, her ex-fiancé Adam?"

"That's the one," Clarissa confirmed. "Hey guys, by the way."

We said quick "hellos" before getting back to the issue. Without thinking, I reached over and took Dream's hand and gave it a squeeze. Maybe it wasn't the most appropriate thing to do given what had gone down that week, but I didn't give a shit. She squeezed my hand right back, then gave her head a quick shake as she came back into the moment. The stunned expression faded, replaced by a determined one.

"OK, tell me what happened. Where is he? He's not here at the market, is he?"

Clarissa shook her head. "No, thank God. He came to the apartment and asked about you. It was crazy – I was sitting in the living room watching Netflix and I heard a loud banging knock at the door. I had no idea who it was, and when I saw that it was Adam, part of me wanted to call the cops."

She sighed and went on.

"Anyway, I opened the door and right away he's looking over my shoulder – the prick doesn't even say 'hi' first. He asked if you were there, saying he was in town visiting and thought you might be staying with me." She raised her palms. "Don't worry – I lied and said I didn't know where you were staying."

Relief washed over Dream's face.

"Thank you. I mean, I don't expect you to lie on my behalf, but..."

"This is a major exception to that rule," she said. "Only thing that matters is keeping Adam as far away from you as possible."

"That was the smart move," Jay told her. "But it's a temporary solution. If he came all the way from Chicago looking for you, not a chance in hell he's going to leave just because you weren't at Clarissa's."

"Did he say anything else?" Dream asked.

"Yeah. I asked him if there was anything I should pass along if I happen to see you. Thought it'd be a good way to find out what the hell he wanted."

"Smart move," I agreed.

She nodded toward me then looked back over at Dream. Clarissa pursed her lips and appeared conflicted, as if she weren't sure if she should say what she was about to.

"Say it," Dream demanded, her tone stern. "I need to know everything."

Clarissa nodded quickly before speaking. "He said that he'd come to apologize. He said that he'd come to tell you he'd been a real jerk and that..." she trailed off but another hard glance from Dream put her back on track.

I had to hand it to Dream. No doubt that this crap with Adam had her all kinds of shaken up, but while that might've been how she felt on the inside, she sure as hell didn't show it on the outside. She seemed calm and in control, like all she wanted was the information so she could decide her next move.

Dream was tough like that – one of the many things I loved about her.

"He said that he wanted you back." Clarissa blurted out the words, like there was no easier way to say them than to just do it.

Silence fell over the table. All of us put down our beers and burritos and simply sat for a moment, taking in what we'd just heard. Then Jay and Duncan and I glanced at one another, having the kind of silent conversation that only three brothers as close as us could have.

"You can't do it!" Clarissa said, her eyes wide and her tone pleading. "He's the worst asshole in the world and if you take him back after the way he treated you...you just can't!"

"Right," Duncan piped in. He sat back and crossed his arms over his chest. "This is classic prick behavior – do something out of pocket, treat someone like shit, then expect to get back on their good side with nothing more than a few nice words and a fake apology."

Jay nodded in agreement, leaning forward. "Bet you anything he's got this whole speech planned, got a bunch of over-the-top things to say, all designed to get you to let your guard down. I wouldn't trust that asshole as far as I could throw him." Jay's voice got angrier as he spoke, and by the end I was sure that if Adam were there with us right now, Jay would've stomped his ass into the ground.

"Why give that jackass a second of your time?" I asked. "He's a shithead, that's all there is to it. You're back here in town to start fresh and turn the page on your life, right? Seems like the last thing you'd want to do is to go back to a guy who treated you the way he did."

Dream closed her eyes and raised a palm, letting us all know it was time to stop.

"Guys, I appreciate it, but please don't tell me what to do."

"Just giving some friendly advice," Clarissa put in.

Dream opened her eyes and reached for her beer. "I know. And I appreciate it like crazy. But there's no need for any of that. There's not a chance in hell I'd give Adam another opportunity to ruin my life. The engagement's off, and that's all there is to it."

When she was done, she took a sip of her beer and set the bottle down.

The guys and I shared a quick smile, one that showed we were all happy with what she had to say. I wouldn't have thought Dream would get sucked in by Adam for another go round on the bullshit express, but when it came to matters of love it was hard to predict what anyone might do.

"There's something else, too," Clarissa added. "The way I remember Adam from back in the day...he was always cool and calm, you know? Confident in himself."

"Fine line between being confident and being a smug prick," Jay said, a scowl on his face.

"Well, when he came over, he seemed, I don't know, *off*. Like he wasn't quite right in the head, you know? He seemed unstable, really. If I'm being honest, he kind of scared me. It felt like at any moment the smile might vanish, and he'd do something crazy."

"If that's how you felt," Duncan said, "Then you probably had good reason to think that way. The more I hear about Adam, the more it sounds like the side of him that Dream saw was his true nature, and the cool and calm part of his personality was just a show. Could be that Dream telling him to screw off was the trigger that made him not hide who he really is any longer."

"That's exactly how I felt," Clarissa admitted. "Either way, I didn't want to be around him for any longer than I had to. And as soon as he was gone, I hurried here to tell you what was going on."

"Thanks," Dream said, with genuine gratitude in her voice. "And sorry you had to get dragged into my crap."

Clarissa shook her head. "Don't apologize for a thing. I'm your best friend and I've got your back."

"We've *all* got your back," I said. "You're the one who knows what's best for you. But if you want us to make sure this asshole doesn't come anywhere near you..."

I didn't finish my sentence. The look on Dream's face let me know I didn't need to.

"I'm not going back to him – that's not something I'd consider, even for a second. But he's still in town. And Charmed Bay isn't the biggest place in the world. If he wants to find me here, he will."

The guys and I shared another hard look.

I watched as Jay cracked his knuckles – the thing he did when he was itching for a fight. At that moment, I was right there with him. There wasn't a chance in hell we were going to let anything happen to Dream.

If Adam knew what was good for him, he'd watch his back. Some lines, when crossed, couldn't be walked back. It was a lesson that seemed damn likely Adam was going to learn the hard way.

CHAPTER 18

DREAM

The guys and I finished up lunch, and since there was plenty to go around, Clarissa joined us.

Unfortunately, the rest of the meal wasn't nearly as fun and light-hearted as the start. The news about Adam had hit me like a cold spike to the stomach. When we finished up and put everything away, the guys regarded me with the same expression of concern.

"You want us to stay?" Duncan asked. "Because we will."

"No reason you can't enjoy the rest of the market and not have to worry about you-know-who," Jay added.

"Yeah," Evan put in. "We're here for you."

I took in the sight of the Wolf brothers standing in front of me all puffy-chested.

I couldn't help but laugh.

"What's so funny?" Duncan asked, seeming a bit concerned.

"Nothing," I said. "Just that this is how you guys were back in high school, always ready to do whatever it took to make sure I never had to worry about anything. The more things change, you know?"

The guys smiled.

"We're always going to look out for you, Dream," Duncan said. We're always going to take care of you and make sure you're alright."

At those words, Jay and I shared a quick glance, one that spoke volumes. I had to wonder if he'd told the guys about what had happened, what we'd done the night before. Because he'd "taken care of me," alright. But most likely not in the way Duncan had meant.

"Thanks, guys. And don't worry – I'll keep you all in the loop. I like to handle my own affairs, but I'm smart enough to know when three Navy SEALS might come in handy."

"Hey," Duncan said with a wink. "Two SEALS and a Green Beret."

I laughed, always having found the military rivalries between the guys endearing.

"What about your gear?" Jay asked. "Want us to come back and help you pack up?"

"You kidding?" Clarissa piped up as she wrapped her arm around my shoulder and pulled me close. "Look at these guns." She flexed to prove her point. "They can handle all the gear you can throw at them."

Evan gave Clarissa a skeptical look, then reached forward and wrapped his finger and thumb around the thickest part of her bicep, touching one tip to the other.

"Guns, huh?" he asked with a grin.

"That doesn't count! You guys don't have normal sized hands. They're like...huge bunches of bananas."

The guys laughed.

"Seriously," I said. "I think we can handle it. Just a few boxes. And Jay, I'll make sure to get the tent back to you after this weekend."

He waved the idea away. "Keep it for as long as you need."

We said our goodbyes to the boys, and they were off. Despite everything that was going on, I couldn't help but let my eyes dance from one perfect ass to the other. I'd seen Jay's glorious body on full display, and part of me wanted nothing more than to see the others.

"Not a bad team to have on your side," Clarissa commented as she watched the guys head out. "Useful, and nice to look at."

I laughed, giving her a slight shove. "Alright, alright, none of that now."

"You're no fun," she said with a wag of her finger. "Now, you ready to get back to work? I'll stick around and play assistant if you don't mind. Got the evening off from Blueprint."

"Perfect." I was more than happy for the company.

Together, we reopened the stand. It didn't take long at all before customers started streaming in again. Among them were more than a few boys asking where the soldiers had all gone off to. The Wolf brothers had been a hit, and part of me wondered, with a smile on my face, if I ought to bring them back to the stand some other market day to shore up business.

The rest of the day flew by in a whirlwind of face and body painting. Clarissa was a huge help being right there with supplies and cleanup duty. When it was all done, I came across a pleasant surprise as I counted my money.

"This is weird," I said, iPad in my hand, my eyes on the tallies for all the card swipes.

"What is it?" Clarissa asked as she came over. "Did your card reader go down? I had that happen once at Blueprint and it was the biggest pain in the ass to get the transactions back in there. I had to call up the reader company and everything."

"No, that's not it. Look." I held up the pad, pointing out the total amount I'd rang up that day.

It was far, far more than I'd expected.

"Wow," Clarissa said. "I don't know what a good day for painting is, but I'd guess that's not bad."

"Not bad at all," I said, my eyes on the four-digit total.

I found myself replaying in my mind the conversation I'd had with the guys about how I ought to quit my day job and go into painting full-time. I was still confident in my decision, but with a day like this under my belt I couldn't help but wonder...

"Anyway," I said. "I think this is more than deserving of some Thai food from Tuk-Tuk and a little wine to go with it. What do you think?"

She grinned. "Absolutely not going to say no to either of those."

We packed up and carried the gear to Clarissa's Bug, the trunk more than big enough for everything. Once it was all loaded up, we headed downtown and picked up a couple orders of Pad Thai, along with a pair of bottles of white from the nearby liquor store.

As we drove, I knew in the back of my head that Clarissa needed to know about what happened with Jay and me. She was going to get it out of me eventually, so I figured I might as well spill the beans on my own terms.

As we pulled up to the apartment, however, I found my stomach tensing. Fear spread like frost through me, with worry that Adam might be there waiting. He wasn't, though, and the relief was incredible.

"You OK?" Clarissa asked as we parked. "You looked pale as a sheet."

"Adam."

"*Ahh*," she said. "Don't worry – he's a prick, but he's not stupid. He'd know better than to stalk around here waiting for you. A stunt like that would have me on the phone with the cops. I bet he doesn't want that kind of attention."

She was right. Adam wasn't stupid, which was one of the scariest things about him. Another quick look around confirmed that he wasn't there. For the time being, I didn't need to worry about him.

We decided to leave the boxes and tent in the car for now, both of us starving by that point. A few minutes later we were sitting at the coffee table, take-out in front of us, wine in our glasses, and some Joni Mitchell - one of Clarissa's favorites - on the stereo.

"So," I said after steeling myself with a few bites of Pad Thai. "There's something I need to tell you. Something about Jay…"

Her eyes flashed and she leaned in, clearly interested. "Is that right?"

I went into it, telling her about what happened with Jay on the beach the day before. Just as I'd expected, Clarissa hung off my every word with total, rapt attention. I didn't go into complete detail, but she got the picture.

When I was done, her jaw hung open and her eyes were wide.

"That's *crazy*! You slept with Jay!"

She followed this up by putting her hand on my knee and giving me a shove.

"I did. And now I don't know what to do."

Clarissa let out a scoff. "I'll bet you don't! Do the other guys know? Did Jay tell them?"

"Not sure. I mean, I know they're all close, but I don't know that they'd share things like that."

I sighed, sitting back with a glass of wine in my hands.

"It's ridiculous. I knew it would be a bad idea to get involved with any of them, especially with what's going on with Adam and me. But I couldn't resist! When I was alone with Jay it was like I felt...safe, you know? Like there wasn't anything to worry about. The beach and sunset sure as hell didn't hurt, either."

"I remember what you would often say about Adam," Clarissa began. "How he was always erratic, unpredictable. One day he'd be all lovey-dovey and the next he'd be pissed off and then the next he'd be sulking about this thing or that."

"Right. It was the exact opposite of how I felt with Jay. With Adam I'd feel insecure and unsure. I hated it, hated never knowing what to expect from him."

"Then it makes sense you'd be into the Wolf guys. Jay's a little on the gruffer side, but he's still even-keeled and reliable."

"And I never have any doubt that he cares about me. That goes a long way."

I sipped my wine then shook my head, something else occurring to me.

"What's wrong?" Clarissa asked.

"It's silly."

"Nothing's too silly for your bestie. And you might as well spill it now before I get another glass of wine into you and hear it anyway." She followed this up with a warm smile.

I pursed my lips then spoke. "Just thinking about how I used to be with Adam, how I always tried to get him to...you know, look at me a certain way."

"What kind of way?"

"The way someone looks at you when they love you, when they're crazy about you, when you're the most beautiful person in the world to them. Adam was never like that with me. I guess part of me had hoped that marrying him I might finally get that. But now I know it's because his head was always somewhere else."

"Literally," Clarissa said. Then her eyes flashed. "Sorry, that was in really poor taste."

I couldn't help but laugh. "In poor taste, maybe, but still true. All that time I was trying to get his attention, to make him care about me the way I'd always hoped someone might. But little did I know, he was running around town sticking his dick into whatever woman was up for it."

Clarissa's eyes flashed with anger. "And now he has the nerve to come here and try to get you to take him back. What an asshole!"

I sighed. "But the way Jay looked at me, the way the guys all look at me – that's what I'm talking about! It's like I've been searching for so long for a guy to feel a certain way about me, to look at me with love in his eyes."

"And now you've got three of them," Clarissa replied with a nod, understanding my situation. "But hey, you have to admit – that's not a bad problem to have."

I reached forward and grabbed the bottle of wine, topping off my glass. There was so much more to think about. Like what I wanted to do for my career, if corporate graphic design work was a world that I wanted to stay in.

In the meantime, I gave myself a moment to close my eyes and savor that feeling, the way I felt about the guys, and the way they felt about me.

There was something sweet and perfect about it all, and I wanted to see where that feeling might take me.

No matter what.

CHAPTER 19

JAY

I was ten years old again, my heart pounding with rage and fear as I hid behind my bed, Evan sitting next to me with an expression of fear on his face.

"Evan! Where the hell are you?"

My dad's voice always sounded larger than life, like a booming giant who'd stormed down from some forgotten mountaintop to wreak destruction and havoc.

"What's wrong with Dad?" I asked.

Evan, twelve years old at the time, regarded me with an unsure expression. By that point I was well aware of Dad's anger, how he used it to get what he wanted, to keep the household in line through intimidation.

To me, Dad's anger was confusing. Dads were supposed to be loving. Why did our dad get so angry for no reason?

There was more to it than that. Dad hit Evan, hurt him in ways that Evan was always protecting me from. When I was a kid, I'd never been sure why Dad always seemed to choose him as the main target for his rage. Maybe because Evan was never one to buckle under authority, always talking back and questioning his tyranny.

"Dads in a bad mood," Evan said, trying to keep his voice calm. "You know how he gets."

Calling Dad's anger a "bad mood" was the understatement to end all understatements, but what was he supposed to say? That his own dad liked to hit his kids?

"*Evan!*" Dad's voice sounded like the sheer power of it might be enough to bring the house down to its foundations. "Get your ass out here *right now!*"

The thunderous voice was followed by the banging of his heavy boots against the ground.

I had learned by now that if Dad had to come and find Evan, it would be even worse. Not to mention, there was always the risk that any one of us could be brought into the violence.

"Stay here," Evan said, grabbing my wrist. "I don't know what's wrong with Dad, but we need to hide."

I shook my head. "Can't hide. Dad's going to find us."

Evan took his hand off my wrist and prepared to stand.

"No!" I shouted. "You can't!"

"It's just Dad and I arguing about stuff. Nothing you need to worry about. I have to go, Jay. Dad's...he's not fun when he's in these moods."

Evan regarded me with an expression that suggested he knew he had to give up his hiding place, and that he didn't like it one bit.

My heart pounded and my nerves were on fire. Evan had faced down Dad before, so I knew what to expect by that point. However, that didn't make it any easier. Evan placed his palms on the rug and prepared to stand and I braced myself for what was about to happen.

Evan rose and turned just in time to watch as dad threw open the bedroom door. Dad was tall, but in that moment, he seemed even bigger, larger than life. His eyes seemed to be on fire with pure, molten anger.

"Evan!" he shouted; his voice so loud that I could feel it in my bones. "What have I told you about making me come find you?"

Evan said nothing, knowing there was nothing he could say or do that would help. Every word would be used against him. So, he kept silent.

Dad snorted, the noise reminding me of a bull about to charge.

"Doesn't matter. You're in trouble, kid. And you and I are going to have a talk in the garage. Got it?"

I was still huddled by Evan's feet, hopefully hidden out of sight by the bed.

Evan prepared to take a step in Dad's direction. Without even a moment to react, Dad flew across the room with superhuman speed, bent over, grabbed the bed, and flipped it away as if it weighed nothing at all.

I was exposed and Dad's eyes landed on me.

"What the hell are you doing here, Jay?" Dad growled. "Were you two coming up with new ways to ignore my rules, to disrespect me?"

"No!" Evan shouted. "He just wanted to know—"

Dad's huge hand shot out and grabbed Evan by the shoulder. He squeezed hard, hard enough to pull a cry of pain out of Evan's mouth.

"Shut up!" Dad snarled. "You're *both* coming with me!"

"No!" Evan repeated.

But there was nothing Evan could do. Dad reached down and snatched me up by the wrist, yanking me to my feet as tears poured down my face. Together, Dad dragged us from the bedroom, both of us screaming, the only thought on my mind was confusion and hurt. Why was dad treating us this way?

I awoke to the chipper chime of my phone alarm. Without thinking, I shot my hand out and turned it off. A glance down at the white undershirt I had on revealed that I'd sweated through it. It was the typical physiological reaction to the dreams, as if my entire fight-or-flight response were channeled into my sweat glands.

I hated it, hated the dreams about Dad. They were always the same – Dad coming for Evan, and I had the opportunity to do something - but I was too young and scared to stand up to him. I was only ten, I shouldn't blame myself, but I did. I would eventually stand up to our father, but all the times I hadn't were etched in my brain forever.

It was hard to believe Evan didn't turn out more like me. After all, he's the one that lived through the years of abuse. He was the one who suffered the most. But somehow, he was warm, happy-go-lucky and not withdrawn and hard like me. Made me wonder how we turned out so differently.

I needed to push it all out of my head. I checked the time on my phone, seeing that it was a little after seven-thirty. I hurried to the bathroom, stripped off my clothes and jumped into the shower to get my day started. The hot water against my body always helped in washing away the traces of the nightmares when they happened.

When I was done in the bathroom, I threw on a pair of jeans, a black Henley, and a hooded sweatshirt, along with some black boots. The day outside was gray and dreary, a reminder that even though the weather had been warmer than usual, it was still winter. Summers could be hot and clear, but whenever I thought of home the memory was always skies of deep, slate gray and the wind lolling the tops of the trees. For some reason, I always thought of winter.

My place was a cabin outside of town, the property isolated and surrounded by deep green evergreen trees, their height looming up into the sky. Typically, it was my place of perfect solitude, where I went to recharge.

That morning, however, I knew I needed to get out of the house. I grabbed my keys and a book and headed out, deciding to swing by Blueprint for a cup of coffee. I remembered Dream mentioning that she would be working on Monday, and that she had plans to go to Blueprint to grab her morning coffee where Clarissa worked.

I drove my truck into town, a bit of rain sprinkling onto the windshield. Ten minutes later I pulled into the lot in front of Blueprint. Clarissa's Bug was there, but I couldn't see any sign of Dream through the tall glass windows of the shop.

I stepped into the coffee shop, the place bustling with the morning rush. The din of customers mixed with the hissing of the espresso machines and the growling of coffee grinders. Still a bit on edge from my dream, the sounds took a few moments to get used to.

I scanned the tables, not spotting Dream among the people seated. But I did see Clarissa. She was behind the counter with the rest of the Blueprint crew, handing out coffees and taking orders. Part of me didn't want to bother her in the middle of her rush, but when she saw that I was there her face lit up and she waved me over.

"Hey!" she said, placing her hands on the counter. "What's up? There's a little bit of a line but I can sneak you an espresso if that's what you're here for." She winked, tilting her head toward the big espresso machine behind her.

"Sure – I'll take a double Americano."

"Coming right up!" she turned to the machine and began loading the espresso. "Hey – you haven't seen Dream, have you?"

My stomach tensed. "No. I'd actually come in hoping to bump into her."

"We were supposed to do breakfast before she started work. She said she'd get in around eight but it's almost eight-thirty and she's still not here."

Clarissa placed a to-go cup of espresso in front of me, the crema on the top perfect. I slipped out my wallet, taking a five from inside and putting it in the tip jar.

"Have you tried to call her? Text her?"

She shook her head. "Been too busy. You might want to, though. I'm a little on edge when it comes to her on account of the whole Adam thing. And thanks, by the way." She smiled, glancing over at the tip jar.

"Sure. I might try to get in touch with her. Knowing Adam's running around town..."

Clarissa shivered, as if grossed out. "If you do, tell me what you find out, OK?"

"Will do."

I took my coffee and book and found a small table by the window. The sky above roiled with the promise of a winter storm. I slipped my phone out of my pocket, wondering if I should get in touch or give her space.

Things were complicated with Dream, and I had no doubt they'd only become more so.

But Clarissa was worried about her, and so was I. I tapped out a quick message for her.

Hey Dream, just spoke to Clarissa. She asked me to check on you since you two had breakfast this morning and she hadn't heard from you.

I sipped my Americano and waited for a response. Only a few minutes had passed, but I was getting anxious. Decided to see if any of the guys might be with her, perhaps they had kept her from meeting Clarissa.

Hey guys, just wondering if any of you have seen Dream this morning?

Evan responded first, Sad to say I haven't. Should I check on her?

You'd like that, wouldn't you? I texted back. I sipped my coffee again and was pondering heading over to her place when my phone buzzed again. This time, it was Clarissa.

Hey there! Please tell Clarissa I'm just running late and that I'm sorry.

Relief washed over me in an instant. Knowing that Adam was in town set my nerves on edge, and if I'd had my way, Dream would never be out of my sight... but she was a grown woman and had made herself very clear - she could handle herself. So I had to respect her wishes.

As hard as that might be to do.

CHAPTER 20

DREAM

The rain pattered down gently as I hurried along the main street of town. The plan was to have a quick breakfast, after which I could do my onboarding for remote work on my laptop. Once that was done, I'd head back home and start my first real workday out of Clarissa's living room.

The day wasn't getting off to a good start, however when I slept through my alarm. I wanted to text Clarissa, but I knew she was likely right in the middle of the morning rush. Nothing to do but hurry my butt along and get there ASAP.

It didn't help matters that working my regular job was the last thing I wanted to do. The weekend had been so fun. I'd gotten to spend time with Clarissa and the Wolf brothers, making art, enjoying the sun, and earning a little money. Spending the next eight to nine hours plopped in front of my laptop with Photoshop opened seemed like total hell in comparison.

For now, though, it was what I had to do.

I glanced up at the sky as I hurried down the sidewalk, noticing that it was growing darker by the second. I needed to hurry up and get there unless I wanted to get stuck in the downpour. It was looking like I'd need to borrow Clarissa's car to drive home.

"Hey! Deedee!"

A familiar male voice called out to me. I stopped in my tracks, my blood running cold.

There was only one person on earth who called me "Deedee." And it was the last person I wanted to see.

"Deedee! Hold up!"

I looked around, trying to spot the source of the sound. Then I laid eyes on him, getting out of a nearby parked car.

Adam had found me.

"There you are!" He was in the process of climbing out of some luxury car that was likely a rental, a plastic bag in his hands as he shut the door and started over in my direction. I glanced around, as if someone nearby might be able to pull me away from the last conversation that I wanted to get stuck in.

No such luck. He was coming over, and there was nothing I could do.

Adam Myles wasn't a bad looking guy, really. He was tall and slim, his brown hair close-cropped and his overall look on the preppy side. He wasn't big and beefy like the Wolf brothers, his body more like a swimmer's, long and lean. He was dressed in light brown chinos with black dress shoes and a white button-up. His face was trim and clean-shaven, his dark eyes flashing with his typical high level of enthusiasm.

Everything about him on the surface seemed friendly and normal, like any other white-collar guy who'd never spent a day of his life worrying about money. But I'd known him long enough to understand just how quickly that friendly face could turn hard, those eyes narrowing into hateful little slits. There was a dark side to Adam, one that he did a damn good job at hiding from everyone but me. That two-faced nature of his made it hard to get anyone to believe me when I told them what he could be like behind closed doors.

Adam closed the distance between us, a big smile on his face.

Being so close to him for the first time after our breakup made me sick with fright. I did my best to keep calm, to not let it show how scared I was.

"Deedee," he said, looking me up and down, shaking his head. "God, I can't tell you how good it is to see you."

"Wish I could say the same for you." I knew I was playing a dangerous game as soon as I'd said the words. But I didn't care. What would be the point of not letting him know exactly how I felt?

His smile faded for a moment before quickly returning.

"Been looking all over for you," he said. "Where are you staying?"

"A friend's."

His eyes narrowed. "Who? A guy?"

There it was – the jealousy, the anger.

"No. Not a guy. Even if it was, it would be none of your business."

The anger faded, the smile once again returning. "Well, it doesn't matter, I guess. Just so you've got somewhere to crash, right?" He brought in a big lungful of air, let it out, then lifted the bag. "Anyway, I was planning on swinging by Clarissa's again. Figured there was a chance you might be there. And if you were, I got your favorite breakfast – some strawberry pancakes with whipped cream from the Red Kettle."

"Thanks, but I'm not hungry. And I need to get going."

He pursed his lips together, letting the bag drop to his side. "I figured it might be hard to get you to talk with me."

"Can you blame me?" I asked. "After the way we left things?"

He raised an eyebrow. "You mean with you sneaking out without so much as a word? That hurt, Dream. It really hurt. We were supposed to get married."

"Lots of things were supposed to happen," I said. "But things change. People change. Or, at least, they show their true colors."

Adam sighed, nodding as if he were conceding the point. "I have a proposal for you – talk to me for ten minutes. Ten minutes is all I ask, and if you don't like what I have to say I'll leave and go back to Chicago and never bother you again. Deal?"

Part of me wanted to tell him to screw off right then and there. But standing in front of Adam it was impossible not to think of him the way I once did, as a man I loved, a man I wanted to marry. I hated how weak I felt in that moment. I also realized why I'd left without speaking to him in person.

I sighed. "Fine. Ten minutes."

A big, happy grin spread across his face. "You're not going to regret it. But come on – let's get out of the drizzle." He nodded to a nearby corner park across the street. Together we made our way over and sat at a picnic table under the cover of the Bigleaf Maple that dominated the space. The tree cover was thick enough that the rain didn't come through.

He set the bag on the table and placed his hands palm down. Then he took a big, slow breath, let it out, and began.

"I'm sorry. I'm really, really sorry." He shook his head. "What more can I say? I had the most amazing, most beautiful girl in the world living with me and I threw it away because I was greedy and selfish and angry. I was this close to marrying you, to being the luckiest man in the world, and I threw it away because I wanted more."

He shook his head again, this time in disbelief.

"When you left, I was upset. Hell, I was upset before you left – and I've got a good feeling that's why you finally went out the door."

"It was," I said. "But you know there was more to it than that. Don't insult me by pretending you don't know."

Adam nodded, not trying to deny it.

"You're right. The night before you left, the night before we had that awful argument where I lost my temper...I know why I was so mad."

"And I know, too. You were mad because you got caught."

"No. I was mad because you finding out and being a witness to what I was doing made me realize how screwed up and horrible it was to treat you the way I had."

I didn't know what to say. Adam had always been on the arrogant side, the sort of man to do whatever he wanted and if you didn't like it, tough. That's not how he was at that moment. He was apologizing. It was a side of Adam I'd never seen before.

"When you left, when the shock of you being gone wore off, all I had left was my regret, and shame because of how I'd treated you. I never want to feel that way again. More importantly, I never want *you* to feel the way that you did again. I'll never forgive myself for treating you so badly. If you'll give me the chance, I'll spend my life trying to make it up to you."

He went on, a smile spread across his face. "We could pick up from where we left off like nothing happened. We'd plan our wedding, get married, and live the life we'd always dreamed of. And... your art. God, I can't believe how disrespectful I was of that." He shook his head, a determined expression on his face. "Never again. I'd give you all you needed, all the time, the resources, to make your dreams of being an artist come true. All you'd need to do is...say *yes*."

"What are you saying?"

He reached across the table and took my hand. I was too stunned to pull it back.

"I'm saying that I'm sorry. I'm saying that I want you to take me back, to give me another shot. I know I'm not a perfect man." He chuckled wryly. "Hell, I'm far from it. But that's what I realized about you, Deedee – you make me want to be a better man. I don't deserve a woman like you, and when I decided to try this insane plan of coming back to Charmed Bay, I was prepared for the possibility that you might tell me to screw off."

He paused, and I got the impression he was waiting for me to say it.

I didn't, and I couldn't figure out why. I had every right to, in fact, after what he'd done.

"Listen, this is a lot to take in, a lot to process. I'd love it if you opened your arms wide right here under this tree and took me back on the spot, but I'm not naïve enough to think that might happen.

Instead, I want you to take some time. Think about it, alright? You have my number. I can't wait to hear from you, one way or another."

With that, he gave me a warm, understanding smile.

"Have some breakfast. I know you well enough to know you can't turn down some strawberry pancakes. There's coffee in there, too. Talk to you soon, Deedee."

He didn't say another word before getting up and leaving me alone. Not knowing what else to do, I turned to watch him make his way back to his car. The rain had picked up by that point, coming down a bit harder. Adam slipped into his car and drove off, disappearing around the next block.

Just like that, I was alone, left to sit and stew in the insane conversation I'd just had. Before Adam had spilled his guts, I'd been totally prepared to do exactly what he'd said, to tell him to screw off and leave me alone forever. After hearing him say his piece, however, I was...confused

He'd seemed contrite in a way I'd never seen him before, genuinely upset that he'd hurt me, ready to make things right. I wasn't even sure that was the same man I'd been engaged to; it was almost creepy.

It would be easier to just go back with him, to pretend that everything he said was true. But even if it was true, did I want to go back to Chicago, back to that life, after having a taste of what life could be like in Charmed Bay?

And there were the Wolf brothers; the way I felt about them was unlike anything I'd known before – even with Adam. Then again, what the hell was I thinking? There were three of them and one of me. They'd said I didn't have to pick one of them, but what did that even mean? What was I supposed to do, date three guys? Three guys who were brothers?

What the hell would Charmed Bay say about that? God, we'd have to move to Alaska and live in a cabin in the woods or something. As soon as I considered the words, the image of the four of us all living together in some secluded cabin appeared in my mind, the brothers dressed in flannels and boots and rugged jeans, the four of us getting nice and cozy by the fire as the snow drifted down...

I shook my head, putting it out of my mind as I grabbed the coffee from the bag, taking a sip as the rain came down. Things were complicated as all hell, but there was one thing I knew. I took my phone out of my bag and fired off a text to Clarissa, letting her know that I wouldn't be coming in for breakfast.

I had some major thinking to do.

CHAPTER 21

DUNCAN

G oing to Dream's unannounced might've been a bad idea. But I didn't care. After Jay's text asking if we'd seen Dream, I became worried. He later replied it was fine, but without giving any details. I needed to know for myself that she was okay.

I couldn't stop thinking about Dream and Adam and I wasn't sure why. Was I envious? Pissed off at the idea of Adam swooping back in and convincing her to come back to Chicago with him? Or was it something else, maybe me feeling a sense of protectiveness over her? Either way, I knew I'd have to see her to know for sure.

I pulled up to Clarissa's place, seeing one light on inside. After I parked the car and turned off the engine, I gave myself a moment to think it over, to try and figure out if I was about to do something stupid.

Didn't matter. I was there, and as I sat in the lot, the idea of turning the car back on and pulling away was out of the question.

I hopped out of the car and stepped up to the door. My stomach was tense, like I was picking a girl up for a first date. I snorted in amusement, shook my head at how much of a dumbass I was being, then knocked.

Music played from inside, and I focused for a moment to hear that it was The Smashing Pumpkins. Before I could make out the song, the door opened.

Dream stood there, looking as gorgeous as ever. She was dressed in a gray pair of cotton lounge shorts, and a half-shirt that showed off her toned middle. Her hair was in her usual ponytail, and she didn't seem to have a drop of makeup on her face – not that she needed it. She regarded me with an expression of surprise.

"Duncan?"

"Hey!" At that moment I realized just how freaking weird it was to show up unannounced. Who, in the age of text messages, did something like that?

Me, I guess.

"What's up?" I asked.

She cocked her head and looked over my shoulder, as if there might be a camera crew or something.

"Nothing. Just hanging out and going over some work stuff for tomorrow. What's up with *you*?"

That was a damn good question. What *was* up with me?

"Uh, I was in the area coming home from some errands. I don't live too far from here, so I figured I'd drop in to say hey.'"

She smiled. "Very retro of you, Duncan Wolf."

I laughed. "I guess retro works."

A moment passed. It wasn't an awkward moment – it was something different, as if we were simply enjoying one another's company before getting into the reason why I was there.

She scoffed and shook her head, as if something had occurred to her that she couldn't believe she'd forgotten. "What's wrong with me? Come in!" Dream stepped aside and eagerly gestured for me to enter.

I did and took in the sights of her place. Or Clarissa's place. The couch was piled with Dream's bedding and pillows, the coffee table covered in sketches, a half-drunk glass of white wine close at hand. I shut the door behind me and watched as Dream stepped around the kitchen island.

Dream took her phone out of her pocket and turned down the music. "Want something to drink? I've got a bottle of wine open, but there's beer too."

"Wine's fine. Where's Clarissa?" I asked as I stepped over to the kitchen bar.

"She's working at Blueprint today."

"Oh, I thought you two were having breakfast this morning, I didn't realize--"

Dream flashed me a curious smile and shook her head. "Word sure gets around fast in this town. Let me guess, Jay sent you over to check on me?"

"Well he didn't send me over, but he did ask if we'd seen you this morning, and it had me a little worried."

"Ahh the joys of small towns," Dream chuckled before turning around to grab the bottle of wine. She had to bend over to retrieve it, and my eyes went right to her backside, to the bottom of her ass poking out of her shorts as she bent over. My cock shifted, the idea of stepping over to Dream and taking her from behind flashing in my mind.

Get it together, dude, I told myself. *You didn't come here to admire the way she looks in a pair of short shorts.*

She turned, standing on her tiptoes to pull down a glass then filled it with the wine.

"Something tells me you're not usually a white wine kind of dude." Dream stepped around the kitchen island and came over to me.

"What, just because I'm a Green Beret you think I can't enjoy a crisp glass of white every now and then?"

Dream laughed as she placed the glass in my hands, her fingers grazing mine.

"You're just full of surprises, aren't you, Duncan?"

"Happy to keep you on your toes."

She tilted her head toward the couch, and I followed her over.

Once she was there, she began frantically pulling pillows and blankets away to clear space for me.

"Sorry – this is kind of my bed and workstation all in one."

"No problem. Glad to see that you are working on your art."

Once a space had been cleared for me, I sat on the couch and leaned forward to look at the sketches. They were amazing, of course, with pictures of the Charmed Bay coast done in spectacular detail.

"You know," I began. But I didn't finish the sentence – no doubt she knew what I was going to say.

"I *do* know," she said, nodding and pursing her lips. "I should be doing this full-time. But it's trickier than that."

"Scary, sure. Tricky? I'm not so sure. A woman with talent like this...I can't imagine you having to grind for too long before you get a good thing going."

She smiled warmly. "That's nice of you to say. I mean it. But for the time being I've got so much on my mind. Figuring out my art career, if I'm even going to have one, isn't even close to the top of my priority list." Her expression turned grave, as if whatever had been troubling her appeared in her thoughts at that moment.

Part of me wanted to not let up, to give her some more words of encouragement. But the better part of me knew that I needed to get to the point, to the reason I'd come.

"Anyway," she said, shaking her head as if coming out of a trance. "I could tell from the moment I opened the door that you had something on your mind. What's up?"

I took a sip of my wine, trying to decide where to begin. It was bizarre. I'd spent the drive going over in my head exactly what I wanted to say to her. Now that I was there, now that we were alone, my mind was totally blank. There was something about Dream that made it hard to think straight.

Or maybe it was just those tiny shorts she had on, the way she was sitting with her legs crossed that put her full, luscious thighs on display.

I cleared my throat, deciding to start with the name at the center of the issue.

"Adam."

The smile vanished from her face the moment I said the name. She glanced down, quickly taking a sip of her wine, her thumb rubbing up and down the glass's stem.

"I've been thinking about what happened at the market, what Clarissa said. Just the idea of Adam coming back here after what he pulled and trying to get into your good graces...it makes me mad, to put it really, really freaking lightly."

"Well, he certainly tried," Dream said, her voice lower than usual.

"He what?" My fists balled up at my sides. "If he hurt you again, I'm going to--"

"Calm down, he just found me in town and tried to apologize for all the bullshit," she said, her facial expression making her seem more distant, as if she wasn't really there with me. It was clear that what-ever happened earlier had really upset her. "He tried to tell me he was a different man, that he would change."

Anger boiled up in me, and I clenched my jaw hard for several seconds to try and let the rage pass. It did, and I went on. "And did you tell him to fuck right off?"."

"Well-- not exactly, no."

"Listen, I know that I have no right to tell you how to live your life, but please, Dream. I care about you, and there's no reason why you should waste even a second more with someone like him."

She listened attentively, the warmth in her eyes suggesting that she was more than receptive to what I was saying.

I could've stopped there. I'd made my point, that she shouldn't be with Adam. What more needed to be said?

But I didn't stop there, and what came next seemed to have left my mouth of its own accord.

"You shouldn't be with him. You deserve better. In fact, if I had my way you'd be with me."

I finally managed to shut myself up, but it was too late. The expression on her face let me know that I'd possibly crossed a line that I wouldn't be able to come back from.

"You want me to be with you?" she asked.

"That's right. You're the one I want, Dream. I get that this might seem out of left field, and it might make you uncomfortable to hear, and if that's the case, I'm sorry. But it's the truth, and it's how I've felt for a long time."

As soon as I finished speaking, I felt...*relief*. I wasn't regretful, I didn't feel like an idiot. OK, maybe a little bit of an idiot, but I was relieved as hell that I'd finally gotten it off my chest. Years and years I'd carried around the true nature of my feelings for Dream and now they were out in the open.

She broke eye contact with me, turning her attention to the glass of wine. Her hand shot out and she grabbed the glass by the stem, bringing it to her lips and taking a quick sip.

There was a damn good chance I'd screwed up, that I'd ruined things between us. As happy as I was to have put it all out there like that, I reminded myself that there was no guarantee she felt the same way. For all I knew, she was trying to come up with a way to tell me to screw off.

I had to give her an out.

"Listen, this is a lot to take in, I get it. You're here trying to relax after what you heard about Adam, and here I am, making it even more complicated. So, if you want me gone, just say the word and I'll leave without protest."

She took another sip of wine and nodded. Then Dream set down the glass and continued staring ahead.

Finally, she shook her head. "I don't want you to go. I want you to stay. And I'm glad you're here." She turned to me, her expression softening, a small smile forming on her lips.

My heart skipped a beat, and when she reached forward and placed her hand on mine, I had a damn good feeling that things were about to get very interesting.

CHAPTER 22

DREAM

Duncan had said what, deep down, I was hoping he'd tell me from the moment I'd answered the door.

But it was more complicated than a simple matter of liking him back – which I did, of course. There was the little, teensy detail of my having slept with his brother. What the hell was I supposed to say, that sure, I dug him too and we could see where it took us so long as he didn't care that I'd had his brother inside of me less than forty-eight hours ago?

Looking into his eyes, however, seemed to make it all appear so simple. I wanted him, and he wanted me. The longer my hand lingered on his, the more turned on I became, the wetter I grew between my thighs.

Once more, the words I'd heard that first night at the bar played in my mind.

"You don't have to pick one of us..."

But were they just words? How the hell could I be certain the brothers would be totally fine with me having all three of them? Wasn't that a recipe for anger and jealousy?

"It's fine," Duncan said, slipping his hand from underneath mine. "No pressure, alright? Last thing I wanted to do is come over here and give you one more thing to worry about."

He placed his hands on his legs and prepared to get up. But the instant my hand was no longer touching his I knew that I didn't want him to leave.

"Wait," I said. My hand shot out toward his. I grabbed it harder than I'd anticipated, my squeeze making Duncan's eyes flash with surprise.

He turned, not saying a word. Duncan had been good about it all, letting me know that the ball was in my court. I'd been indecisive for long enough.

I rose standing in front of him. Duncan, like his brothers, was tall enough to loom over me, to make me feel tiny in a way I liked.

"Yeah?" he asked.

"I want you to stay. I want you here."

I reached down and took his hand, wrapping my fingers around it. Duncan smiled, stepping forward and placing his huge hand on my shoulder. He brought me close to him, his solid muscles feeling like I'd just pressed myself against a brick wall.

"Then I'll stay," he said.

"Good."

I opened my mouth slightly, tilting my chin up as I wordlessly invited the kiss I'd been craving since he'd arrived. Thankfully, I didn't need to say what I wanted. Duncan leaned down and placed his fingertips under my chin, holding me in place as he put his lips on mine.

As soon as the kiss began, I was filled with the same electricity that had flowed through me when I'd been with Jay. But there was a subtle difference in the way Duncan touched me, the way he held me, the way he kissed me. Jay was aggressive in exactly the right way, which I'd loved. But Duncan seemed different – tenderness and passion all at once.

Our mouths opened at the same time, his tongue probing for mine, the sweetness from the wine trickling across my palate. I wrapped my arms around him, savoring the sensation of his solid, powerful body, his back a wide "V" underneath his shirt. We kissed more and more, my pussy clenching, soaking through my panties.

Right when I was about to lose myself in the kiss, thoughts of his brothers returned. Evan and Jay had been the ones to tell me that the three of us could be together, but how did Duncan feel about all of this? I had already slept with his brother; did he know about that? How did he feel?

And even if he was okay with it in the moment, what if it caused a rift between the three of them?

Duncan seemed to sense my hesitation. He placed his hands on my upper arms and pulled back, regarding me with an expression of concern.

"What's wrong?"

What the hell was I supposed to say? Did I need to tell him the truth right then and there? What even was the truth to tell? That I had feelings for him and his brothers, that I couldn't pick just one over the other?

"I just have a lot going on. Sorry. I'm getting distracted and it's a total buzzkill."

He smiled, a smile that was warm and sexy and hungry all at once.

"How about this – you and I go back to what we were doing, and I promise I'll give you a damn good distraction from the distraction." Duncan followed this up with another one of those same smiles, making the offer even more enticing.

"Duncan, it's about you and your brothers, I--"

"Shhh," he said, tracing my lips with his fingertips. "You don't have to worry about that. You don't have to choose."

"But--" I didn't even know how to finish my sentence. Should I tell him it felt wrong? Because that would be a lie. It felt right, so totally right. But it could also complicate things between all of us, and that was something I did not want.

It was my last chance to back off. Because if I were to let him put those gorgeous lips on mine one more time, there'd be no taking them off.

"No buts," Duncan said, his hands stroking my cheek ever so tenderly. "Everything will be fine, Dream."

Screw it. I couldn't deny it anymore.

I smiled up at him and closed my eyes.

He brought his mouth to mine, speaking with his touch instead of his words.

We kissed, our hands moving all over one another's bodies, his tongue wrapping around mine, his cock pressing through his jeans. I couldn't help but wonder what he had going on underneath the denim, if Duncan's towering height and striking good looks weren't the only thing he had in common with his brother.

I grabbed the bottom of his shirt and pulled it up over his head. His body was shredded, just as I'd expected. A few scars marred his otherwise perfect physique, but I didn't mind them one bit. If anything, they reminded me that his body was built for action, that he wasn't simply some gym-sculpted pretty boy.

Everything about him turned me on like mad. My shirt came off, Duncan pulling it up and tossing it to the side of the living room. Next, his hands swooped down the curve of my back, resting on my ass through my shorts. He squeezed my rear hard enough to make my eyes go wide with surprise. The way he touched me made it clear beyond a shadow of a doubt that he wanted me like crazy.

His hands still on my ass, he lifted me off my feet. I let out a happy squeal as he hoisted me off the ground, loving how effortlessly he carried me. I wrapped my legs around him, letting his cock press against my pussy through my shorts as he strode from the kitchen to the living room. Once we were there, he set me down gently on the edge of the couch, dropping down to his knees and spreading my legs.

Duncan moved his hands under my ass once more, this time taking my shorts by the waistband and pulling them down. I squeezed my legs together just enough to help him lower my shorts. A glance down revealed that I was wearing a simple pair of black hipster panties, and I made a mental note to try and get in the habit of putting on sexier underwear. .

The panties didn't stay on for long, however. He swept his big palms over my thighs, tingles spreading through my body at his touch. I watched eagerly as he slipped his fingers underneath the waistband of my panties, rolling them down to my ankles.

Once I was bare, Duncan put his hands on my hips and moved me back further, my legs dangling over his shoulders, my soaked pussy right in front of his face.

"You know," he said, the fingers of his right hand inching closer and closer to between my legs. "I've always wondered what you tasted liked."

His deep, low voice saying words like those was enough to push me to the brink.

"Now's your chance to find out."

Duncan flashed me another smile, then lowered his head between my legs. He spread me open, teasing my clit before pressing his tongue against me. The sparking pleasure was so immediate, so intense, that all I could do was let my head hang back and sigh. Duncan pressed against my clit with the flat, wet surface of his tongue, dragging it slowly over my most sensitive of spots. As he worked his magic with his mouth, he moved into me with his fingers.

The sensation of him inside me that way was intense, throbbing delight making me shake and quiver.

"Feel good when I do that?" he asked, lifting his head while still moving his fingers in and out of me, his lips glistening with my juices.

"Feels so damn good," I said, my hips tightening as he curled his fingers in a come-hither gesture, hitting my G-spot as he brought his lips back down to my womanhood.

I sighed and moaned, my hips rolling up and down like waves as the sensation of total ecstasy roiled through me. Duncan soon changed his technique, using the tip of his tongue to make slow circles around my clit as his fingers worked in and out of me.

It was enough to take me over the edge. A hot, pulsing orgasm rocked me from toe to top. I slipped my hands into Duncan's thick hair as he continued to eat me.

Duncan sensed when the orgasm was done, placing his hands on the edge of the couch and raising himself up. He quickly removed his jeans and boxer briefs, then moved toward me, stopping when he was directly over top, his spear-straight cock pointing directly down at me. His lips still glistened, and I couldn't help but ask him the question he'd begged.

"Well?" I asked. "Did I taste like you were expecting?"

"Even better." He grinned, and I did the same.

As amazing as the orgasm had felt, I needed more. I reached down and wrapped my fingers around his cock. He was warm and stiff and just as big as I'd been hoping, as big as I'd been craving.

He closed his eyes, savoring the sensation of my touch. I stroked his long thickness up and down, my fingertips lingering on the contours of his member, growls of pleasure rumbling from his mouth. It wasn't long before he couldn't take any more. His eyes flashed open, his expression one of intense hunger.

I guided him down, opening my legs and wrapping them around his narrow, powerful hips. His head pushed my lips apart, and I bucked upward to give him the angle he needed to plunge deeply into me. Duncan pushed inch after inch inside, giving me the sensation of being split in two in the best way imaginable. When he was buried to the root, I forced my eyes open, glancing down and burning into my memory the sight of him between my legs.

I swept my hands to his ass. Duncan raised his hips up and pushed into me, my wetness making his cock slick, letting him glide into me effortlessly. It wasn't long before he was in a steady rhythm, his length vanishing into me over and over, my pussy stretched to accommodate him, my modest breasts rocking back and forth from the unrelenting penetration.

The next orgasm was more powerful than the first, my entire body clenching, my arms and legs wrapped around him. He drove into me through the orgasm.

And when it was done, I still wanted *more*.

"Lie on your back," I said, a sly smile on my lips. "Now it's my turn to taste *you*."

CHAPTER 23

DUNCAN

The lust in Dream's eyes was about the sexiest damn thing I'd ever seen in my life.

At least, that's what I thought right up until the moment she wrapped her plump, sensual lips around my cock.

She teased me at first, stroking my member slowly, dragging the backs of her nails against my length in a way that drove me absolutely wild. After a bit of this, she kissed me up and down, from root to head. And after she'd had enough of that, she took me into her mouth.

Dream's mouth was warm and wet and inviting, her tongue circling around my head as she sucked me slowly, deeply.

She went down, down, until Dream had half my length inside of her. And when she looked up at me with those eager eyes, her mouth full of my cock, it took all the restraint I had not to unload down her throat.

Dream repeated the process, and when she was done my cock glistened from the hard work.

"Don't finish just yet," she said.

"Wouldn't dare."

I rose, slipping my arm under her trim belly and flipping her over. Dream's body was something special, but her ass was on another level. Perfect and plump and heart-shaped, it was the kind of booty that could make a grown man weep.

I placed a hand on her left cheek, wrapping the other around my cock and placing it at her opening. Once I was in position, I slid into her, watching my cock vanish inside of her. She moaned as I penetrated her, pressing her ass against my crotch as if she wanted to make sure I put every last inch inside of her.

I did just as her body asked, burying myself as deeply as I could. Once I was fully pushed into her, I took a moment to savor the delicious pleasure of Dream's warm, velvet walls wrapped around my engorged prick. Seeing her bent over in front of me, waiting for more was, well, a dream come true.

I pulled back and pushed into her, watched as her lips stretched to grip me. One more thrust, and then another, and then another, and soon I was bucking into her with wild abandon, my hands caressing her ass and hips and reaching around to cup her perfect breasts.

Dream looked back at me as I worked, glancing at me with hungry eyes before wincing into a tight expression of total pleasure. I focused on her body, drinking in the sight of her muscles working, her ass bouncing, her breasts swaying back and forth underneath her.

"Come inside of me, Duncan," she moaned, yearning in her words. "Come right as I do—!"

She didn't manage another word. Her womanhood cinched around me as she came, the tightness pushing me over the point of no return. With a hard grunt I came, my cock pulsing as I drained myself into her willing walls. She moaned and bucked, writhing against me.

We rose together and we fell together. Dream collapsed forward and I fell on top of her, rolling off as quickly as I could so as not to hurt her. We laid like that for a long while, saying nothing and simply staring into one another's eyes. She was so damn beautiful that it almost hurt to look at her.

Finally, after several moments, I couldn't help but break the silence.

"I can't even tell you how long I've been thinking about that."

"Well, I'd be lying if I were to say I hadn't been thinking bad thoughts like those about you, Duncan. And believe me, when you're an awkward kid in high school, having three hot as hell brothers looking out for you, well, it was almost too much for me at times.'."

"Well looks like you got your wish, Dream," I said with a grin.

Dream smiled back at me, but before she said another word, her eyes flashed as she realized something. She sat up, and I was half convinced she was about to say that she'd just realized what a horrible idea this had been.

"*Crap.*"

"What is it?" I asked.

"Clarissa," she said.

"When's she due back?" I asked.

She checked the clock on the wall. "In twenty minutes or so."

"Shoot. Then I should get out of here."

A look of longing appeared on Dream's face, one that suggested she didn't want me to go anywhere. I wasn't exactly thrilled to go, either. However, the last thing we needed was Clarissa coming home and finding out that Dream had just slept with me. It took all the effort I had, but I managed to put both feet on the ground and get off the couch.

"Wow," Dream said. "Not going to get tired of that view."

"Huh?" I glanced over my shoulder and realized that I was standing buck naked, my rear only a few feet from her. I couldn't help but laugh.

Together we threw on our clothes and did our best to make the couch look like it hadn't just had two people screwing on it. When that was done and we were dressed, the two of us hurried out of the apartment. It wasn't that late, but the sun was already disappearing on the horizon. The evening was still and cool, the evening quiet.

The storm from earlier had passed. Off in the distance the waves crashed on the shore in soft hushes.

"One of those nights that makes you glad to live in a place like this, huh?" I asked.

"Yeah. One of those nights that makes you wish you could spend it with a certain someone and not kick them out into the cold." She followed this up with a sly smile.

"Don't make leaving any harder," I said, returning her smile.

When we were near my car, Dream and I turned to face one another. The silver light of the moon gave her already beautiful features an unearthly glow. It was impossible to stand there in front of her without planting one last kiss on her lips.

So, that's what I did. I leaned forward and kissed Dream, her mouth melting into mine, our tongues intertwining for several long moments. I didn't want it to end, but knew it had to. I took my lips from hers and backed up.

"See you around, Dream," I said with a smile as I opened my car door.

She said nothing in response, simply smiling and gently waving her fingertips, as if nothing needed to be said.

She was right.

I woke up bright and early that next morning with the biggest damn smile on my face I'd had in a long, long time. Dream was on my mind, of course – the only subject of my thoughts from the moment I woke up and beyond. A quick check of my phone revealed a text from Evan asking if I was planning on heading to the gym for a morning workout, that he and Jay wanted to meet me there. I replied with an affirmative.

I decided to skip the shower, figuring I'd get one in at the locker room at Jake's. After throwing on some gym clothes and making myself an iced coffee mixed with some pre-workout protein powder, I was on my way.

The morning was perfect. The air was cool, but still warmer than most winter days, and the sun came up in stunning colors over the eastern horizon. I pulled up to the gym next to Evan and Jay's cars, the place already alive with activity. After checking in and chatting for a few minutes with the front desk employees, who I was on a first name basis with, I found Evan and Jay by the leg press machine switching off sets.

Evan, who was leaning against the machine while Jay worked, regarded me with an expression of curiosity.

"Whoa," he said, smirking a bit. "Someone had a good night's sleep."

"What're you talking about?" I asked as I made my way over to the guys.

Evan gestured toward my face, a bottle of light blue Gatorade Zero in his other hand. Jay, in the middle of his set, greeted me with a quick flip up of his chin before turning his attention back to the task at hand.

"You rolled up with the biggest, most shit-eating-grin on your face. I mean, you look like you got the best news of your life, man."

Jay pushed the weights back up one last time before locking them into place with the safety catch. Then he glanced up at me, his curiosity piqued.

"Yeah," he said as he hopped up, wiping his face with his towel. "You look all bright-eyed and bushy-tailed."

I hesitated for a moment. Part of me wanted to keep to myself what had gone down last night. Not because I didn't trust my brothers, but more out of respect for Dream, thinking that she might not appreciate having her sex life up for open discussion.

Ultimately, my brothers won out in my internal debate. The guys and I told everything to one another, and I wasn't about to start keeping secrets now.

"It's Dream," I said, rubbing the back of my neck as I spoke. "Last night...she and I..."

"You serious?" Evan asked. "You hooked up with Dream?"

I glanced around, making sure we hadn't caught anyone's attention. The music was loud and the gymgoers around us all had headphones on or earbuds in.

"How the hell did that happen?" he asked.

I leaned back against the machine. "Went over to her place yesterday. Just dropped by."

Jay was confused. "You just...went over? Like, you strolled over unannounced?"

"That's what texts are for, dude," Evan said with a grin.

"That's what she told me. But I hadn't been planning on doing it. After Jay's text asking about her, and knowing Adam was in town, I just had to see for myself that she was okay.."

The mere mention of Adam was enough to make Evan and Jay's faces darken.

"And how was she?" Evan inquired.

"Must've been distressed out of her mind if she ended up jumping into bed with this dumbass." Jay gave a grin, letting me know he was only messing around.

"Hey, asshole," I said with a smirk of my own, shoving him in a joking around sort of way.

"Seriously," Jay said. "That Adam thing must've had her thirty different kinds of shaken up."

"She seemed fine, really," I replied. "Dream's tough as hell. But no doubt she had it on her mind."

"Anyway," Jay prodded. "So, one thing led to another and then another and then..."

I shrugged. What else could I say?

"Pretty much."

After I said the words, a strange expression took hold on Jay's face. It was an expression I couldn't puzzle out, like he had something on his mind but wasn't sure how to say it.

"Alright, out with it," I said.

"Dream and I...the other day at the farmer's market...we, well..."

It didn't take any more explaining than that.

"You're kidding!" I shouted. Despite the music and everyone's headphones, my voice rose loud enough to catch the attention of damn near everyone there. I winced, waiting a few seconds for the rest of the gymgoers to go back to their workouts.

"Not kidding," Jay replied. "And it's not like I went out to seduce her or anything like that. I agreed to help her with her stand at the market and we ended up going for a walk and..."

"One thing led to another," I said. "Yep, know exactly what you're talking about."

Jay nodded. "The woman's hard to resist. And it doesn't help that she's into all three of us."

Evan shook his head in disbelief. "Man, both of you guys hooked up with Dream? You know what I did last night? I played *Modern Warfare* until midnight. Meanwhile you guys are getting it on with the girl of our dreams." We looked around, but thankfully no one was paying that much attention.

Jay flashed a smile. "Well, bro – guess we're just better than you."

I laughed. "Right. That damn middle child syndrome. But don't screw it up by bragging about your *Call of Duty* killstreaks. Kind of a turn-off."

Evan shoulder-checked me with a laugh. "Pricks!"

But the joking around didn't go on for very long. Up at the front desk I spotted a familiar face.

It was Adam Myles. He was dressed in high-end, colorful Nike sneakers, tight black bike shorts and a matching sleeveless shirt, one that showed off his lanky physique. I could tell by his posture that he was in the process of hitting on the front desk girl who, judging by her expression, didn't seem interested in his overtures in the slightest.

It was Adam summed up – rich and arrogant and entitled.

"Shit," Jay said. "Adam's here."

The anger boiled in my belly. Knowing what he did to Dream

made me see red. When he was finally done flirting with the clerk, seeming to have accepted that she wasn't into him, he stepped onto the gym floor, a pleased smile on his face as if he'd done the favor of a lifetime by showing her some attention.

I couldn't resist.

"Don't do it, dude," Evan cautioned. "I know what you're thinking and it's not worth it."

Maybe Evan was right, but there wasn't a chance in hell I was letting Adam off the hook.

Without another word, I started over to him. He was wrapped up in his phone at first, but as I drew closer, he glanced up and regarded me with that shit-eating, condescending expression I'd seen on his face countless times, the one that made it clear he knew he could get away with whatever he wanted and that if he ever did fall into any trouble Daddy would be there to bail him out.

"If it isn't the Wolf boys," he said, looking me up and down as I came to a stop. "As strapping as ever. Very cute that you're all here to spot one another, clean up one another's sweat and all that."

He hadn't changed a bit, but I knew better than to get baited by his bullshit.

"Here's the deal, Myles. I don't know what you said to Dream to upset her. Not a doubt in my mind it involved you pouring some major amounts of bullshit into her ears. But that stops now. I know the way you treated her and there's not a chance in hell I'm going to stand by and let you do it again."

He arched his eyebrows. "Are you...*threatening* me?"

"Yeah, I guess I am. You come near her again and I'll make sure you regret being in the same state as she is."

He narrowed his eyes. Adam was an arrogant prick, and nothing made an arrogant prick madder than someone not respecting whatever it was he felt like he deserved to be up his own ass about.

"Now, I don't know how they do things in the service, big guy, but here in civilization we don't talk like that unless we're ready to back it up."

"Oh, I'm more than ready to back it up. Just say the word and I'll stick the nearest bench bar up that arrogant ass of yours."

His eyes formed into hateful little slivers. We were close, close enough that I could feel the fight about to happen.

"Alright, that's enough. I'm the hot-headed one, remember?" Jay appeared on one side of us, Evan on the other. Each clapped a hand down on my shoulders and led me back, putting enough distance between Adam and me to ease the tension.

"Lucky your keepers are here, Duncan," Adam said. "Can't wait to see what happens when they're not."

With that, he slipped his Air pods into his ears, flashed me one more cocky smile, then walked away. I watched as he went over to the nearest Elliptical machine, not a care in the world.

Evan, his hand still on my shoulder, led me away from where I stood.

"Dude, I know you want to kick his ass. *I* want to kick his ass."

"Same here," Jay added. "You have no idea how badly I want to kick his ass."

"But we can't start shit like that in the middle of the gym. Unless you want to get all of us banned from here, that is."

I clenched and unclenched my jaw, doing my best not to glare at Adam.

"Yeah, you're right," I said.

"And that's not all," Jay reminded us. "This isn't our battle to fight. We can be there for Dream, sure. But we can't solve it for her. If she wants Adam gone, she's got to be the one to send him packing."

I took in one more slow breath. "And we need to trust that she'll do it."

"Exactly," Evan agreed. "I know it goes against all of our natures to step back and let things happen, but it's the right thing to do. We've got to give Dream a chance to work through her problems on her own."

I looked over at Jay. "When did you become the level-headed one, huh?"

"Trust me, it's not easy. I wanted to knock the smirk off his face the moment I saw him, but I knew I had to respect Dream's wishes. She just left an abusive situation with an aggressive man, the last thing she needs is three more hot-heads starting trouble for her."

And he was right. Jay was absolutely right.

CHAPTER 24

EVAN

The near fight had been on my mind for the rest of the workout, and well into the afternoon.

There was no getting around it – part of me wished that Duncan would've gone through with it. I couldn't put into words how satisfying it would've been to see my big brother cock his fist back and slam it hard right into Adam's smug face, to send him ass-over-teakettle into the squat rack.

Sure, we would've gotten banned from the best gym in town, but it would've been worth it. More than that, it could've sent the message to Adam that he needed to stay far, far away from Dream.

I thought it all over during lunch at the Red Kettle, popping fries into my mouth one after another, wishing I could do something to make it easier for Dream. But what the guys and I had decided was right – this was her decision to make. We would be there to support her, but that was the best we could do.

I hated it. I was sure Duncan and Jay were feeling the same as I was - we wanted to solve the problem. I wanted to set Adam's smug ass straight, to make it so Dream didn't have to worry about a damn thing. I pondered it all as I chomped through my bacon cheeseburger.

"Doing alright, Ev?"

I glanced up to see Melody, the manager, standing at my table-side with a fresh glass of Sprite.

"Just girl stuff," I said. "You ever get in one of those situations where you want to do something for someone else, but know you can't?"

"Oh, yeah," she said, taking my empty glass and replacing it with the new one. "That's what growing up is all about – finding out that sometimes the best thing to do is to let go, realizing that it's not your responsibility to make sure everything works out."

"I hate it," I said. "I joined the service to *do things*, you know? And now..."

She smiled. "The other part of it is trusting people, giving them the space to make their own decisions. You'll find that sometimes they surprise you in the best ways."

Her words mellowed me out.

"Yeah, you're right." I glanced down at my plate, which was empty aside from a few fries. "Mind putting another one of those in?"

Melody chuckled. "See? If you've got your appetite things can't be that bad. And you've *always* had an appetite. I'll throw on some extra bacon this time."

She was off with a smile and the moment I was alone again, my phone lit up with a text from Dream.

My heart skipped a beat when I saw her name on the screen.

Hey! What's up?

I grinned and typed my response.

Not much. Just about to start on round two with a burger at Red Kettle. You?

A smiling emoji started the sentence. *I wanted to send out some text invites for the Christmas party we're having at Clarissa's. You in?*

You kidding? Of course I'll be there! I followed this up with some fire emojis.

Nice. I figured you'd be down. But I wanted to make sure I got your RSVP all the same.

Speaking of plans, I typed out. *What're you doing tonight?*

Tonight? Working now, but nothing later.

Let's get some dinner. This awesome Ethiopian place opened up near downtown that I've been dying to try.

The three dots that meant a text in progress appeared. Then they disappeared. Then they appeared again.

I couldn't help but laugh. No doubt she was unsure of how to handle me asking her out when she'd already hooked up with Duncan and Jay. Part of me wanted to tell her that I knew and didn't care. If anything, I was happy for the guys. But I wasn't about to overwhelm her too much.

That sounds nice, actually. Work's kind of annoying today and it'd give me something to look forward to.

I wanted to pump my fist with excitement, but I kept myself in check.

Great! You're working from home, right? I'll pick you up at five-thirty.

She replied with a thumbs-up emoji and a smiley face next to it. To make the moment even better, Melody arrived with my burger, setting it directly in front of me. It looked perfect, extra juicy, the crispy strips of bacon sticking out the sides.

I lifted it up and took a big bite.

It was hard not to smile like an idiot on the way over to Dream's. I loved spending time with her. Really, she was my favorite person to hang with outside my brothers.

When I pulled up to Clarissa's apartment, Dream stepped out wearing a pair of tight-fitting slacks and a blouse that hugged her curves. I was reminded that she did things to me no other woman could. I mean, how the hell could I even lay eyes on a woman like her without noticing how beautiful she was? When she turned to lock the door, giving me a glimpse at her perfect, round ass...God, I went from nothing to hard in a second flat.

As she approached the car I pinched my upper thigh, doing the old trick to make a hard cock go soft. Once I was ready, I hopped out and made my way over to the passenger door of my Jeep, opening it for her.

"Such a gentleman," she said with a cheeky grin. "Good to see you, Evan."

We hugged; her petite body pressed against mine.

"When am I not a gentleman?" I asked with a wink. As we hugged, I couldn't help but imagine what other things I could do with her, what her body would feel like totally naked, my arms wrapped around her. I pushed those thoughts out of my head before they grew too out of control.

Moments later we were on our way to the restaurant.

"How's work?" I asked.

Out of the corner of my eye, I saw Dream biting her lower lip before turning to look out the window.

"It's fine."

I couldn't help but laugh. "Dream, that's about the most unconvincing 'it's fine' I've ever heard in my life. Even if we hadn't known each other since we were kids, I'd spot it as BS right away."

She turned back toward me, a small smile on her face that suggested she was relieved that I'd called her out.

"Sorry, not trying to lie. It's more that I don't want to dump boring stuff about work on your lap while we're going out to have fun."

"I didn't ask just to fill the air," I said. "I asked because I want to know. You moved to a new town, and you're doing your job remotely. I'm curious how it's all going."

"It's going the same," she said. "Once I did the online onboarding and got used to handling all my communication with the rest of the staff in Slack and on Zoom, I was fine. Hell, if anything it was a little better. Now I don't have to worry about commutes or rush hour or anything like that."

She sighed. "But once the novelty wore off, I realized it was... well, it was the same old job it's always been. I click around in Photoshop, I touch up ads, and that's about it."

"You're not sounding all that enthused about it."

"That's because I'm not. And it makes me feel like a spoiled brat, you know? There are people who'd kill for my job, for the sort of stability I have. But all I can think about is...well, what you guys all talked to me about."

"Quitting your job to pursue art full-time?"

"That's it," she said with a smile. "I'd always dreamed about it, right? But when I did, it only lived in my head. Talking about it with you guys, having you encourage me, that made it real in a way it hadn't been before. And now it's all I can think about."

"Here's something else," I said with a smile, beyond happy to hear that she was still thinking about going for art as a full-time job. "You said that you feel spoiled having your job when other people could, right?"

"Right."

"Then...why not give it to them? If you were to quit, that'd mean your job is open. And that would mean someone else, someone who's passionate about the work, or just wants a steady job, could take it."

She opened her mouth to speak, as if there were some point I'd missed that she was about to refute.

"That's...that's actually a good point. Here I am, whining about the job and talking it up all at the same time!"

We reached downtown by this point, and I pulled in front of the Ethiopian joint. The interior was dimly lit, the scents of bread and spices in the air. A host led us to a table near one of the front windows, the view of downtown Charmed Bay on display. We ordered some tea and sambusa appetizers, and once that was done the conversation picked up right where we'd left it off.

"But where would I even begin?" she asked. "I can't just set up a booth at the farmer's market every weekend and hope for the best. I'd need to think about my art like a businesswoman, turn it into something that could grow, something I'd be able to live off one day."

"All good stuff to think about. You've got a good head for this, Dream. Plenty of people think they can drop everything and chase their passions and that it'll all work out in the end. You, on the other hand, know it takes more than that."

She smiled, glancing down for a moment before turning her attention back to me.

"Thanks. I mean it. Having you and Jay and Duncan all believing in me the way you do...it's really something."

"And you know we'd call you out if you were talking nonsense," I followed this up with a smile. "Like if you said you wanted to drop everything and join the WNBA."

She was confused for a moment. Then her eyes flashed with indignation when Dream realized what I was getting at.

"You guys can never pass up a short joke, can you?" she said after giving me a playful shove.

And I could've been imagining things, but it really seemed like her hand lingered on my arm for longer than normal.

I put it out of my head. Talking about Dream's future was a hell of a lot more important than my attraction to her.

"Hey, you can make fun of us for being tall whenever you want."

"Tall jokes don't hit the same," she said. "Besides, what is there aside from 'how's the weather up there'?"

I laughed. "Good point."

The waiter arrived, placing a plate of sambusas on the table. Dream and I happily dug in.

"But seriously," I said. "You don't have to come up with your business plan all at once. You can start small. Like..." My eyes flashed as an idea occurred to me. "Like, you could start a website!"

She cocked her head to the side in consideration as she chewed her sambusa.

"Are you serious? A website?"

"Yeah! You could put something up and advertise your services, have a place for your work. Then you could get in touch with other festivals in the area and give them a spot to check out your stuff. Trust me, once they see what you can do, they'll be begging to have you work their fairs."

Dream took another bite, the words having an effect.

"Think about it – you made good money at the farmer's market in town, right?"

"Very good money."

"Now, imagine it in the summer you could have all kinds of fairs lined up. Maybe one on Monday, another on Tuesday...you get the idea. You could drive around the state making cash, take breaks whenever you want."

She set down her sambusa, appearing to be so involved in what I was saying that she didn't want to eat.

"But outside of Charmed Bay, are there a lot of festivals and fairs in the fall and winter? Farmer's Markets are all usually on the weekend, in most cities, and I can't be at all of them at the same time. There's only one of me."

She had a good point. "You don't need to have your business model worked out right *now*," I said. "Work the summers all over the state, work the local Farmer's Market in the fall and winter, then get the rest planned out down the road. You don't want to focus *just* on the future or *just* on the present. Do a little of both and guaranteed you will be able to succeed."

She popped the rest of her sambusa into her mouth, chewing it thoughtfully.

"You know, you've got a pretty good mind for business, Evan."

I chuckled and shrugged. "It's all about attitude, you know. Stay positive, and don't let things get you down. If, and when you come across a bump in the road, don't let that distract you, learn from it and move on."

"That's how you've always been," she said. "Always looking on the bright side of things."

"I try. Jay likes to bust my balls about being naïve, but I don't think this way because I haven't been through things – I think this way because I have. Life's going to throw some crazy stuff your way. And if you can take it with a smile, not let it wear you down, then you've got a major advantage."

She said nothing at this, instead smiling at me as if I'd said something she'd been waiting to hear.

We went back to the topic of her work, brainstorming some ideas for her blog, how to get her business off the ground. I got so wrapped up in the conversation that I hardly noticed when the food came.

"Uh, you going to eat that?" asked Dream, pointing to my big plate of meat and lentils all served on a flat circle of unleavened bread.

"Shoot!" I replied, turning my attention to my food. "How the hell did I miss this?"

"That's got to be the first time I've ever seen you ignore food," she said. "I've more than a few memories of us having to order a separate pizza just for you back in high school."

I laughed. "What can I say – I like to eat!"

We worked through our dinners. Afterwards, the two of us were so wrapped up in conversation that we decided to grab some drinks at the Surefire Inn, a place that I loved, situated a little out of town. Over beers, we talked some more about her job plans, even doing some research on other festivals and farmer's markets up and down the coast.

About halfway into our second pitcher, however, Dream sat back with a despondent expression on her face.

"What's wrong?" I asked.

"Nothing. Just that this is...well, it's exciting. But it's scary too, you know?"

I grinned. "That's how you know you need to do it. It's important to shake things up every now and then, do something that scares the crap out of you."

"You know, you sound like one of those novelty mugs you can

buy at Marshalls – ones that have expressions like that." She gave my leg a warm squeeze.

I laughed. "Maybe I do. But it's how I live my life, and that attitude has taken me to some pretty great places. It's got me sitting at a bar with just about the hottest woman on the west coast." That last part sort of slipped out. But it was true.

Her face went red, but she kept on smiling. "Thanks, Evan. You're sweet. You've always been like this, always had such a big heart."

I winked. "Thanks, Dream. But now I'm thinking about mugs… maybe we need to get you one. I'm thinking one that says something like 'Girlboss,' all one word, with a hashtag."

She laughed. Just then, the music picked up in the bar. A quick glance to the main floor let me see that the place had nearly filled up. Dream and I shared a confused look, both of us wondering what the hell was going on. The bartender, seeming to pick up on our bewilderment, tapped a flyer that hung from one of the mirrors behind the bar. It read "Honky-Tonk Night" with the date on the flyer being today.

Despite how much I was enjoying the conversation, a little dancing sounded nice. But I wanted to make sure Dream was in the mood. Before I could say a word, I glanced down to see that she was moving her hips from side to side where she sat, the music moving through her as she watched the crowd.

"Miss Dream," I said, hopping out of my seat and extending my hand in a jokingly over-the-top gesture. "May I have this dance?"

She broke out into a huge smile as she glanced down at my hand. "That sounds quite wonderful, good sir," she said, imitating my joking formality.

With that, I took her hand and helped her out of the seat. I gestured to the bartender, and then to the napkins we'd written on, and he got the message and took them out of sight. Once that was settled, we were on the dance floor.

The crowd was crazy, the music moving through us as we shook our butts. Dream was impossible to keep my hands off, her toned, curvy body grinding against mine as we worked our way from one song to the next. When the first song ended, we hurried to the bar to throw back a couple of whiskey shots, the booze burning just right on the way down.

"This was exactly what I needed, Evan!" she shouted over the music. "You've always been good at this, taking my mind off of things."

"My pleasure!" I said, shouting right back. "And you're not such bad company yourself!"

She winked and I winked right back, Dream grabbing my hand and leading us back out to the dance floor. There was something in the air, something unleashed by the music and the dancing and the booze...it was like we were both giving in to what we'd both wanted.

We were lost in the music, my hands on her hips and her ass against my crotch, the bass thumping. By this point the crowd was so thick we could barely move, our bodies pressed against one another's. I grew bold, moving my right hand from her hip to her belly then under her shirt up to the bottom of her bra.

She didn't stop me. Hell, not only did she not stop me, but she placed her hand on mine and held it there. My cock went stiff in my jeans, my left hand on the front of her waist, pressing her back against me, making sure she felt it.

I wanted her, and there wasn't any doubt in my mind that she wanted me.

Then the song ended, relative quiet returning to the room.

We went back to the bar, leaning against it as we caught our breath. And damn, damn, *damn*, did she look good. Her body glistened with just a bit of sweat, her chest rising and falling as she undid her ponytail, letting her hair hang loose on her slender shoulders. I wanted her so badly it *hurt*.

But she seemed pensive. I leaned in and asked, "You alright?"

She flicked her eyes up at me, and I could sense the conflict.

"Dream, ever since you were a kid you've always been a thinker, you know? Smart and sharp, but always up in your own head, always thinking about what you *should* be doing instead of what you *want* to be doing."

She smiled slightly, and I could sense I'd hit onto something.

"Now," I said, preparing myself for the million-dollar question. "Let me ask you this – what do you want to be doing right now?"

CHAPTER 25

DREAM

Evan had worked his magic on me. I'd been stressed about work and Adam and everything else. But just one evening with him had been enough to melt my cares away.

And more than that, the dancing and music had made me realize just how attracted to him I was, how much he turned me on. So, when he asked me what I really wanted, I had to do my best to keep myself in check.

After all, I knew what I wanted. It was to be on my back being used by all three of the Wolf brothers at once. I didn't dare say that out loud. Then again, Evan had been the one to tell me I didn't have to pick between all three of them. But all of them at the same time couldn't have possibly been what he'd meant...right?

However, there was one Wolf there with me. And if he desired a taste of what I wanted, I'd give it to him. I reached forward and took hold of his collar, pulling him down toward me. Evan had a sly grin on his face as we moved closer and closer together, as if he knew we were both about to get exactly what we wanted.

The moment his lips touched mine I had no doubt I'd made the right call. The sting of whiskey washed over my mouth, the musky scent of his sweat wrapping around me, pulling me closer to him as surely as a third arm. I pressed my body against his, feeling the hardness of his chest and middle and, well, everything else.

Evan put his hand on the small of my back, bringing my body completely against his. Just like with Jay and Duncan it felt right to be held by Evan, as if it simply made sense. And as our tongues teased one another's, all I could think about was how much *more* I wanted.

The music started again, whoops and hollers sounding from the crowd as everyone hurried back onto the dance floor. The noise was enough to remind both of us that we were still in public, that we couldn't get *too* hot and heavy where we were.

Sure, we could've danced some more. But I wasn't in the mood for dancing. Nope – I was in the mood for a different sort of physical activity. And judging by Evan's hardness down below, so was he.

"We should get out of here," I said.

He grinned. "I most definitely agree with that."

Evan stood up straight. And when he did, a strange expression took hold of his handsome face.

"You alright?" I asked.

"Just...a little tipsy. I mean, I'm fine. But I don't think I should be driving."

I felt a little wobbly myself. Those whiskey shots had done their work, and although I felt clear-headed and with it, driving likely wasn't a good idea.

"How about an Uber?" I asked.

"We could do that. But Jay's not too far from here. I'll give him a call."

My eyes flashed wide. Jay? He was going to call his brother to... what, have him pick us up then drop us off at Evan's place? What would Jay think about that?

But Evan, seeming to sense the unease I felt, put his hand on my shoulder. The moment he touched me I felt better, the tension melting away. The Wolf brothers were a little magical like that.

"It's fine," he said. "Trust me."

Before I could respond, he slipped his phone out of his pocket, dialed Jay, and stepped away from me with his other hand covering his free ear. I watched as he spoke, unable to hear what he was saying over the noise of the crowd.

Whatever they talked about didn't take long. Evan put his phone back in his pocket and came back over to me.

"He's actually on his way home from getting a drink down the way. Says he'll be here in a couple of minutes."

My heart began to race. What was going to happen when Jay got here, saw that we were both a little tipsy and spending time together? Jay was as sharp as they came – no way he wouldn't be able to read between the lines, to pick up on subtext. I bit my lip as Evan retrieved the notes from the bartender then came over to take my hand.

"Come on," he said. "Don't want to keep little bro waiting."

I nodded, not saying a word as we weaved through the crowd and made our way outside. The evening air was calm and still with a touch of briskness, a few bar patrons out there smoking cigarettes and chatting amongst themselves. There was so much I wanted to ask Evan – where were we going? Did he tell Jay what had happened? Had Jay told him what had happened?

But we didn't get a chance. Two big beams of light that I recognized right away as belonging to Jay's truck cut through the dark of night. His truck grumbled to a stop in front of the bar, as Jay looked both of us up and down.

"You kids need a lift?" he said with a grin.

"Took you long enough!" Evan shouted jokingly.

"Ha, ha," Jay replied dryly. "Get your drunk asses in here."

Jay gave me a nod as I approached, his eyes moving up and down my body in a way that turned me on like wild. I stepped around the truck and Evan already had the door open for me. He placed his hand on the small of my back to help me in. Once I was seated next to Jay, Evan climbed inside and shut the door.

I was sandwiched in between the brothers, two massive, muscular men on either side of me. Just their nearness alone was enough to make my chest rise and fall like wild, for my pussy to clench and soak through my panties.

We said nothing, as grunge music played too loud for conversation. And I wasn't sure, but I could swear the guys were looking at one another, sharing knowing glances.

It didn't take long before I noticed that we weren't heading into town, but out of it. I looked around to see the trees surrounding us, tall pines that stretched into the sparkling night sky. I turned down the stereo.

"Where are we going?" I asked.

"My place," said Jay. "Figured we could hang there for a bit. Closer than Evan's."

"That cool with you?" asked Evan. "Because it's no problem to have Jay take us back into town."

Just like with Duncan, Evan was giving me the choice, making sure I knew that what we were doing, whatever it might be, was up to me. And there was no pressure.

"No," I said. "Jay's place is fine."

The guys shared another knowing look, and this time it most definitely wasn't all in my head. We drove on, taking the weaving road deeper into the woods until we reached Jay's cabin, a charming little place that looked like something out of a rustic dream.

Jay parked and we made our way into the house, my heart beating so quickly with excitement that I could hardly think straight. Jay opened the door and flicked the lights on, revealing an interior that was just as cozy as the outside suggested. There were rugs and a fireplace and books – so many damn books. Jay stepped over to the fireplace and squatted down in front of it, quickly getting a fire burning.

"Get me a little of that whiskey, would you Evan?" asked Jay, glancing over his shoulder. "And whatever you guys want."

Evan raised his eyebrows at me, wordlessly asking for my drink choice. Right then I was at the perfect level of tipsy. But a little something to sip on sounded nice.

"Mind if I share with you, Evan? I don't want a drink of my own."

"Of course," said Evan with a grin. "We're big on sharing."

The brothers exchanged another look. The fire crackled, the space filling with warm, toasty air. Evan made a couple of drinks, handing one to Jay and one to me. I took a small sip, curious what was going to happen next.

"So," Jay began, leaning against the back of his couch with his drink in hand, his posture cool and casual and effortlessly sexy. "Evan tells me that you guys were having a pretty good night over at the Surefire."

I grinned, my mind going back to the dancing. "We were. It was just what I needed to take my mind off some things."

"Glad to hear it. Evan said that you were getting pretty close on the dance floor."

Redness tinged my cheeks. What else had Evan told him?

"That's true, too."

Jay nodded, Evan standing next to me.

"Let me ask you this," said Jay. "If I put on some music, would you be able to demonstrate what he was talking about?"

My heart skipped a beat. What was he asking, exactly?

"I think we could," Evan said with a smile. "What about you, Dream?"

The choice was clear. "Yeah, I believe we could."

"Excellent," said Jay. "Let me turn something on."

"It was country music," said Evan. "If you really want to set the scene."

Jay grinned as he slipped out his phone. "I'll just put 'country music' into Spotify and see what happens."

Evan laughed as he sipped his whiskey. Then he set the glass down on a nearby side table and turned to me. Evan loomed large over me as he stepped closer, upbeat country music like what we'd heard in the bar coming from Jay's speaker system.

"Now," said Evan as he put his hands on my hips. "Where were we?"

Jay dimmed the lights a bit, and after swallowing how strange it all was, that Evan and I were going to dance and Jay was going to watch, I closed my eyes and moved to the music. I was surprised how quickly it happened, how comfortable I felt moving my hips against Evan's cock, a smile forming on my mouth as I felt his hardness return.

Evan turned me toward him. I opened my eyes just in time to see him move in with another kiss. And just like at the bar, I fell into it the moment his mouth touched mine, closing my eyes and savoring his taste. Our tongues met and his hands traveled all over my body, my nipples going hard through my shirt as he caressed me.

I opened my eyes just enough to see Jay watching, sipping his drink. What was he thinking? Was he envious that Evan had me in his arms, and he didn't? If he was, he didn't show it. He simply watched and sipped his drink. I found myself wondering if he was turned on, if his cock was as hard as his brother's.

Maybe I'd find out.

I closed my eyes again and focused on the kiss. I placed my hand on Evan's, which at that moment was on my breast. I wanted more, and so I guided his hand down lower and lower, over my waist and down between my legs. I sighed through the kiss once he began to rub me through my slacks, my pussy tightening and tingles spreading through my body.

I wanted more.

"We're not on the dance floor anymore," said Evan, his voice low and sensual in my ear. "You don't have to hold back. We can do whatever you want."

I licked my lips, my hand on his cock, my fingertips tracing his outline.

I knew what I wanted. I dropped to my knees, his cock now at eye level. I moved my hands over his torso, up under his shirt and across the solid grid of his abs. Then I went to work undoing his belt and opening his jeans. Once that was done, I yanked them down, his black boxer briefs and the bulge of his cock in front of me.

Jay. What the hell could he be thinking? I glanced over to where he was sitting and saw that he was in the middle of another sip, watching us with narrow-eyed interest. It was always hard to tell what Jay was thinking, but in that moment, I could sense he liked what he was seeing.

So, I kept going. I rubbed Evan's cock through his underwear, and when I was ready, I pulled down the waistband and reached inside, taking hold of his long, warm, hardness. After a bit of teasing, I took it out, his perfect, gorgeous cock right in front of me.

It was going to be tough, just like with Duncan the other night. But I was ready. I started with slow kisses, placing my lips on his head, and covering every bit of it with a press of my mouth. Then I let my tongue come out, the tip drawing slow circles over his salty, delicious flesh.

It was insane. I was about to take Evan into my mouth while Jay, his brother, was watching. But knowing that, knowing how taboo it all was, just turned me on even more. Once again, I gave my attention to Evan, opening my mouth and taking his head into it. Evan groaned with pleasure, his hand moving into my hair and guiding me down further. I took more of him in, every inch as delicious as the last.

Once I was in a steady pace, my lips moving up and down his shaft, I placed my hand on his balls and squeezed them gently, pushing them up into his root. He loved it, a smile spreading across his face as I pleasured him.

Then I saw something out of the corner of my eye. Jay threw back the last of his whiskey and set the glass down, then pushed himself off the couch and started toward us. He came to a stop next to me, gazing down as I sucked Evan.

Evan gently placed his hands on the side of my head and guided me off him, his length glistening. He turned me to Jay, whose own cock strained against his jeans. I knew what they both wanted. I was ready to give it to them.

With a few quick, deft movements I had Jay's pants open, that now familiar cock springing out to greet me. Two Wolf cocks were out, both so tantalizingly close. I opened my mouth and took Jay, wrapping my lips into a tight seal. My right hand went to Evan's cock, stroking him as I sucked his brother.

I did this for a time before switching back over, taking Evan into my mouth again and working Jay with my free hand. It was intoxicating, the feeling of knowing I was bringing them both pleasure, knowing I had them both right where I wanted them. My desire was to keep going, to drain one into my mouth and then the other.

But the brothers had other plans. Evan reached down as I sucked him, bringing me up to my feet. Without a word he began undressing me, Evan taking off my shirt and bra and Jay undoing my pants from behind and pulling them and my panties down my legs. The two sets of hands had me naked before I knew what was happening.

And I loved it. It was like I was caught up in a force of nature, two massive men ready to use me for their pleasure.

"So," said Jay, his hands sliding up and down my bare curves. "You've slept with me; you've slept with Duncan. But you haven't slept with Evan."

"Right," Evan said with a smile. "Have to admit, I'm feeling a little left out."

I smiled right back at him. "Then we ought to take care of that, shouldn't we?"

"We should," he replied.

Before I could react, he turned me around. Evan placed his big hand on the top middle of my back, guiding me down into a bent-over position. Once I was there, I felt his head drag against my opening, a pleasured sigh pouring from my mouth as he did. It was hard to stand like that, but luckily Jay was there to put my hands on.

Evan pushed into me, his thickness filling me with ease. He sheathed himself with a groan, burying himself to the base. He held fast for a moment before pulling back and driving into me again, the sound of flesh colliding with flesh filling the air, my breasts shaking underneath me. Evan did this again and again, and it didn't take much before an orgasm exploded through my body. I moaned and bucked against him, urging him not to stop.

When the orgasm faded, I was ready for Jay in front of me, his cock still stiff, urging for attention. I moved forward just enough to reach him, opening my mouth to take him inside. And when my lips were wrapped around him, I savored the forbidden pleasure of having two brothers inside of me at the same time.

I sucked Jay as Evan pounded me from behind, another orgasm building. Evan, seeming to sense this, withdrew from me and turned me around, scooping me off the ground and placing me on the back of the couch. Once I was seated Evan dropped to his knees, placing his mouth on my pussy. Jay approached me from the side, wordlessly bringing me into a kiss as his brother carried me to another orgasm, his tongue on my clit and his fingers deep inside.

When the orgasm rose and fell, Jay picked me up. We kissed as he carried me to the bedroom, only breaking our lips when we reached the bed. He laid me down carefully, positioning my body so my legs were spread open at the end of the bed. I was mad with passion by this point, wanting nothing more than to make both brothers come.

Jay wrapped his big arms around my legs, spreading me open and splitting me in two with his cock. His thrusting was relentless, my eyes wide with shock at how damn good it felt. Evan joined us, stepping to the side of the bed, and kneeling to bring his cock to eye level. Seconds later I had both inside me once more, Jay in my pussy and Evan in my mouth.

Jay brought me to the brink of another orgasm, the hot waves of pleasure crashing through me as he came too, his cock pulsing. At the same time, I brought Evan over the brink with my mouth, his salty, warm seed splashing into my mouth. Eagerly, I swallowed every drop, the sensation of his cock throbbing in my mouth as he groaned the perfect accompaniment to my orgasm.

And then it was over. I laid there stunned, hardly able to wrap my mind around what had just happened – I'd slept with two of the Wolfs at the same time.

If either of the brothers felt bad or awkward about it, neither of them said a word. Jay crawled to one side of me, placing his hand on my belly. Evan moved to the other, kissing me gently on the shoulder. And there, nestled between two of the most gorgeous men I'd ever seen in my life, a post-coital contentment flowing through me like I'd never known before, I slept.

CHAPTER 26

JAY

I woke up the next morning with the biggest damn smile on my face. Dream was sleeping next to me, Evan nowhere to be found. With my eyes half-open I grabbed my phone from the nightstand to see that it was a little after eight.

And there was a text from Evan.

Yo! Dipped out early, figured Dream had enough of a wild night without the shock of waking up next to both of us. Gym later?

I thumbs-upped the message before setting the phone back down. I wouldn't have minded Evan sticking around. But he'd probably made the right call by giving Dream a little breathing room. I seriously doubted she'd ever done anything like what she'd done last night.

She was still asleep, and I laid there for a time watching her, the sheet pulled over her gorgeous body as her chest rose and fell. I was glad she'd been down for sharing – a woman like her was too special to be tied to only one man. What the future held, I couldn't say. But at that moment, I was damn glad she was there in my bed.

Part of me wanted to rouse her, to wake her up in the proper way. But I didn't. She needed rest, to be able to get up when she was good and ready. And more than that, I was hungry as hell. I'd spent the evening working around the property, cutting some firewood, and cleaning up some brush. After that I'd gone out for a drink, Evan calling me before I'd had a chance to order some food.

So, I was starving. I took one last, long look at Dream before carefully rolling off the bed as not to wake her. Carefully, I left the bedroom and shut the door behind me. The morning looked pleasant enough, the sun shining, the wind lolling the pines outside. The fire in the fireplace still smoldered, and I shut the doors in front of it to smother the flames before opening the window to let the heat out. Then I gathered Dream's clothes from the ground and put them into the bedroom, so they'd be there when she got up.

Once that was done, I went to work in the kitchen. My pantry and fridge were stocked with meats and eggs and dairy from local farmers, just about everything fresh and sourced to within fifty miles of Charmed Bay. Eggs sounded good, so I took out the necessary ingredients and went to work, scrambling the eggs with some cheese and cutting a few slices of bread I'd made myself the day before. After that was in the works, I started some coffee.

It didn't take long before the smells and sounds roused Dream. The bedroom door opened, and she stepped out, dressed and ready for the day. Sure, her hair was a bit messy, and it was apparent her clothes had been pulled off in a hurry. But she still looked so damn gorgeous I wanted to scream.

"Hey," she said with a smile as she shut the bedroom door behind her.

"Morning."

She craned her neck to see what I was making. "Look at you, Mr. Up-and at 'em."

I chuckled as I moved the eggs around on the cast iron pan. "Figured you'd need some replenishment after last night." Maybe it was a mistake to bring up last night so soon. But I wanted to gauge her reaction to it, to see if she felt strange, or if she just wanted to talk.

Dream's eyes widened for a moment, then she let out a sigh as she came over to the small table near the kitchen.

"Oh yeah," she said. "Last night."

I offered a small smile as I prepared her a cup of coffee, setting it down in front of her along with a bit of milk.

"You doing OK?" I asked, turning my attention back to the food. I sprinkled some more cheese on top of the eggs.

"Yeah." She nodded, confident in her answer. "I mean, it's insanely weird what happened. But the good kind of weird, you know? And I must admit, it'd been on my mind since that night at Red's."

It was a major relief to hear her say that. The last thing I wanted was to make Dream feel uncomfortable.

"Good," I said. "And it goes without saying that we've all been thinking about it too."

She smiled slightly. "No offense, but that's a little strange to hear. I'm glad for it, of course, but knowing you all have been talking about me like that...not sure what to make of it. Guess I should be a little flattered."

I chuckled as I placed the toast on a plate, bringing it over to her along with some butter.

"We didn't talk about you like you were a piece of meat, or a toy that we were all fighting for time with. Most of the conversations were about making sure you were cool with what might happen. We definitely didn't want to make you upset or anything."

That got another smile. "I appreciate it. But...you guys are cool with this? With me...doing what I'm doing."

I shrugged. The eggs were done, so I pushed the fluffy mounds onto some plates, the cheese perfectly melted.

"We've never been like that. Jealousy's just never been a part of our relationship. Besides, we've shared women before, though not so directly."

"So, I'm the first that you two have...been with like that?"

"Yep. So don't worry – that was a first for us, too."

"And how do *you* feel?" she asked as I brought the rest of the food over and sat down across from her. "I appreciate that you guys are thinking about me, but whatever this thing is we've got going, there are four hearts involved."

I opened my mouth to speak, but nothing came out. I had a hard time finding the words. And as I struggled for them, I realized that she'd asked me something that no one else ever did– how I felt. Sure, my brothers had my back, no doubt in my mind about it. But other than them...

I shifted in my seat. "It's fine. I mean that. We're all crazy about you, and you're here with me right now. And that's it." The words came out with a harder tone than I'd intended. Dream must've picked up on it because her attention was more on me than the food.

"You've always been kind of cut off, closed off from people. I noticed it the second we met when we were kids. And I always wondered why." She reached across the table and took my hand, her touch making me feel better instantly. "You know you can tell me anything, right?"

I chuckled nervously, slipping my hand from hers. "It's...I don't know. Just dad shit, I guess."

"Your dad?"

I couldn't believe I'd said it. Heat rose inside of me, and all I wanted was to be able to take back the words.

"It's nothing," I said. "Forget about it."

But I knew Dream well enough to understand that there was no way she'd be letting it drop that easily.

"Tell me what you mean, Jay," she said, her voice braced with kindness, understanding. "I've known you for years, yet you've never let me in."

"Well, I kind of did last night." I smiled slightly and Dream returned it. It was a lame joke, but the tension eased enough to be bearable.

"Funny," she said. "But seriously...what happened between you and your dad?"

I shifted in my seat, taking a sip of coffee to give myself a second to get ready for what I was about to say. I'd never told anyone what I was about to tell her. But there was something about Dream that made it seem OK.

"When we were growing up, my old man rode Evan hard. Not sure why. I guess Duncan was the older one, knew his place. I was the baby, my dad always having a soft spot for me. But with Evan...it was different. He demanded the best, whether it came to school or part-time jobs or anything else. And when he didn't get the best..."

I trailed off, taking one more drink of my coffee. Dream reached over once again and took my hand. This time, I didn't pull away.

"He was physical with Evan, hitting him whenever he didn't live up to his standards. It started when I was barely ten, Evan was twelve. It finally stopped one day when Evan was sixteen and brought home a 'C' on a geometry test. He got up in Evan's face, telling him that he'd be a failure unless he got his shit together – the usual stuff. By this time, I was fourteen and already on my way to being taller and bigger than my dad. I had enough of him bullying Evan, so I stepped in between them, balled my hand up and slammed him in the face."

"Oh my God," she said. "What happened?"

"Nothing. He stood there with a little bit of blood trickling down his nose. Then he smirked a little, wiped the blood with the back of his hand, and walked off. He never came after Evan like that again. Looking back, I figured it was because he realized we weren't kids anymore, kids that he could easily smack around and overpower. Any one of us could kick his ass if we wanted to. Whatever the reason, he gave all of us our distance."

"That must've been a relief."

"It was and it wasn't. My biggest fear, the thing I'd lost sleep over since I was little, was that one day he was going to really hurt Evan. And then turn his fists on me. I was getting furious just thinking about it, one hand under Dream's and the other clenched hard under the table. "But it never happened. All the same, I was a bundle of nerves until Evan and me were gone, shipped off for the service."

I wasn't quite sure how to describe how I felt after I'd said what I had.

"Things are rough with my mom," she said. "But that's a whole other level."

"I know your mom," I said. "She's...got her faults. But she loves you and wants the best for you. Hell, maybe my dad's the same way. But never in my life will I regret doing what I did."

"And you shouldn't," said Dream. "You stuck up for yourself and your brother, and you're a stronger person because of it. And I understand now why you are the way you are. But you don't need to be that way with me."

I shook my head. "Funny thing is it actually makes me feel weak."

"You're not weak – you're one of the strongest people I know and what you just told me only makes me more certain of that. You stayed strong not just for yourself, but for your brother."

I didn't know what to say.

"I never told any of this to anyone for obvious reasons. But more than anything, I was worried I'd explain it to someone, and they'd feel pity for me. Pity's the last damn thing I want."

"I don't pity you, Jay," she said. "I admire you. Life handed you something difficult and you worked through it. Now, all you need to do is let that anger go."

"I know. Just not sure I'm ready to yet."

"You don't need to do it now," she said. "Take your time and think about it. But if you ever decide one day to confront your dad about all this, let me know. I can give you some backup." She followed this up with a warm, loving smile.

The idea of looking the old man in the eye and telling him how I felt about what happened...it was too much to process. But knowing Dream had my back went a hell of a long way.

"Thanks, Dream. I appreciate it." I slipped my hand from under hers. "Now, eat your damn food – it's getting cold."

She smiled one more time before turning her attention to her breakfast. As I took a bite, I realized that there was a hell of a lot more to what was going on with me and Dream than just sex. It was fulfilling on all levels, mental, physical, and spiritual.

I couldn't wait for whatever was next.

CHAPTER 27

DREAM

The events of that evening and the morning after were more than I could process all at once. My evening with Evan and Jay had been like nothing I'd ever experienced before. And my morning with Jay had been special and unexpected. I felt a true connection with him, one that I'd never shared with anyone else.

Jay dropped me off at Clarissa's, leaving me with a kiss and a promise that he and the rest of the brothers would see me again soon. As I watched his truck disappear around the bend, I found myself thinking something odd.

Last night had been great. But I didn't want only two of them at once – I wanted them *all*.

It was a scary thought. Was I becoming some sort of addict, some perved-out sex freak who'd need more and more extreme acts to get me off?

I couldn't help but laugh at the idea as I stepped inside the apartment. That wasn't the case, and I knew it. It was more that I was crazy about the Wolf brothers, and only having two at once, while nice, reminded me that there was a third, one who could make the pleasure even more exquisite.

"Morning!" I shouted into the apartment. But there was no response. "Yo, you here?"

I glanced outside, spotting Clarissa's car. But as far as I could tell, she wasn't home. A quick check of her bedroom revealed that she was gone. And I knew her well enough to know that it meant she was either pulling a morning shift at Blueprint, or that she was currently in the bed of her latest paramour.

I plopped down on the couch, knowing that I needed to get to work before too long. But the conversation I'd had with Jay stuck with me. He'd dealt with some serious shit with his dad, problems that made what was going on with me and my mom seem like nothing.

I made myself some coffee and thought it over. And by the time I had the mug in my hands I was certain of two things. I needed to stand up for myself with Adam. I needed to make it clear that we were over, once and for all, and to tell him to screw off like I had wanted to when he confronted me in town. And secondly, I wasn't sure where things were going with the Wolf brothers, but I was excited to see what laid ahead for us. It made what I was about to do even easier knowing what it felt like to be truly cared for by not just one man, but three.

I took out my phone and pulled up his number. It was time to pull the trigger, to get it all over with as soon as possible. Sure, I could've done it with a text. But I wanted to speak to Adam and make sure he got the picture.

"Hey!" said Adam. There was friendliness to his voice, the same friendliness I'd noticed the other day when we'd spoken in person. But after being around the Wolfs, guys who were authentically warm and kind, I could detect a fakeness to it that I hadn't noticed before.

I took a deep breath and began. "Hi, Adam. I've been thinking about our conversation."

"Yeah?" The friendliness turned into eagerness.

"And...no."

"No?"

"No. We're done. And truth be told, I'd be happy if I never saw you again. I think it'd be best for you to fly back to Chicago sooner than later."

There was silence. And then a weak, "oh."

For a moment, I felt like I was being too rough on him.

"I'm sorry if this is coming off cold or rude, but I want to be as clear as possible. What happened between us is over, and I'm starting my new life here in Charmed Bay. And you're not going to be a part of it. Do you understand?"

More silence.

"I...I understand."

"Good. I don't want to see you again before you leave, so please respect my wishes. Goodbye, Adam."

"Goodbye." He said the word with a strange, almost robotic tone.

If he felt anything other than the odd detachment I was hearing from him, I didn't care. I hung up the phone feeling victorious; I had conquered a difficult task and won. Sure, there was still the matter of him getting his ass out of town without bothering me. But I'd cross that bridge if I came to it.

I went over to the window that looked down onto where the ocean met the bay, the scene peaceful and inspiring. I sipped my coffee with a smile on my face, happy beyond measure to have finally put the Adam situation behind me. It was almost as if the closer I grew to the Wolfs, the more strength I found within myself.

But I didn't want to think it over too much. Besides, it was time to get to work.

And Christmas was coming up, something that I kept forgetting due to everything else going on, but I finally allowed myself to be excited about the upcoming holiday.

Coffee in hand, I stepped over to the coffee table and sat down, opening my MacBook. Once the screen was open, however, I realized there wasn't a chance in hell I'd be able to get anything done. I was too distracted thinking about the Wolfs, about the conversation I'd had with Jay concerning his father, and Evan regarding all the work stuff we'd had planned.

So, instead of working, I opened Slack and typed a quick message letting the group know that I was going to be out for the day, but to be in touch if there was an emergency. As soon as I hit "enter" a profound relief washed over me.

That taken care of, I picked up the notebook that I'd jotted down all of the ideas that Evan and I had discussed and flipped through it. There were so many great thoughts inside. All I wanted was to get started, maybe to go over some more concepts with Evan soon.

But I had to begin somewhere. So, after doing a little bit of research I found a great website builder and signed up for a plan. I could fill it in later with my portfolio and all that good stuff, but the important thing was that I'd taken the first step.

When that was done, Mom appeared in my mind. I felt like a hypocrite, having given the advice that I had to Jay about his dad when I still had a sore relationship with my own mother.

I wanted to do something about it. Not only that, but she needed to know about Adam. It'd been no secret that she'd been holding out hope of me and him patching things up. It was time I made it clear to her that it wasn't going to happen.

After throwing back the last sip of my coffee, I picked up my phone and typed up a text to Mom asking her what she was doing. I could tell by her response that she was curious as to what I wanted.

Come on over, she said, following up her first message. My lunch with the girls got canceled, Janine is still recovering from her tummy tuck.

After taking a quick shower and changing out of last night's clothes, I grabbed my things and hurried out the door. Moments later I was behind the wheel of Clarissa's bug. I had a big smile on my face the entire drive. I felt strange, different. It was like I was starting off on a new adventure, one where I'd be filling my life with things that *I* wanted, rather than what I was expected to want.

It was a little scary, sure, but what was an adventure without some uncertainty? Either way, I was totally confident in my ability to see it all through, to make my life into something worth being proud about. Mom needed to know how I felt. She needed to know that whatever my life might hold, it wouldn't involve Adam.

When I pulled up to Mom's house, however, the excitement faded a bit and was replaced by fear. As I parked in front of the sleek mansion of glass walls, I realized that I was going to have to do something, rather than just imagine it.

I took a deep breath and got out, entering the house without knocking.

"Is that you, dear?" asked Mom, her carefree voice drifting through the open space. "I'm in the back. Grab yourself something to drink and meet me out here."

"OK!" My throat was tight as I spoke – I was nervous.

I went into the kitchen and pulled a bottle of sparkling water from the fridge. That in hand, I made my way out to the back patio, the view looking out over the large, rectangular pool and to the ocean beyond.

I had to give it to Mom – she really knew how to live.

She was seated at the small four chair table near the doors, and as I approached, she glanced back at me with a smile on her face.

"So happy you decided to come by!" she said. "Sit, sit!"

I hurried over and sat down next to her. For several moments the two of us said nothing to one another, and I found myself wondering if Mom knew something that I didn't.

"So!" she said. "I'm sure you've heard the good news!"

"What's that?" I already didn't like the sound of it.

"Adam is back in town!"

Uh-oh.

"But I'm sure he's gotten in touch with you already, right?"

"He has. How did you know he was here?"

"Because he told me, of course!"

I sighed and sat back, opening the bottle of sparkling water with a hard twist that mimicked what I wanted to do to Adam's scrawny pencil neck. Him getting in touch with my mom wasn't because he liked her. Nope. I knew Adam well enough to understand that if he let my mom know that I was in town she'd put the pressure on me to get back together with him – his usual underhanded bullshit.

"You...don't seem happy about this," said Mom. "I can't imagine why. You ask me, this is a perfect opportunity to sort things out between the two of you. Why you broke up to begin with, I still have no idea. But he's handsome and wealthy and from a good family, and in my opinion he—"

"It's *not* happening!" The words came out of my mouth like a thunderclap. Mom stopped speaking, her eyes going wide. "Not now, not ever. Mom, I didn't tell you this because I didn't want to worry you. But, one night when Adam and I were arguing, he got really pissed at me and punched the wall only a few inches from me."

"He...he what? Adam *Myles*?" She said his name as if I might've gotten him confused with some other Adam.

"The one I dated, Mom, yes" I said. "And yeah – there's a side to him that you don't know about. He gets angry when he doesn't get his way. I put up with it for years. I mean, everyone always talked about him like he was the catch of Charmed Bay. So, I believed that if I thought there was something wrong with him it was my fault."

Mom said nothing, watching me with concern. Tears formed in my eyes, and she didn't waste a second in reaching into her purse and taking out some tissues.

"Thanks." I wiped my eyes, feeling like a crazy person having gone from on top of the world to down into a pit. But I knew I had to get all of this out. Mom needed to know. "I tried, Mom. I really did. But when I decided to come back home, I didn't do it lightly. I did it because I was scared of what might happen if I stuck around and Adam took things to another level."

I wiped my eyes again, shaking my head and staring at the water.

"And then he came back, followed me here, tried to tell me he'd changed, that things would be different if I just gave him a chance. He was a totally different person, that calm, nice guy that everything thinks he is... but I now know that's just an act, and I'm not falling for it like it did when we started dating.."

Mom took my hand into hers and squeezed it tightly. I wiped my eyes one last time, not wanting to shed another tear over that little creep.

"It's not going to happen. I'm not going to get back together with him. I'm here to live my life on my own terms, and if you don't want to cheer for me, that's fine. I can cheer for myself." I didn't mention that I had three great guys who were also ready to cheer for me. The Wolfs, whatever was happening with me and them, was a subject for another day.

Mom said nothing at first, turning her eyes to the ocean as if collecting her thoughts.

Then she squeezed my hand one more time.

"I...I didn't know all of that," she said. "I didn't. Here I was, thinking Adam was some great catch. But I had no idea he had this dark side. And that you were suffering through it, thousands of miles away!" Mom shook her head as if in total disbelief, as if she had no idea how to even begin processing it all. "It's over now, baby. You're here, you're with your mom, I'm not going to shame you into dating an awful man just because he looks good on paper."

Relief washed over me. "Thanks, Mom."

"I know it might feel like your life is over coming back here. But you're brilliant and beautiful and talented and the world is there for you to reach out and grab it! And I know I haven't been the best mother when it comes to supporting you the way I should. But I promise to try if you'll let me."

I smiled. Tears were still in my eyes, but for a different reason.

"I'd like that, Mom."

She squeezed my hand once more. It was going to take work for me and Mom to have something like a normal relationship. But I was more than ready to get started.

Together we watched the waves come in, as mother and daughter.

CHAPTER 28

JAY

What do you think?

I couldn't help but smile as I looked over the text from Dream. It was a picture taken in a very nice townhome, a two-bedroom place where she was planning on moving with Clarissa. The shot was over a big, open living room, the sun pouring into the empty space, the ocean visible off in the distance through the tall, rectangular windows.

Another text followed. *Twelve-hundred square feet, two floors, and it's even got an awesome rooftop that'll be perfect for the Christmas party. And you can see in the picture that it's right by the beach.*

The place looked great. We'd been chatting over the last day since we'd seen one another. Evidently, she and her mother had a conversation where they'd patched things up a bit between them, her mother insisting that she help her with a new place now that she was going to be staying back in Charmed Bay long-term. No daughter of hers would be sleeping on a couch, had been her words according to Dream.

Looks amazing. But the real question is – do you have to sleep on a couch? I grinned as I sent the text, knowing already that the answer was a likely "no."

The reply came a few moments later as I was filling up my coffee mug in my kitchen. It was a shot of a big bedroom with its own private balcony.

Does that answer your question? This was followed with a tongue-sticking-out emoji.

I let my eyes linger on the picture of the bedroom, imagining what it'd be like to have her alone in that room underneath the covers of some big, comfy bed. Maybe even up against the wall. Or even on the balcony with no one watching but the sea.

Well, what do you think?

I shook my head, snapping back into the moment.

Looks amazing. Can't wait to see what you do with the place.

There was no doubt another question coming, one that she hadn't asked yet. I decided to beat her to the punch and answer it in advance.

And yes, I'll help you move. Don't even worry about it.

The response was immediate. *Hahaha! I was going to ask, but you know. There's one thing about that. We're prob going to be signing the lease today, but the only good day to do the moving in for the big stuff is on the 22nd. We can get all the small things, so it'd only be the furniture and beds. I figure with you all helping we could have it done in a few hours. Then we can party a couple days later!*

There was no thinking about it – I was ready to help. The date was the twenty-second, so that gave them a solid day to get the rest of the stuff. Moving during the holidays came with some extra challenges - and deadlines - but my brothers and I were more than willing to help.

You know we'll help. I'll check with the guys, but I seriously doubt they'll say no. And let us know if you need help with any of the other stuff. We can carry more than just couches, you know.

I know, but I don't want to wring too much out of you guys. And thanks so much. You three are the best.

Happy to do it.

I had a big smile on my face when the conversation was over. I wanted the best for Dream, for her to hit the ground running with this new life of hers, to go after the success and happiness that she seemed destined for and certainly deserved.

Sure, there was still the matter of that prick Adam being in town. But if he knew what was good for him, he'd give Dream a wide berth. Because if I caught even the slightest whiff of him giving her any trouble...

Just the thought of Adam doing anything to make her upset was enough to make my hand clench into a diamond-hard fist. I pushed it out of my head as best I could, not wanting to get myself pissed over something that hadn't yet happened. Still, I was on guard.

And there was something more that I'd been thinking about, something I couldn't shake – the conversation we'd had about her mom had made me so badly want to talk to Dad. Just the idea was enough to make my stomach tighten. I hated that he still made me feel this way, that even as an adult I was scared to tell him about how what he'd done to me still stuck.

I sipped my coffee and stared off into space, wondering what it would be like to look my father in the eye and give him a piece of my mind. The scary part? The more I thought about it, the more I wanted to do it. Something about bringing it up with Dream had turned my relationship with Dad from a distant thought that floated in the periphery of my mind to something concrete, a problem that I could deal with.

And most importantly, a problem I could solve.

I shook my head as I continued to sip my coffee. Was today going to be the day that I spoke to him? After all, Dad lived less than twenty minutes from my place. It'd take nothing more than a quick drive.

By the time I was done with my coffee I'd made my decision.

I was going to do it.

I picked up my phone, my heart thudding. I pulled up my text conversation with Dad, seeing that the last time I'd talked to him had been over four months ago, a quick exchange about when my leave was over.

I typed.

You busy today? Want to talk to you about something.

I set down my phone. Dad wasn't exactly the techiest guy in the world and hated using his phone for anything but necessary calls. To my surprise, his reply came only a few minutes after I sent the text.

About what? Just text me with what you want.

Knowing dad, that response surprised me. Did he really not want to see me that badly?

Something I want to talk to you about in person. We both hate texting.

He replied a few moments later.

Fine. Got things to do this afternoon, so you want to come by, do it sooner rather than later.

Nothing warm or inviting about Dad's message. Not that I expected anything else – Dad was about as warm as the north pole in the dead of winter.

I typed up one last text. *Be over in thirty.*

Fine.

When I set down the phone, I couldn't help but wonder if Dad knew the reason I was coming. Maybe he'd even been expecting it. But the chances were just as good that he didn't give a damn about me, that he had no idea why I was coming and wanted to get it over as soon as possible.

Didn't matter. I was going to speak to him, to tell him what was on my mind and in my heart. After taking a few moments to psyche myself up, I grabbed my keys and hurried out the door and into my truck.

The day was overcast, one of those days where you might expect snow if the temperature dropped low enough. I spent the drive over rehearsing what I was going to say, trying to get all the words right. But ten minutes into it I realized that there was no point in doing that. Showing up with some speech would only leave me open to getting caught off-guard when Dad came at me from an angle that I wasn't expecting.

And he was good at that.

Our childhood home was in one of the nicer parts of Charmed Bay, on the southern side of downtown where all the pre-war houses were. The house was three-story and brick with white columns in front, the lawn the best looking on the block. Dad's white Land Rover, spotless as ever, was parked in the driveway.

I pulled in behind him and killed the engine. My stomach was quaking with tension. In the service I'd learned a trick to managing last-minute nerves – close your eyes, clear your head, and focus on your breathing. A simple trick, but it worked. And as I sat there, I found myself wondering what it might be like to have a normal childhood, what it would be like to pull up to the home where you grew up and felt happiness.

I pushed that out of my head as quickly as I could. Whatever that might be like, it wasn't my reality. No sense in dwelling on it.

I grabbed the keys and hopped out of the truck, making my way to the front door. I opened it and stepped into the large entry room, the view from the front looking all the way down the main hall through the living room, the stairs going up to the other two floors. The place was as spotless as I remembered it being – Dad had always been big on neatness and order.

"Dad?" My voice echoed through the silent home.

"Kitchen." His deep, booming voice called out to me.

I swallowed one last time before making my way to the kitchen.

Dad was seated at the kitchen bar, a newspaper in his hands and jazz playing lightly on the stereo. A tall glass of a protein smoothie, his preferred breakfast, was close at hand. Dad was tall and broad-shouldered, and one look at him made it clear as day that my brothers and I were his sons. He had a shaved head and neatly trimmed silver beard, his eyes a piercing blue, his expression hard. Dad wore a white polo, gray slacks and brown boots, a faded Army Ranger tattoo poking out from the armband of his shirt.

He flicked his eyes up to me as I entered, neatly folding his paper then setting it down.

"You're just marching into the house, huh?" he asked. "No knock?"

"Most parents don't make their kids knock on the door of their own homes."

"This isn't your home," he reminded me. "It ceased being that when you became a man and moved out. Now that you have your own place, you need to show *my* home respect." He sighed, shaking his head. "But that doesn't matter. What is it you wanted to talk to me about?"

Right to the point, as always. Dad was all business, never one for small talk.

"I want to talk to you about the way you treated us. Back when I was a kid."

He cocked his head to the side and folded his arms over his big, barrel chest.

"You...what? About when you were a kid? Why the hell would you want to talk about that?"

I couldn't tell if he was playing dumb or if he genuinely didn't know. Either way, I wasn't about to back down.

"About your style of discipline."

Dad let his eyes rest on mine, his gaze burning, for several long moments. Then he snorted, looking away and shaking his head.

"Figured you'd come sulking in here one of these days whining about that. I was hoping, however, that you'd get over it and move on with your life."

Anger boiled in me, and I did my best to keep it in check.

"Are you serious? You abused us and you hoped that I'd just never mention it?"

"Abuse? You call that abuse? I swear, what is it with your generation that makes you all soft as hell? My old man hit me when I got out of line, and his old man did the same to him. You think any of us ever went whining to our dads about getting a smack every now and then? God, look at you, all geared up to really have a moment with me. Does it feel good? Do you think you'll get some nice movie-of-the-week resolution from confronting me?"

"You're unbelievable," I said, shaking my head. "Look at yourself – fronting like you're some pillar of the community when you used to get off on hitting helpless children, and later you cheated on your wife with a younger woman - a woman who is younger than your own kids. You're no hero dad, you're nothing but a hypocrite."

Dad's eyes flashed with anger, and for a moment I worried he might rush over to me and hit me right then and there.

"You're out of line, kiddo," he said, standing and leaning against the counter.

"Does it bother you that I'm ashamed of you, of the childhood you gave me? That I joined the military to escape from you, that we all did?"

Rage burned in Dad's eyes. But this time, it didn't go away. He stepped closer to me with determined footfalls, his boots against the ground echoing through the kitchen. It took all I had to stand firm and still, to not back down.

"You've got a lot of nerve, kid," he said. "Coming into my home and speaking to me like this."

"And you've got a lot of nerve ruining my childhood and not even having the decency to apologize."

"So, what're you going to do? Tattle? Spread gossip around town like some teenage girl?"

"No, because I don't care what everyone in town thinks about you. I know what kind of man you are, and I don't need to remind my brothers of the trauma you inflicted upon us. But know this, I will not repeat the sins of my father or your father before you. My brothers and I are bigger and better men than you could ever dream to be."

There was nothing more to be said. Dad let his eyes stay on mine for several moments. There was conflict in his stare, as if he hadn't been expecting me to stand up to him like that, to show him that I wasn't afraid.

"Do it," he said, a small smirk forming on his lips. "I bet you've fantasized about slugging your old man again, really teaching him a lesson. Do it. Do it unless you're a pussy."

The temptation was there. But more than that, I didn't want to be like him. Hitting Dad now would put me on his level, making me no better than he was.

I turned, striding out of the kitchen.

"Good!" he shouted after me. "Be a coward! You had your chance to stand up to me and you *failed*. Now get the hell out of my house!"

Moments later I was back in my truck, my heart racing. Dad had tried to goad me into a fight, and I'd resisted. I'd wanted to hit him so damn badly, but I knew it wouldn't make a bit of difference.

As I pulled out of the drive, I realized it was a victory, however small.

CHAPTER 29

DUNCAN

"Yo, dude! Turn it the *other* way!"

"I am turning it the other way!"

"Not *your* other way! *My* other way!"

I could barely see Evan over the massive couch that we were in the process of carrying up the small flight of stairs that led into Dream's new place. But with some doing, Evan and I managed to turn the thing and fit it through.

"You got it!" shouted Clarissa, clapping her hands and jumping up and down as we made our way over the threshold and set the couch down on the ground.

"That...that was surprisingly heavy for an Ikea couch." I glanced down at the long, pink piece of furniture. "What is it, filled with bowling balls?"

Clarissa laughed. "That's not Ikea, believe it or not. That's some vintage piece my parents got me as a birthday present. I guess they made stuff sturdier back then."

"I guess so," I replied.

"You guys want something to drink?" Evan called to us from the kitchen, his voice carrying through the mostly open space of the home. Most of the furniture had been brought in, though it hadn't been arranged. And the small stuff was still in stacked boxes here and there.

"I'll take a beer!" I shouted back at him.

"Make that two!" said Clarissa.

"Three!" Dream trotted down the stairs, a big smile on her face. She looked smoking hot dressed in her tight yoga pants– good enough that I wanted to be the one to give her the first orgasm in her new room.

"Got it!" shouted Evan.

A grunt sounded out behind me. I turned to see Jay coming in, the girls' huge, new TV in his hands. It was still in the box, making for an awkward carry. I hurried over to help him.

"I got it," he said, flashing me a hard look, one that made it clear he didn't want any help at all.

"You sure?"

"I'm sure."

"Fine."

Clarissa was busy moving furniture into place, but when I glanced over my shoulder, I saw Evan standing at the entrance to the living room, beers in his hands and an expression of concern on his face. We met eyes, and there was no doubt that we were thinking the same thing, that Jay had been prickly all day, more than usual. And out of the corner of my eye I could see that Dream seemed to be thinking the same.

Something was wrong.

Jay carried the TV over the far wall and set it down, Clarissa hurrying over to help guide him.

"Perfect!" she said, giving Jay a pat on the back when he was done. "Now you just need to set it up and plug it in!" Clarissa grinned, letting him know she was only joking.

But Jay's expression stayed stony. Not like he'd ever been the kind of guy to break out into wild laughter for the sake of being friendly, but even he could crack a smile every now and then.

Clarissa, realizing she wasn't going to get any kind of reaction, scrunched her face and turned away.

Clarissa caught my attention as Jay slouched out of the house back to the truck.

What's wrong with him? she mouthed the words.

I shrugged, making a "your guess is as good as mine" face.

"Anyway," Evan said, coming around to pass out the beers. "Only a few more things and then we are done."

Clarissa, beer in hand, let out a squeal of happiness. Then she rushed over to Evan and threw her arms around him, pulling my brother into a tight hug. When she was done with him, she came over to me and did the same.

"You guys have been amazing," she said. "You know, if you ever decide to retire from the military, you could easily open a moving company. Call it 'Three Hot Brothers Moving' or something like that."

"Clever name," said Evan with an ironic wink.

"OK, I can do better than that. How about 'Muscleman Moving,' or maybe 'Beefcake Budgers!' There's got to be something."

The three of us laughed. But as we were in the middle of it, Jay came in with a side table in his hands.

"You guys taking your break already?" he asked. "More work to be done."

I turned and looked over his shoulder. Nothing remained in his truck but a small bookshelf. And that was the last of it – we'd gotten everything from the old place.

But I could tell Jay wasn't going to stop until he'd gotten everything. Thing about that was, if any of us needed a beer and some relaxing time, it was him. I really wanted to know what was going on with my brother. However, I knew him well enough to understand that if there was one way to get him to close up even further, it was to try to make him share his feelings.

"I'll get it," I said. "Jay, you've earned a beer."

"Yeah," added Dream. "Sit down, Jay. Take a load off." Her eyes flashed. "Oh! If you still want to help you can put the pizza order together."

"Yeah. Sure." Jay said the words with a grouchy tone, but I could tell he was happy to have something more to do. Jay was the sort of person who liked to transfer his bad feelings into action, even if it was something as simple as ordering pizza.

"We doing Gianni's?" asked Evan. "If so, give them my name. They've got my usual order – an extra-large works with extra bacon and extra cheese. Oh, and an order of cheesy garlic rolls."

Jay went to work on the order, with Clarissa and Dream looking at the online menu for Gianni's. And as they did, I went outside and grabbed the final piece of furniture. It was a gorgeous day, and some pizza and beer on the girls' new back patio sounded just right after an afternoon of moving. I made a mental note not to get too carried away – the girls' Christmas party was in two days, after all. Hard to believe it was Christmas with the weather warmer than usual this year.

"Order's in," said Jay as I entered and set the bookshelf in an open spot. "Got a little bit of everything." He sipped his beer after he spoke, staring off into the distance. I couldn't tell what was on his mind, but it was clear he was hurting. And I hated to see either of my brothers hurt. Dream wore an expression of concern, and once more I could sense she was thinking the same thing as me.

She cleared her throat and spoke. "OK, guys, I know I've told you a million times already, but thank you all so much for helping us move in. I have to add it to the ever-growing list of times the Wolf brothers have been there for me when I needed them. I appreciate it, and I love you all like crazy."

"Sure!" said Evan as he flopped onto one of the open couches.

Dream pursed her lips together, giving some thought to what she had to say next.

"Let's do this on the back patio," she said. "I've got a little announcement for you guys."

All of us shared a glance of confusion. What sort of announcement did she have in mind?

After grabbing some fresh beers, we headed out onto the back patio. The space was big and open, a wooden deck perfect for the party tomorrow. And the beach was right there in sight, just a few hundred feet away. The rest of the group came out, Evan bringing an iced bucket of beers with him.

I leaned back against the deck railing, eager to hear what Dream had on her mind.

"Alright," she said once all attention was on her. "So, as all of you guys know, I've been giving some serious thought to my future. I've recently made some huge changes in my life, and so far, all of them have worked out for the best. I'm so happy to be back in my hometown with my friends and family, and there's not a doubt in my mind that I made the right call."

"And we're glad to have you back!" said Clarissa, raising her beer.

Dream smiled, then went on.

"Well, I did some thinking about my work and what I want to do for a living, where I see myself and what might make me the happiest. And as I did, I figured well, what's one more life altering change on top of the rest? So, I want you guys to be the first ones to know that I'm going to be a full-time artist!"

"What?" asked Evan, springing out of his chair with excitement. "Are you serious? You're going for your art full-time?"

"Yep!" said Dream. "I know it's going to be hard, and I know it's going to have some ups and downs. But I've got a solid financial cushion from my current job that'll carry me for a while, and if I need to get a part-time job at Blueprint to help make ends meet, I'll do that too."

"Dream!" I said, "This is so awesome!" I couldn't put into words how happy I was to hear the news. Dream was beyond talented, and knowing she was going to devote herself fully to bringing her art to the world...God, it was, well, awesome!

Evan set down his beer and hurried over to give her a hug, Clarissa letting out a squeal of excitement. We embraced all around. Even Jay, distant as he was that evening, gave his congratulations.

It was a perfect cause for celebration. Clarissa put on some music, the pizza showed up, and together we talked eagerly with Dream about her future plans. However, as the sun began to dip, I noticed that Jay was gone. His truck was still out front, but he was nowhere to be found.

Something was wrong. I didn't want to pry. But I needed to know my brother was OK.

CHAPTER 30

DREAM

"You hear anything back?" There was a touch of worry in Evan's tone.

"Nothing so far." My eyes were on the text conversation with Jay. When we'd realized he'd left, leaving his truck parked in the driveway, all of us began wondering where the hell he'd gone off to.

Hey! Just wanted to make sure everything was OK. That had been my message. Knowing Jay, knowing he wasn't the kind of guy to just dump his feelings out, I understood that asking him if he was OK had been a risk. But what else could I do?

He hadn't responded. It'd been clear from the first minute I'd seen him that day that he'd been preoccupied with something. And as much as I wanted to respect his desire to keep things to himself, I hated knowing that he was suffering in silence.

Right as I began to get really worried, however, the noise of an incoming text sounded out and a message appeared.

Hey. Sorry, just needed some fresh air. And I'm not being very good company today. Didn't want to put a damper on the celebration. I'll be back in a bit when my head's right.

Relief moved through me like a cool wave. I read the text to the group, and it was clear they were as relieved as I was to know Jay was OK.

"That's just like him," said Duncan. "Always vanishing when he's got something troubling him. I understand needing some time to process...but I wish he'd get that his brothers are there for him, you know?"

"More than his brothers," said Clarissa. "We're *all* here for him."

Evan reached for another slice of pizza. "Well, Jay would also hate to hear that we were all sitting around talking about him, right?"

"No kidding," said Duncan.

"How about this instead," suggested Evan. "Dream, why don't you tell us about the website? We went over a ton of stuff when we last met up. I bet these two would be great to bounce ideas off of."

"Yeah!" said Clarissa. "Let's hear the business plan!"

"Well, it's not much. But..."

Evan went in to grab the notebook we'd put together and I walked Duncan and Clarissa through it. There wasn't much done, and plenty more work ahead of me, but it was a good way to change the subject. Another hour went by, and right as I could sense we were all starting to think of Jay again, another text arrived.

Stopped for a drink – I'll be there in twenty. Tell the guys not to wait up for me.

I read the text to the group.

"I hope he's doing alright," said Clarissa.

Duncan's brow was furrowed in thought. "Well, we all want to know what's going on with him. And I can tell you this much, that if he comes back here and all of us pounce on him with questions, he's going to lock up tighter than a bank vault."

"What're you saying?" I asked.

"He's saying," Evan jumped in. "That it's probably a good idea for us to peace out. I'm thinking I need to get going anyway – got to be well-rested for the party tomorrow, right?"

He stood up, putting together a pizza box made up of the various kinds of slices.

"A little midnight snack, you know?"

I smiled as he and Duncan got up. "Thanks again, guys. For the moving and the support and the *everything*."

"Happy to do it," said Duncan. "We've always got your back. Never forget it."

There were hugs all around, and I made sure that the boys would be the first ones to arrive for the party. The guest list was huge, and I couldn't wait.

Once Clarissa and I were alone, we started the work of putting away the pizza. But it didn't take long before Jay showed up.

"Hey," he said as he stepped through the door. "Guys gone? Didn't see their cars out there."

"Yeah, they're gone," I said.

Clarissa's face tensed up. I could tell she was feeling like a third wheel.

"Um, well, I've got some major unpacking to do upstairs. Good seeing you, Jay!"

Without another word, and without giving Jay a chance to say anything, she zipped up the stairs and was gone. Jay and I were alone.

"I should probably get going too," he said. "See you later—"

"No," I said, cutting him off and shaking my head. "You're not getting out of here that easily."

"Huh?"

I went to the fridge and grabbed a couple of beers. "Come on, Jay. We're going back outside, and I want you to tell me what's wrong."

"Nothing's wrong," he said. "Just had a lot of stuff on my mind."

"I'm not buying that for a second. Now, let's go."

I held the two beer bottles in my left hand, grabbing Jay's hand with my right and leading him back out to the patio. Sure, he could've stopped me if he really wanted to, but he didn't.

"Clarissa's room is on the other side of the house," I said. "Mine's over top. So, you don't need to worry about anyone listening in."

He chuckled as he sat down next to me on one of the benches. "Am I that predictable?"

"Not predictable," I said with a smile. "Just...I know you by now. You don't get to be in someone's life for over ten years and not have them understand you a little – even with your best efforts to keep your emotions hidden."

Jay sighed and shook his head as he cracked open his beer. "Sorry for acting like a cranky little kid today. Had some shit on my mind and I didn't want to make a thing about it. I'm happy as hell that you're moved in and starting your new career. Knowing that you've got such a bright future waiting for you to take hold of it...it does me some good. I can't wait to see what life has in store for you."

His words made me feel great. But I hadn't brought him outside to get myself puffed up even more than I already was.

"Thanks, Jay. Really. But tell me, what's going on with you? It's like...a switch flipped."

Jay shifted in his seat and looked away. "It's hard to talk about."

"Try. Because I don't want you keeping it stuffed up inside if you don't have to. We might not technically be family anymore, but that doesn't mean we can't still be open with one another."

"It's Dad." I could tell that merely saying the words had been difficult for him.

His dad wasn't a happy subject for anyone. Knowing what he did to my mom was enough to send a flash of anger through my body at the mere mention of him, and then after hearing what he'd done to Jay and his brothers? Saying I despised the man would be the under-statement of the year.

"What happened?"

"I confronted him. About what happened all those years ago."

"You *what*? Jay, I told you that if you needed me to be there for you when you talked to him, I'd do it! Why didn't you call me?"

"Because it was my battle to fight. You didn't need to be there for it."

"But what if I wanted to give him a piece of my mind, too? He's hurt many people I care about."

. . .

I stopped myself before I said another word. Speaking of selfish, *I* was being selfish. Jay had summoned up a ton of courage to confront his father, and there I was already questioning how he did it.

"Sorry," I said, collecting myself. "It's just that...I have history with him too, you know?"

"I get it. And I appreciate you making the offer to be there for me. But I did what I needed to do."

"And what happened? What did you say?"

He took a sip of his beer, tension forming on his face. "I called him out for what he did, told him how wrong it was the way he abused us. It was hard, but I said what I needed to say."

"How did he take it?"

Jay let out a grim snort of a laugh. "Not well. Tried to make me feel like shit for bringing it up, like it was no big freaking deal. But that doesn't matter. I went to give him a piece of my mind. It was stupid as hell for me to expect that he'd have some change of heart on the spot."

"And...how do you feel now?"

"Better. I know I was being moody tonight, but I feel better. Something I've learned in life is that you can't control everything and everyone. Sounds obvious, but when you're a kid it's easy to think you're the main character in life, that whatever you want is going to work out in exactly the way you want it. But you do have control over yourself. When I told Dad how I felt, I wasn't expecting much from him. I did what I did for *me*. How he reacted was his own damn business. I didn't have any control over that shit."

He shifted in his seat, rubbing his mouth with the back of his hand before taking another sip of beer. His words made sense. But I couldn't help but wonder if he had been hoping for a different outcome. None of that mattered, however.

Jay set down his beer and turned to me.

"And most importantly, what happened made me realize how lucky I am to have someone like you in my life. You and my brothers

– you're the world to me. And you listened when I told you what was troubling me; you gave a damn. So...thanks."

I smiled, turning to him. "I'm always here for you."

Without thinking, I wrapped my arms around him and pulled him close into a tight hug. Jay's body stiffened in the way it always did when he was on the receiving end of some unexpected physical affection.

Then he hugged me back, wrapping his powerful arms around me.

"Thanks, Dream," he said. "Thank you for being there."

"Always."

We held each other close, and when the hug ended our hands stayed on one another's bodies. He regarded me with a strange expression, one that suggested he was trying to decide how he felt about me in that moment.

The expression didn't stay for long, however. Slowly, he leaned in close for a kiss.

It was a kiss that, deep down, I'd been wanting like crazy. Our lips touched and the usual electricity exploded through my body, my muscles tightening and my pussy clenching. All it took was a touch and a kiss from him to drive me wild with desire.

He opened his mouth, and I did the same. Our tongues found one another's, and the kiss carried so much passion, so much intensity, that I felt as though I might melt on the spot. His hands fell onto my breasts and mine onto his solid chest, and in that moment, there was nothing in the world but our kiss.

My chest rose and fell, my arousal building by the second. I wanted Jay, I needed him. And the longer our kiss went on the more likely it was that I would give in to him right then and there.

"We should take this upstairs," I said, his kiss traveling from the curve of my jaw down to the slope of my neck. "As much as I'd love to have you outside, there's a roommate situation to worry about."

"Good call."

He rose, his cock straining against his jeans and begging for my attention. Almost as if I didn't have control over myself, my hands flew to his zipper and button. With a flash of motion, I had them open, his cock pulled out in front of me.

With a flicker of a smile, I took him into my mouth and formed a tight seal around him with my lips. Jay groaned with pleasure as I glanced up at him before giving my full attention to his manhood. I brought my lips down then up, down then up, letting his musky, delicious taste flood my senses. The idea of him spilling into my mouth was divine. But I wanted more than that. Besides, there was still a very much awake roommate upstairs to worry about.

I took him out of my mouth, placing my lips on his head one last time before standing, tucking his cock back into his jeans.

"A little hint of things to come," I said with a sly smile.

He matched my smile with one of his own. And when he did, I took a moment to appreciate the way his face looked when he smiled, the dimples in his cheeks and the slight crinkling around his eyes. It was beyond sexy it was...something I couldn't explain as I stood there with his cock in my hand.

Once he was decent, the two of us hurried through the first floor and up to the second. Sure, Clarissa likely heard the twin sets of footsteps as we went up the stairs, one soft and quick and the other big and booming, but that didn't matter. Soon we were in my room, nothing there but the bed and the stacks of boxes and the bags of my clothes.

We kissed more, this time slipping one another out of our clothes. Jay's big hand grabbed my bare inner thigh, moving up and undoing the button and zipper of my jean shorts. When they were open the baggy shorts dropped to my feet and he placed his hand on my pussy through my panties, touching me in a way that made my knees weak.

I soaked through my panties in record time, Jay slipping his fingers underneath the thin strip of fabric between my legs and entering me. He placed his thumb on my clit and two main fingers inside. It took only a bit of this before I came, the orgasm like flashes of white-hot light bursting through my body.

When it was over, I was ready for more. Jay pulled his shirt off over his head, revealing his powerful, muscular body. I did the rest of the work, getting him out of his jeans and underwear. Once we were both naked, he scooped me off my feet and set me down, opening my legs and moving between them. My eyes stayed locked onto his thick, deliciously long manhood as he brought it down closer to my sex.

Once he was close, I took hold of him, rubbing my clit with his stone-solid head, each touch sending pulses of pleasure through me. I bucked and moaned, bringing myself to another orgasm using him in such a way. But I needed more. He gently took my hand from him and grasped his cock, placing it at my entrance and gliding into me like he was made for me and me alone.

I let out a long, pleasured sigh as he plunged into me, his inches vanishing until there were no more to give. My back arched and I wrapped my arms and legs around Jay, drawing him close, feeling his solid warmth both in me and against me. He lavished me with kisses as he moved inside, kissing my lips and face, neck and breasts. The more he pushed into me, the more he touched me, the more I wanted.

It was nearly impossible to open my eyes through the intensity of his lovemaking. But I did, desperately desiring to watch his perfect, powerful body at work. His flawless, toned muscles flexed and tensed with each penetration, our breaths and moans growing louder and louder. He wrapped his arm around me, making my body flush with his.

We gazed intently at one another. And as we did, I felt something more than what I was used to. There wasn't simply affect, not simply attraction, there was something so much more.

I gasped when I realized what it was.

Love.

The word didn't have time to settle in my mind. Another orgasm ripped through me, and for this one Jay joined. He grunted hard as he released deeply into my walls, his cock throbbing as he filled me with his seed. When he was done his muscles went from tight and taut to slack, the pulsing of him inside of me making the last ebbs of my own pleasure even more delightful.

He collapsed to my side and once he did the word returned. It flashed in my mind like a neon sign, and I knew there was no sense in denying it.

"I love you."

Jay knitted his brow, as if he weren't sure that he'd heard me correctly. He rolled onto his side and gazed at me.

"You...you what?"

"I love you. I love you like mad."

I meant the words as I said them. But as soon as they were out, I realized that they weren't...*enough*. At first, I was confused by how I felt.

Then I realized why I was uncertain.

I didn't just love Jay.

I loved all of them.

"I love you," I said. "And I love Duncan. And I love Evan. And I have no idea what to do with any of this."

I was worried about his reaction. Jay had been through so much and there I was, dumping more onto his lap. But he wasn't mad. Instead, he smiled broadly, a warm, inviting smile that was so rare on his usually hard features.

"Well, I love you too. And I can't speak for my brothers, but I'd bet you anything they feel the same way."

He pulled me close and planted a soft kiss on my forehead.

"But don't worry," he said with a mischievous grin. "We're very good at sharing."

CHAPTER 31

EVAN

It was the evening of the party, and Dream's place was filled with the sounds of people laughing. Christmas music played softly in the background, and somehow, she managed to set up a tree in the short amount of time since moving in two days before.

The un-moved-in house ended up being the perfect venue for a Christmas. The bottom floor was packed with tons of people from town, people we'd known for years since all the way back in high school. The back patio and rooftop terrace was full too.

It was *the* place to be in Charmed Bay for Christmas Eve. And I was having the time of my life. Still, there was only one guest there I really wanted to get some one-on-one time with.

"How does she manage to look hotter every day?" I asked Duncan, who wore a cheesy Christmas sweater with Rudolph on the front, complete with a glowing red nose. I felt a little underdressed in a red Henley and jeans compared to him. Maybe I should have tried a little harder to be festive with my attire.

My eyes were on Dream, of course. She wore a fitted emerald green dress that hit her at mid-thigh. Her hair was down, not in her usual ponytail, and she wore a Santa hat on top of her head, making her the sexiest Mrs. Claus I had ever seen in my life.

There was also a lightness to her, an ease that hadn't been there before. Made me wonder if her decision to finally go for what she wanted had changed something inside of her.

"Maybe you should go ask her," Duncan said with a grin I could spot out of the corner of my eye. "Unless you're planning on spending the whole party gawking at her from across the room."

I laughed nervously, rubbing the back of my head.

"I suppose I could do that," I said. "But what about you?"

He seemed confused. "What *about* me?"

"Aren't you going to want some time alone with her tonight?"

"I mean, yeah. But she's with all three of us, right? We're going to have to learn to share some time. So, I'll be the big brother here and let you get some time alone with her."

I laughed before taking a sip of my beer. "Aren't you a real sweetheart?"

He grinned. "I have my moments. Besides, there's tons of people here I want to catch up with from back in the day. Now, go talk to her before she starts wondering why not one of us is with her."

I was ready. I moved through the party, weaving between the knots of people, saying my "hellos" to familiar faces and doing some back-patting here and there. I wanted to make time for my friends at the party, but there was the whole night ahead for that.

Dream – she was the only one who was on my mind.

Her face lit up as she saw me walking over, her beauty like nothing else. She was in the middle of chatting with a couple people who I didn't recognize. As I drew near, she ended the conversation and saw them off with friendly waves.

"Don't give your friends the boot on my behalf," I said as I approached.

"Oh, it's nothing. Those were some people from the farmer's market I met the other weekend. Evidently, a bunch of people from town do a little circuit with the other markets in the surrounding towns. We were talking about me joining them."

I couldn't help but smile like crazy, totally thrilled at the news.

"You serious? That's awesome! When do you start?"

"Well, nothing's set in stone just yet. But if I can get things wrapped up with my other job in the next month or two, I might be able to join them starting after the New Year. And then there's the spring market season after that." She sighed and shook her head, as if she was having a hard time wrapping her thoughts around it. "I know there's going to be a ton more work to do. And I haven't even gotten started. But already I'm feeling so damn lucky. More than that, I've got *you*, Evan Wolf, to thank for helping me get things off the ground."

"Happy to help. But this is all your talent and your ambition and your passion. All I did was point out what's obvious to anyone who's known you for more than a few minutes."

She squeezed my arm, her touch making me want more.

"Don't sell yourself short, Evan. I was uncertain and a little scared about going for my dreams. But you were there to talk me through it. If it weren't for you, I might still be looking down the barrel of years and years at some soul-sucking graphic design job."

"My pleasure." I couldn't resist any longer and didn't care if we were in public - I slipped my arm around her waist and pulled her close.

She laughed as she came near, her body against mine.

"Evan!" she said. "You know, if you touch me like this, people are going to start wondering what's going on between me and you. And if *Duncan* touches me like this too, and *Jay* does it too..."

She trailed off. I could tell by her tone that Dream was a little thrilled and scared all at the same time.

"There's plenty of time to roll out what's going on with all of us. In the meantime, what do you say we get a little moment to ourselves?"

"A little what?" Dream said it with a slightly scandalized tone, but I could tell she was intrigued.

"Upstairs – the second-floor bathroom. I go and you meet me there."

"That...that's such a bad idea."

"Bad? Or really, really fun."

She smiled slyly. "Maybe just for a few minutes."

"Then I'll see you there." I gave her butt a quick, secret little squeeze before slipping away and heading up the stairs.

The second floor was off-limits aside from the bathroom and the stairs to get to the roof, so no one was there to see me enter. I stepped inside and glanced in the mirror to see a big, excited smile on my face. I'd never been one to have a hard time being positive about life. But this thing with Dream was taking it all to another level. I couldn't wait to see what was in store for me, her, and my brothers.

I didn't have to wait long before a soft knock sounded at the bathroom door.

"Occupied?" asked Dream, her voice slightly muffled.

I hurried over and opened, letting her in and shutting the door behind her.

And the moment we were alone the fireworks began. It was like we'd time-traveled to midnight on New Year's Eve. I put my hands on her hips and brought her against my body, kissing her fast and hard. Dream kissed me right back, her tongue finding mine and her taste washing over me.

Our mouths still together, I lifted her off her feet and set her down on the two-sink counter, her legs opening and wrapping around my waist. I was stiff as steel by this point, grinding my cock against her as we kissed hard and deep.

She moaned through the kiss, gently bucking her body against mine, rubbing her pussy on me. I felt myself losing control by the moment. All I could think about was bending her over, flipping that dress of hers over her lower back, and—

Buzz Buzz Buzz

Her cell phone ringtone went off. Dream's brow furrowed as she pulled her phone from her clutch, and with a sigh, she said, "Ah, Clarissa is looking for me."

I nodded. "Shoot, I told Clarissa I'd help get the bonfire going as soon as it was dark enough, so she's probably looking for me too."

She smiled. "Well. Between that and my hosting duties, I think we're both being a bit neglectful right now."

"True, true. Then how about we put a pin in this, as they say. Come back to it a little later?"

"I like that idea. I like it a lot."

She hopped off the counter, then stepped up on her tiptoes and kissed me one last time. As her lips played on mine the urge to make it more than just a kiss came over me once more. But I put all that aside. Something told me we'd have plenty of time for all that in the days and weeks to come. Not to mention, who could say what the evening held?

I opened the door and let her out, stealing one last kiss on her neck as she slipped past me and left me in the wake of her delicious scent. When she was gone, I gave her a minute or two to go back downstairs before I did so as not to draw too much attention to the both of us. And then when I was ready, I left.

I was all smiles from the hot-as-shit make out session. After rejoining the party, I grabbed a fresh beer from the keg on the patio and started making the rounds. The time flew by as I caught up with some of my old friends from high school, mostly guys from the wrestling team.

It wasn't long before Clarissa found me, leading me down to the beach where I helped her, and a few other guys get the bonfire ready. It wasn't quite dark yet, but it wouldn't be long before the sun started dipping low.

But a half-hour or so later, when we were back up at the house, I noticed something strange. That is, I noticed someone wasn't there – Dream. From where I stood on the patio, I glanced around at the couple dozen people filling the space. Dream wasn't among them.

"Hey, Clarissa," I said, getting her attention. "You know where Dream is?"

She shrugged, not seeming to think it was a big deal. "Not sure." Clarissa craned her neck to look inside the house.

"Hmm, don't see her. Maybe up on the roof?"

It was the one part of the party I couldn't see from the patio. A set of stairs outside of the house led to the roof, and I didn't waste any time getting up there. My gut felt tense, as if my body sensed that something was wrong.

When I reached the roof, I spotted Duncan and Jay chatting with one another. They met my eyes as I approached, their expressions taking on a serious tone as if they could sense how I felt.

Duncan greeted me with a nod. "Yo. You look pretty tense for someone at a Christmas party."

"Yeah, what's up?" asked Jay.

"I don't know – might be being stupid. But I haven't seen Dream anywhere. Either of you guys know where she is?"

They shook their heads.

"I'd been downstairs for the last half-hour or so," said Jay. "Didn't see her there."

"And I've been jumping from conversation to conversation," added Duncan. "Feel like I would've seen her at some point."

I felt a little vindicated. "Right, so you guys don't think I'm being out of line here? Just seems strange that she'd go AWOL at her own party."

"Let's check downstairs," said Jay. "And I'll hit the bathroom on the second floor to see if she's in there."

"Good plan," said Duncan. "Let's move."

Together we headed down to the patio, Duncan making his way to the crowds now gathered around the bonfire while me and Jay headed inside. Dream was tiny, sure, and not the easiest person to spot in a crowd, but it wasn't like the place was so huge that it was unreasonable to think we could find her right away.

"Can you believe he showed up?" The voice of a woman nearby

caught my attention. I turned to see two college-age women speaking with one another, looks of disgust on their faces.

"I know. And he looked really wasted and out of it too. The guy's a freaking mess."

"Yeah. I mean Adam should've gotten the hint that if he wasn't invited that meant Dream didn't want him here. But he crashed the party anyway."

"Hey," I said, joining the conversation. "Sorry to interrupt. But are you two talking about Adam Myles?"

The woman to my right, a tall blonde nodded.

"That's the one. He just rolled in here with a little bottle of vodka in his hand trying to talk to Dream. He was getting super annoying about it, and she finally just went off somewhere with him to get him to calm down."

"What?" I couldn't believe what I was hearing.

"Yep," said the other girl, a cute redhead with a pixie cut. "Something's wrong with that dude."

"Do you two have any idea where they went?"

"No, sorry," said the blonde. "It was really cringe and embarrassing to watch so I didn't want to stare, you know?"

"Thanks."

I stepped away from the girls and ran my hand through my hair.

Adam was there. And he was alone with Dream.

There was no doubt in my mind that only bad would come from this. I had to find her, and fast.

CHAPTER 32

DREAM

*Y*ou should've known. You should've known.

The words repeated in my head over and over again as I watched Adam pace back and forth in my bedroom. Fear tensed my stomach. I was scared.

Why did you think meeting him this time would be any different? You knew the kind of man he was deep down. He showed you, remember?

I quieted the voice in my head, trying to get a sense of how I needed to handle this. Adam was drunk and unstable. And more than that, he was in front of the bedroom door. The party was downstairs, and with Christmas music and the sounds of people talking, I knew that it was unlikely anyone would hear if I called out to them.

Going someplace alone with Adam when I could smell the booze on his breath had been a bad idea. But scolding myself for it was about the least productive thing I could do now.

"I don't get it!" he said after taking a frantic pull of his vodka bottle and twisting the cap back on. "What did I say? What did I do? I told you that I'd change, and I meant it. Why don't you believe me?"

He leaned against the door when he was done, staring off into space with a stunned expression. Adam ran his hand through his hair, sweaty strands draping down over his glistening forehead. It looked like he hadn't slept a wink since the phone call when I'd told him we were done.

Adam took another sip of the vodka. I wanted more than anything to get that bottle out of his hands. Each drop he had would only make a bad situation even worse.

He tucked the bottle into his jeans pocket and looked up at me.

"OK." Adam said the word as if he'd just come to a very important realization. "OK. I think I know what's going on here. I did something at some point that you're still feeling uncertain about. And I think I know what it is." He laughed and scoffed. "It's when I punched the wall. You're still upset about that."

"Adam..."

His eyes flashed with anger. "Don't, *do not*, take that tone with me. Do *not* take that tone with me where you talk to me like I'm a kid. That's the last thing I want to hear. Got it?"

There was real rage in his voice, rage that scared me. When Adam had punched the wall back in Chicago, he'd been sober. Now he was drunk and unhinged, and I had no idea of how far he'd go.

"So, here's what we can do. It's a great plan. I'll move back here to Charmed Bay. I've got plenty of money, and we can get whatever house you want." He swept his hand dismissively around him. "Dream, there's no reason you have to be living like this."

"Living like what?" I asked. "Living on the beach with my best friend?"

It was a bad idea to antagonize him. But there wasn't a chance in hell I'd simply sit back and let him talk to me like that.

"Living in a rented place with a roommate. You get back together with me, and you don't have to worry about any of that! You can live your life with financial security and whatever else you want. I'm rich, don't you get it? I mean, well, I'm not rich yet, but I will be. But my family's rich, and we can provide for you whatever you want."

I shook my head. "Adam. After all this time, I can't believe you think that all it'll take is promising me money. How, after knowing me for this long, can you still think that's what I want?"

"Isn't that what everyone wants?" he asked. "I mean, why are you doing all this art stuff if you're not planning on making a ton of money from it?" Adam quickly slipped out the vodka and took another pull.

Adam said the word *art* with the same disdain that he'd used for *roommate*, the same disdain with which he spoke about anything he felt was below him. And on top of it all, he was beginning to slur his words. With each moment that passed he seemed to become more and more unstable.

I wished I had said something to the guys, that I'd told them about Adam before I'd agreed to speak with him alone. I glanced down at the nearby window, the view of the beach and the deck below. Everyone out there was having fun – a total contrast to the fearful situation I was in.

"Adam," I said. "If you want to keep having this conversation, can you please stop drinking?"

His face tightened into anger, and I understood right away that I'd made a major misstep.

"Are you serious?" he growled, taking the half-drank bottle of booze out of his pocket and shoving it toward me. "You put me through all this bullshit and now you want to tell me not to drink? Dream, I have to drink to deal with you, to deal with how badly it tears me up inside that you won't give me another chance!"

He pushed himself off the door and started moving toward me.

"I don't get it!" he yelled, shaking his head. "I don't get why you won't give me another chance! What is it, Dream? Is it...is it someone else?"

As soon as he said the words he stopped in place, an expression of terrible realization taking hold.

"There *is* someone else," he said. "And I know who it is!"

"What?"

"It's that fucking prick Duncan Wolf!" He practically spit out the words, so intense was his disgust.

I had no idea what to do. He was right, of course. But what was I supposed to say? Was I supposed to tell him the truth, that it wasn't only Duncan I was into, but all three of the Wolf brothers?

He took one more long pull from the bottle of booze, finishing it off and throwing it against the wall. It shattered, the glass spilling onto the ground. A scream of horror shot from my mouth.

"I should've known that you'd end up treating me this way. You know what? All this time I worried I wasn't good enough for you. And now I know it's the total opposite – that *you're* not good enough for *me*!"

Adam stepped closer toward me, closing the distance.

"You know what you are, Dream? You're nothing more than a disgusting little slut. I wouldn't be surprised if you were fucking all the Wolf brothers."

As soon as he said the word "slut", my body moved into action on its own. My hand shot up and I brought it hard across his face. The sound of my skin against his filled the room with a sharp *crack*. When my hand fell back to my side, I couldn't believe what I'd done.

Neither could Adam. He stood stunned, his eyes wide and his mouth slacked open. A red imprint was on his cheek where I'd hit him. I'd crossed a line, I realized. And there would be no more diffusing the situation.

"What...what the hell did you just do, Dream?" he asked. Adam was angry and hurt all at once. "You...hit me."

"It's what you deserved," I said, venom in my words. "Not a chance in hell I'm going to stand here and let you talk to me like that. Get out of my room, Adam. Get out of my room and my life. I never want to see you again."

But he didn't move. Instead, he narrowed his eyes into those hateful little slits. I watched as his hand formed into a fist. And before I could even think of how to react, he slammed his hand into the wall.

A low *boom* sounded out as his fist dug into the wall, his blow denting it and sending bits of plaster falling to the floor.

It was just like back in Chicago. And this time, I knew he wouldn't stop himself from doing more.

"I'm going to make you very, very sorry you did that, Dream," he said, a quiet menace to his voice, the scent of booze on his breath making me want to retch.

He took his fist from the wall and pulled it back.

But he didn't have a chance to do anything else. The door to the bedroom flew open, Adam spinning around on his feet.

Someone had arrived.

Several someone's.

CHAPTER 33

DUNCAN

There were no words to describe how I felt when I threw open the door to Dream's bedroom to see Adam seconds away from hitting her.

So, I didn't use words.

Instead, I strode across the bedroom and clapped my hand down hard onto Adam's shoulder. I turned him in place, spinning him around on his feet.

"Duncan!" he said, doing this pathetic tone of surprise, as if he were about to tell me there'd been some kind of misunderstanding. "What are you—"

I wasn't in the mood to hear a single word from him. I pulled my fist back and brought it forward, connecting with his jaw and sending him flying backward, hitting the wall next to Dream. She let out a sharp scream, her hands going to her mouth and her eyes flashing wide.

I glanced over my shoulder to see Jay and Evan standing there. The hard expressions on their faces made it crystal-clear that they were ready to join the fight. But as mad as I was, I could at least think clearly enough to know not to make this a three-on-one brawl.

Adam was stunned, but he wasn't out. Blood trickled down his nose and he placed his fingertips on it, glancing down at his now blood-covered hand.

"You'll pay for that!"

His face flashed with anger, and he stood up, rushing toward me. I could tell by his movement that he was three sheets to the wind, and all I had to do was step out of the way as he lumbered across the room. He took a few steps forward before he realized he'd overshot the target. And then it took him a few more steps after that to course correct.

Adam slammed into Evan, who didn't move an inch.

"Going somewhere?" he asked.

Adam pushed off Evan's chest and turned toward me. Out of the corner of my eye I saw the broken shards of glass from his booze bottle on the floor. The sight reminded me that, while Adam was outnumbered, he was still dangerous.

"You OK, Dream?" I asked over my shoulder.

"Yeah," she said. "Just...just shaken up."

Jay stepped over to her, making sure to keep an eye on Adam as he did.

"I'll get her out of here," he said. He placed his hand on her shoulder, regarding her with an expression of love and concern. "Come on, OK? Let's go to the roof and get some fresh air."

She nodded, his words allowing her to snap out of the daze-like spell she was in. Jay led her through the room. But before he could take her out, Adam glanced up to see that the door was open. With a panicked look on his face, he broke into a surprisingly quick sprint and rushed past Evan and down the stairs.

"Damnit!" shouted Evan. "We need to get him, make sure he gets escorted out of here."

"Good call," I said, frustrated at myself for letting Adam get away. "Jay, take care of Dream. Evan, let's finish this with Adam."

"Come on," said Jay, his voice exuding a warmth that I couldn't remember ever hearing from him.

Dream, still shaken, left the bedroom with Jay. Once that was done, Evan and I hurried out and down the stairs.

"Get the hell out of the way!" shouted Adam, as he ran past the guests.

We reached the first floor just in time to watch as he pushed his way through the crowd, people making noises of surprise as he did. He nearly toppled over the Christmas tree as he stumbled into it.

"Where the hell does he think he's going?" asked Evan, the two of us watching as Adam struggled through the crowd on the way to the back deck.

"Don't know. But we need to make sure he gets thrown out on his ass."

"Gladly."

Together, Evan and I weaved through the crowd. Everyone there seemed to understand that we'd arrived to handle the Adam situation, the guests moving out of the way to let us through. Evan and I reached the back deck just in time to watch as Adam slammed into the crowd back there.

And this time, no one moved.

"Get out of the way, assholes!" snarled Adam as he struggled to get past. "Move it!"

When everyone there realized what was going on, that Evan and I had come to fetch him, the party was on our side. Adam tried desperately to work his way through.

"So," said Evan. "You got one shot at him. But it's looking to me like he might need one more lesson. What do you think?"

I smirked. "Right there with you, bro."

Without another word, Evan stepped toward Adam. Once he was close, he pulled back his fist and brought it in a sharp arc against his face. Adam dropped to his knees; the blow having knocked him into a state of submission.

"You know Adam," said Evan. "It's a damn shame we need to explain to you that it's not OK to threaten women like that. But what do you say, lesson learned?"

Adam nodded dumbly.

"Good," said Evan, grabbing him by the arm and bringing him to his feet. "Now, let's get your ass out of here, got it?"

Without a word of protest, Adam was pulled to his feet. I came over to take him by the other arm, Evan and I dragging his sorry ass out of the house. Once we were out front, I spotted a slick sports car that I had no doubt was his. Evan pulled Adam's keys out of his pocket, and we checked to make sure the fob worked on the car.

"Now," said Evan. "I'm thinking you're a little too drunk to drive. Because I'm such a nice guy, I'll drop these keys off at your daddy's house when I can, maybe fill him in on what his son's been up to."

"As for you, shithead," I said. "Start walking. And if you're smart, you'll be on the first flight to Chicago once you've slept off your hangover."

"But..." It was all he could manage.

I shoved him forward, and Adam glanced over his shoulder at us, as if to see whether we were serious or not.

"*Now.*" My tone was hard, uncompromising.

He nodded obediently before turning and starting his way down the road. Evan and I watched, making sure he was in good enough shape to march his ass home. When he finally made his way around the bend and was gone, we headed back inside.

The danger was over. But it wasn't finished – we still had to make sure Dream was OK.

CHAPTER 34

JAY

I watched from the rooftop as Adam's sorry ass skulked around the corner and was gone. I wasn't happy in the slightest about what he'd done, but still, the tiniest hint of a smile formed on my lips knowing he'd got what he deserved.

"Alright everyone!" I said, turning back to the crowd on the rooftop. "It's over, let's not let that asshole spoil the festivities, huh?" The crowd let out cheers of agreement before turning their attention back to their drinks and conversation. Thankfully, everyone there seemed not to have allowed the Adam bullshit to bother them.

But they didn't matter as much as Dream. She was seated on the edge of the roof, a faraway look on her face.

"You doing alright?" I asked, placing my hand on her shoulder.

She nodded quickly; her eyes still fixed forward. "Fine. Just...not how I wanted all that to end."

"Yeah?" I sat down next to her. "Sorry if me and the guys made a scene."

"No, that's not it at all." She turned to me with a warm smile. "It's really not. You guys came to help, and I don't even want to think about what would've happened if you hadn't shown up when you did. It's not that."

"Then what's wrong?"

"It's Adam. The guy's a real piece of work and I'm glad he's out of my life."

"We're going to make sure it stays that way," I said. "If he ever bothers you again..."

"I know," she stopped me. "I know you guys will be looking out for me. But all the same, we were together for a long time, right? I never seriously considered getting back with him, but part of me hoped that he might get his act together and put the dark side of his personality behind him. Looks like the opposite happened, though – he let that dark side totally consume him."

"You're right – it is too bad. But maybe he'll be able to turn things around eventually. Until then..."

"Until then...he can screw off. I've got my friends and family and everything else I need. No time for toxic people like that in my life."

There was determination to her voice. I was happy as hell to hear it. Dream had always been a strong woman, and her behavior over the last hour was confirmation of that. She'd been cornered by a drunk asshole who'd made it clear he had no issue with hitting women, and she stood her ground. That was courage.

"Think of this party as a fresh start," I said, pulling her close. "Would've been nice if Adam had gotten the hint a while back, but he had to learn the hard way. Now he's gone for good, and you can finally turn the page."

She smiled. "Happy to have you guys here with me for it."

She snuggled her head into my shoulder. A few people around regarded us with glances of uncertainty, as if they weren't sure what was going on between me and Dream. I couldn't blame them. Over the course of the party, all three of us brothers had been close and cozy with Dream in our own ways.

Things were heating up between me, my brothers and Dream. It was only a matter of time before people started asking questions.

But I didn't give a damn – it was a bridge we'd cross when we came to it.

"Shoot." She sat up, taking her phone out of her pocket. I watched as her screen filled up with texts. "You'll never guess who it is."

"What a prick. What's he saying?" I didn't want to pry into her business, but at the same time I needed to make sure he wasn't saying anything I needed to worry about.

"He's in whiny mode; begging me to take him back." I watched as she made a few swipes here and there. "Done. He's blocked."

"Hopefully he wakes up and makes the right call. But if he doesn't...my brothers and I will just have to teach him another lesson."

Dream smiled up at me, wrapping her arm around my body once more and giving me a tight squeeze. At that moment Clarissa poked her head up from the stairs that led from the deck to the roof, concern all over her face.

"Oh my God!" she shouted, running over to us. "Are you OK? I'm so, so, sorry that I didn't do a better job making sure that asshole didn't show up and ruin things."

"It's fine," I said. "That wasn't your responsibility. And the guys were here to send him packing."

Clarissa sent a warm smile in my direction.

"Thanks, Jay. You know, you've always been kind of a hard ass. But even so I've always suspected that deep down there was a real sweetie pie waiting to come out."

I laughed. "A 'sweetie pie,' huh? Let's not go crazy."

Dream laughed. "Maybe a slice of sweetie pie."

"Let me get you guys some drinks," said Clarissa. "God knows I'd be needing something after all of that. "Eggnog OK?"

"As long as it's spiked with some rum, it sounds great," I said.

Clarissa smiled. "Do you think we'd have non-alcoholic eggnog? What kind of woman do you take me for, Dream?"

The two women shared a smile, and she was gone, hurrying down the stairs. From the other flight of steps, the one that led to the second floor of the house, Duncan and Evan appeared. I stood up as soon as they arrived, ready for whatever news they might have.

"What's the word?" I asked.

"He's gone," said Duncan. "And it doesn't look like he's coming back. I put in a call with one of my buddies at the station to keep an eye out for him wandering around town. If he's still out causing trouble, they'll throw him in the drunk tank for the night to sleep it off."

"And I took care of the mess in your room," said Evan. "Got all the glass from that bottle he threw. The hole in the wall's going to need some patching up but shouldn't be a problem."

"Awesome," I said.

Dream stood up and moved next to me. "Wow, I'm really starting to see some advantages in dating three men. A problem comes up and you guys can tackle it from all angles." She flashed a sarcastic grin after she spoke.

"See?" asked Evan, a big smile on his face. "This arrangement is already paying off."

"Is that what this is, Dream?" I asked. "Are you dating all three of us?"

Her eyes flashed with surprise, as if she'd said something that she hadn't intended to.

"That…just kind of slipped out," she replied. "But I don't know, now that I'm thinking about it, the better it sounds. Like it was meant to be. What do you guys think? After all, you were the ones talking about how you don't mind sharing."

Evan didn't waste a second before speaking. "I'm down as hell."

Duncan smiled. "Same here. This bullshit with Adam wasn't fun, but it did show that we all work well together."

Everyone turned to me, waiting for my response.

It was a no-brainer. "Of course, I'm cool with the three of us sharing you. Dream, you're a one-in-a-million woman. How selfish would any *one* guy have to be to think he should have you all to himself?"

Just like that, it was decided. Me and Duncan and Evan and Dream would all be together. It was a strange arrangement, no doubt about it, but it felt right.

"So," she said. "What's the plan for this fantastic foursome?"

"I think maybe we should have some eggnog first," Dream said, her voice soft, "Then join everyone down at the bonfire for some S'mores before we do the gift exchange game."

"Right," said Evan. "I think that sounds like a hell of a plan. Of course, we'll have to share our gifts for you in private later." He followed his statement up with a wink.

"Yes, I think some alone time later would be good," said Duncan with a smile and a nod. "Well, as *alone* as four people can be."

"It's a good thing you bought a king-sized bed," said Evan.

"Then it's settled," said Dream. "Let's make this a Christmas to remember."

CHAPTER 35

DREAM

It didn't take long to put the Adam unpleasantness behind us. Clarissa showed up with a round of eggnog, and together we made our way down to the bonfire for some toasted marshmallows. It was a picture-perfect Christmas Eve surrounded by friends and loved ones. The air seemed to grow colder, and before long, white flurries of snow fell from the sky. We were far enough North to get some snow, but it was still rare enough to feel special.

Me and the guys spent time sitting together, cuddled close for warmth, watching the bonfire crackle. It was already one of the best nights of my life. And it wasn't over yet.

"I think people are beginning to head home," Evan said, his hand gently stroking my hair as I rested my head against his chest. "The fire is about to go out too, unless you'd like me to re-start it."

"No, I think it's fine," I said, lifting my head to see who was still left. It was getting late, and most of us had Christmas day plans bright and early. I was surprised the party had already gone as late as it had, but grateful that everyone seemed to have had a good time. "But maybe we should move somewhere more--well, private."

The matter didn't even need to be discussed. We all rose and, drinks in hand, made our way back into the house The few party-goers that were left all wrapped up in their own fun, drinking hot cocoa and enjoying the light snowfall on the beach, none of them seemed to notice me and my three boyfriends, God, that felt good to say, leaving the party.

The deck was empty, so we took the stairs up to the roof where we were alone. The view was wonderful. From where we stood, we could see the ocean to the west. And to the north was the bay, the circle-shaped body of water dotted with boats, houses around its border. Snow still fell softly around us, not really sticking, but adding to the festive atmosphere, nonetheless.

I dropped into one of the cushioned benches, my arms stretched out across the back. I'd only had a couple of drinks over the last few hours, so the buzz swimming in my head was absolutely perfect. The badness with Adam was a distant memory. In those moments, it was as if I didn't have a care in the world.

Duncan sat to my right, Evan to my left. And Jay took one of the nearby chairs, moving it closer so he wasn't left out

"Are you ready?" Jay asked.

"Ready for what?" I asked, as Duncan covered me with a throw he had grabbed on our way to the roof. I thanked him and curled up underneath it, feeling warmer and toastier.

"Your gifts," Jay said.

"You actually got me presents? You guys, after all that you've done for me, from helping me move to dealing with Adam, you really didn't have to get me anything."

"What kind of ex-stepbrothers - would we be if we didn't get you a little something?" Evan said with a teasing smile.

I rolled my eyes playfully. "You guys were never my stepbrothers."

"For five minutes there, we were technically, by law at least," Evan continued to tease.

I pretended to groan, but I couldn't hide the smile from my face either.

Just being alone and near the guys was enough to start a tingle between my legs. I bit my lip and glanced from Evan to Duncan, the sexual tension building by the moment. Evan's hand was on my thigh, Duncan's arm wrapped around me.

But still I wanted more, and I didn't mean presents, unless that present was each of them naked and pleasuring me

"Well, I got all of you something too, but you're going to have to wait until tomorrow. I left the gifts at my mom's. Didn't know we'd be exchanging them tonight."

"Oh, we have gifts for you for tomorrow too, but some things... well some things we'd like to give you, we can't give you in front of your mom, if you get what I mean." Evan winked at me playfully.

Heat rose inside of my body, and I felt like I might not need the throw for long.

But before we went even further, I wanted to be sure of something.

"So, guys," I said. "We're all together now, right? Not just physically, but we're *together*."

"That's right," said Duncan, turning his attention toward me with a twinkle in his eye that suggested he was having similar thoughts. "And I don't know about you all, but it feels pretty damn good to me."

"Same here," said Evan.

Jay nodded, his gaze focused directly onto me.

"So, if we're to do this, we're going to have to learn to share. Where do we even begin?"

The guys glanced at one another, each with the same smile on his face.

"How about...," began Evan, a thoughtful tone to his words. "We start with a kiss?"

"Sounds perfect to me," I agreed.

Evan placed his hand on my chin and turned me toward him, looking deeply into my eyes before bringing his lips to mine. He tasted so good, so perfect, that the mere pressure of his lips on mine was enough to make me lose myself in the moment.

We kissed and kissed, Evan's mouth opening to give me his tongue. The kiss alone would've been enough to drive me wild. But as it went on, I felt pressure on my thigh. A quick glance over my shoulder revealed that the pressure was from Duncan, who was moving his hand under the hem of my dress and rubbing the skin in such a way that I felt wild with desire.

After some time on my thigh, he brought his hand up to my breast and slipped it under the top of my dress, teasing my nipple underneath my bra as I kissed Evan deeper and deeper. Jay sat up from his chair and dropped slowly to his knees, opening my legs and placing his hands on both thighs, pushing the dress up, up, up until the lilac-colored panties I had on underneath were visible. He placed his lips on my thighs, kissing me softly as he hooked his fingertips underneath the waistband of my panties, rolling them down over my legs.

Duncan slipped the shoulder of my dress down and then the other, expertly removing my bra once it was out in the open. He teased my breasts a bit more before leaning in and putting his mouth on my left nipple. I took a moment to appreciate the fact that I had *three* mouths on me. And they hadn't even begun getting to work.

Jay moved his lips closer and closer to my center, moans pouring out from my mouth as the brothers did their work. And when Jay finally placed his lips on my pussy it was nearly enough on its own to give me the first of what I hoped would be many orgasms.

He opened me, spreading my lips and licking my clit slowly and firmly. Each warm, wet drag of his tongue over me sent spasms of pleasure through my body, my hips writhing where I sat. When it became clear that the moans weren't making kissing me easy, Evan took his lips from my mouth and placed them on my other breast. Evan and Duncan licked and sucked and teased my nipples as Jay ate me, his fingers inside as the orgasm built and built.

But he only took me to the brink. As the brothers sucked my breasts, Jay rose and stood looming in front of me, his cock straining against his pants. With a smirk on his face, Jay pulled off his shirt and slipped off his pants, his beautiful cock springing out in front of me. I wanted to take it into my mouth, but Jay had other plans. He lowered his body and spread my legs, placing his cock at my opening, then entering me. The sensation of the brothers licking my breasts while Jay pushed into me was almost too much, and when Jay began to move inside of me the orgasm came immediately. Hot flashes of pleasure coursed through my body as I came. All I could do was moan and savor it.

When the orgasm faded, I watched as Jay thrust into me over and over, my breasts shaking with each full push.

"I think it's time," I said through the pleasure. "For you two to get as naked as your brother."

It was strange to hear the words come out of my mouth with such certainty, such confidence. Sleeping with Jay and Evan together had been strange. But it'd been the perfect warm-up for what was about to happen.

"What the lady wants...," Evan said with a cheeky smirk as he stood.

Jay slipped himself out of me and stood up as Evan and Duncan flanked him, stepping out of their clothes. It only took a few moments before all three brothers were in front of me, all of them naked and hard, their cocks stiff and long, just for me.

The only question was, where to begin?

But the brothers didn't give me a chance to answer. They wanted me as badly as I wanted them, after all. Duncan leaned down and wrapped his arm around my waist, lifting me up and putting me in the doggy position. Once I was on all fours, he climbed behind me onto the couch and positioned himself where he needed to be.

My face was right in front of Evan's cock, only inches away. The sight was so enticing that I couldn't help myself from wrapping my fingers around his length and taking him into my mouth. Duncan moved into me as soon as Evan was inside, and soon we had a wonderful, rocking rhythm going. Duncan's thrusts moved me forward, taking more of Evan into my mouth. And when I pulled back to suck on his head, Duncan pushed deeper into me.

But Jay wasn't left out. It took some coordination, but I was able to take him into my hand and stroke him as Duncan pounded me hard, my lips around Evan's cock. The fact that I was pleasing all of them at once was almost too much. Another orgasm began to build, and it promised to make the first seem like nothing at all.

The ecstasy was so much that I couldn't focus on Evan's cock. I let it fall out of my mouth as Duncan's steady thrusting, his hands on my hips holding me into place, sent another roiling orgasm through me. I fell forward, my face buried in the cushion.

Duncan took himself out of me as the pleasure faded, and I gave myself a moment to recover.

"Is it all that you'd hoped it would be?" asked Duncan, his voice a low, sensual growl.

I considered the question for a moment. As I did, I realized that what was happening, all three of the Wolfs at the same time, had been my fantasy for as long as I could remember, ever since I was a teenager. And it was finally coming true. More than that, it wasn't going to be a one-off – we were all together, and this night was only the beginning.

I pushed that out of my head as Evan stood in front of me, his cock glistening from my work. He reached behind my head, placing his hand on the couch back and giving it a push. Something in the couch unlatched, the back falling and forming into a flat, bed-like surface.

"Perfect," he said. "Because you're going to need to be laying down for this."

Before I could ask what he meant, Evan moved in front of me and grabbed my legs, slinging them over his broad, round shoulders. He placed his cock at my opening and pushed inside, his thickness stretching me out as surely as his brothers. I laid back, Duncan moving to the side of the bed and bringing his cock toward my mouth.

I took him into me as his brother screwed me from the front. And all I had to do was lay back and enjoy it.

I could sense by the sounds he was making that Evan was getting close to an orgasm. But he didn't cross over the brink. Instead, he withdrew from me and moved to the side so Jay could take a turn. Jay leaned forward, putting his hands on both sides of me as slid inside and thrust like a machine. My body writhed underneath him as he worked, and I slowly grew closer to yet another orgasm.

In the middle of it, however, I felt Duncan's cock slip out of my mouth. Then I watched as he stepped to where Jay was, Jay moving back and letting Duncan stand where he had been. Duncan grabbed my ankles and leaned forward, plunging into me, and picking up my orgasm where Jay had left it off.

It was exactly what I'd fantasized about – to be on my back, being used by the brothers in only the way they could. I smiled, soon feeling Evan's cock against my lips. I eagerly opened my mouth and took him into me, sucking him like mad while Duncan filled me.

Evan's breaths grew faster, and he soon let out a long groan as he finished, his cock throbbing as he spilled himself into my mouth. His seed was thick and sweet, and I eagerly drank down every drop through his orgasm. When he was done, he fell back, his huge chest rising and falling.

. Duncan relentlessly thrusted into me, and when I sensed he was getting close he withdrew. I reached forward and wrapped my fingers around his cock, pulling on him and feeling the orgasm move down his length. His prick emptied itself, splashing onto my breasts and belly in hot spurts.

When he was done, Jay took his place and entered me. I was so close to another orgasm that I could hardly stand it. Evan's taste was still on my lips, my body glistening with Duncan's seed. And then Jay came, finishing inside of me with several hard thrusts. The sensation of his orgasm pushed me over the edge, and I came hard, the third orgasm igniting every molecule of my body with pure delight. My back arched and I let the moans flow.

Then I was nothing more than a puddle of pleasure, my arms and legs dropping onto the flattened-out couch. Luckily, there was more than enough space for all the boys to join me. The boys wrapped their bodies around me, making sure I was warm. We laid there together, one big tangle of limbs.

I was certain we were all thinking the same thing, that we loved one another. And that we couldn't wait to go on this next journey, whatever it might hold, together.

"Oh, we still have to give you your gifts," Evan said sleepily.

"It can wait for tomorrow," Jay said. "Before we head over to her mom's house."

My face hurt from smiling so much, thinking about us all spending the holidays - and beyond - together.

EPILOGUE

DREAM

One Year Later...

"How's right there?"

Three pairs of hands were on me.

I was in total heaven.

I opened my eyes just enough to take in the sight. I was seated on the covered rooftop of my place, the sun bright and brilliant overhead. Evan was in front of me, rubbing my feet. Duncan was to the side, massaging my hands and arms. And Jay was behind, taking out the knots on my shoulders.

Outside, the frost of winter was beginning to set in again, the green of the pines topped with white. But the guys had built a cover for the roof a few months back and even installed a few space heaters.

Hell of a way to spend our one-year anniversary if you ask me. And the guys had done more than a four-way massage. They'd treated me to breakfast in bed, followed by a day trip up to San Francisco for shopping and lunch. After that, back home for an evening of relaxing, followed by a home-cooked meal courtesy of Jay.

A beeping sounded, Jay's hands going stiff on my shoulders.

"Shoot," he said. "Timer for the food. Let me run in and check on it and I'll be right back."

"Make it snappy!" said Evan with a grin.

Jay playfully flicked him off as he rose.

Jay gave my shoulders one last squeeze before running off. I turned to watch as he hurried down the stairs. There'd been something different about Jay these days. After his confrontation with his father his hard attitude had mellowed a bit. He was still his usual self, but there'd been more confidence to him. It was as if telling his dad how he felt had staunched the bleeding of an emotional wound, letting the healing begin.

And speaking of parents, things had been a hell of a lot better with Mom. The last few months had brought some major success with my traveling painting booth, and between that and my relationship with the guys, which had taken her a bit of time to get used to, she'd come around to my new life. We still had a way to go before we had a picture-perfect mother-daughter relationship. But we were definitely on the right path.

As far as the brothers, we'd all been settling into our new lives together. Evan had become my unofficial partner in art business, helping me manage my books and plan my next year on the market circuit once the winter was over.

Duncan had been leading the discussions over the last few months about their lives now that they were done with the service. Last I heard, they'd been considering opening a private security firm to put their skills to use. But for the time being, I was happy to enjoy their full attention.

"Alright!" shouted Jay from downstairs. "Get your butts down here!"

"He's got such a way with words, doesn't he?" asked Evan with a smile as he stood and offered me his hand.

Duncan laughed, the two of them helping me out of my seat. Together, we went down to the first floor.

I was shocked at what I saw.

The guys had been keeping me out of downstairs for the last couple of hours for a reason. The dining area table had been set with four places, a massive, and I mean *massive* bouquet of roses on each end. There was wine and the scent of lasagna and fresh bread that Jay had been cooking was thick in the air.

"Oh my God!" I said, clasping my hands together with happiness as I took in the sight. "This is incredible!"

"Glad you like it," said Duncan. "Only the best, right?"

Everything was perfect. But as I glanced over at the guys, I saw that they all wore the same expression of concern.

"Something wrong?" I asked.

"Where is she?" asked Evan. "Didn't she say she'd be here around six?"

"That's what she said," replied Jay. "Don't tell me there's been a hold-up or something."

"Alright," I said. "Tell me what you guys are talking about."

Before either of them could say anything, a honk sounded out from in front of the house. Then more – honk-honk-*hoooonk*.

I really wanted to know what was going on.

"That's got to be her," said Evan. "Come on!"

"Can someone *please* tell me what's happening?" I asked, excitement creeping into my voice despite not having a clue what was going on.

"A little present," said Jay with a wink as the guys stepped outside. "Come check it out."

I followed them onto the porch, coming to a shocked stop at what I saw. Clarissa was there in the driver's seat of a big van which had the words "Painting by Dream" on the side. I gasped as Clarissa waved to me.

"Hey!" she shouted. "Get your butt over here and check this out!"

She didn't need to talk me into it. I hurried over to the van, looking it over with eager eyes.

"Is this seriously what I think it is?" I asked.

"A ride for your new job," said Duncan as he slapped the side. "We all got to talking and figured you needed something a little more suitable than her beetle to get from town to town when market season starts back up again."

"In other words," said Clarissa as she hopped out. "It was *my* idea."

Evan laughed and gave her a friendly shove.

"Go check out the back," said Jay.

I did, stepping around and opening the back doors. Inside was packed full of all the art supplies I'd need, the walls adorned with samples of my work. Tears formed in my eyes as I took in the sight.

"I...I don't know what to say."

"Say 'I love you'," Duncan replied. "Because hearing those words out of your mouth is really the reason the guys and I do anything these days."

I smiled, turning toward the boys. They stood side-by-side, my men, my loves.

"I love you all," I said. "So damn much."

I kissed Evan, then Jay, then Duncan.

"Now," Clarissa interjected. "I think the least I should get for playing my part is a little of that lasagna you'd been planning on making, Jay. What do you say?"

I laughed and stepped over to give my best friend a big hug. And together we went back into the house, my heart full of a love I'd never known, and eagerness to see what the days ahead held.

THE END

Printed in Great Britain
by Amazon